Wrong Turnings

Wrong Turnings

John Burke

ROBERT HALE · LONDON

© John Burke 2004
First published in Great Britain 2004

ISBN 0 7090 7586 3

Robert Hale Limited
Clerkenwell House
Clerkenwell Green
London EC1R 0HT

2 4 6 8 10 9 7 5 3 1

6925

Typeset in 12/13½pt Times New Roman
by Derek Doyle & Associates, Liverpool.
Printed in Great Britain by
St Edmundsbury Press Ltd, Bury St Edmunds, Suffolk.
Bound by Woolnough Bookbinding Ltd.

1

Anna Chisholm stared at the curtains in outrage. She had not been very favourably impressed by this last family, but had never expected quite such desecration.

'Marmalade!' It exploded with all the fervour of a swear-word. 'Look at it! I mean, did you ever see such . . . I mean . . . *marmalade!*'

The list of regulations in each of the two self-catering cottages was as comprehensive as she had thought necessary, occasionally added to after some unexpected upset. Dogs were banned not merely because her mother-in-law's mongrel invariably went for any such intruder but because the sort of visitors who brought dogs were the sort to go tramping over the countryside and returning with mud all over their boots, ready for transfer to the carpets. Once there had been a party of fishermen who went out one cold morning with dogs, balaclavas and guns, leading to an immediate rumour: 'The IRA's doing a recce.'

No football in the courtyard. And no flying of kites, since one flown by a kid from Covenanter's Cottage had got ravelled round Stables Cottage's TV aerial and ruined the tenants' viewing of World Cup football, making them ask for their money back.

She had not thought it necessary to proscribe physical violence or murder on the premises, because people renting holiday cottages didn't do that sort of thing, did they?

Not nowadays, anyway. There were local legends about troubles in the late Georgian era, when Stables Cottage had really been a stable block, and a villainous laird had horsewhipped a

5

stable lad to death for making unseemly advances to his daughter. After converting the barn on the far side of the yard, Peter Chisholm had named it Covenanter's Cottage after an incident during the Killing Times of the seventeenth-century Scottish Lowlands when the most sadistic of the Persecutors had hunted down two adherents of the National Covenant in Galloway, hacked them to pieces, and left the remains to rot on the hill behind the farmhouse.

Peter's ghost was still vivid in Anna's memory. But ghosts of those other, long-ago sadnesses had never been known to haunt the place.

Marmalade was real and immediate.

'Creative expressiveness in marmalade,' raged Anna. 'I suppose that's how the doting parents see it.'

Stuart Morgan, who had as usual come in to help with the Saturday morning changeover, prodded the curtain with a wary finger. When he tried to pull his finger back, the curtain came billowing with it. He fought his hand loose and lifted the card from the window-ledge below the curtain. 'Getting a bit greasy, isn't it? Can hardly read the house rules any more.'

'That's not grease. It's more marmalade.'

'Better add a new clause. "Spreading marmalade on anything but toast is strictly forbidden."' He looked over her shoulder at the far wall. 'Didn't draw moustaches on your marsh marigolds, did they?'

'What?'

'That painting of yours – you've taken it down?'

Anna couldn't believe it. 'They've nicked it. Nicked my picture.'

'You should be flattered. Never expected your watercolours to be collectors' pieces.'

She attacked a cushion on the sofa, pummelling it into shape and then wrenching it out again. 'That man Ritchie and his letting agency' – a hefty punch into another cushion – 'are going to have some chasing up to do when next I get into town to see him.' She slammed a half-open cupboard door shut. 'I'll have to get another picture from the shop.' And this one, she vowed to herself, would be screwed to the wall. 'And the curtains . . .

we'll have to dig out some old ones to be going on with.'

'Take it easy.' Stuart's voice was at its most lazily reassuring. Often she found it soothing and was grateful to him for just being around. Right now she wasn't in any mood to be soothed. But he went on: 'Come along, let's go into the village. Take the curtains to the cleaners. And you can select another of your masterpieces from the shop to grace these unworthy walls. Something really lurid that *no one* will want to nick.'

There was still this cottage to be cleaned up. The guests in the other, Covenanter's Cottage, had left late yesterday afternoon, so that was fully cleaned and made up ready for the next tenants. Nobody was due in either of them until four this afternoon. Better to go along with Stuart, take the curtains to the laundrette at the back of Brenda's shop, and sort things out from there on.

Trying to simmer down, she went into the bathroom, washed her hands, and peered gloomily into the mirror above the basin.

She had very fine, almost silvery hair, which Peter had urged her to grow long because he found it so delightful to drift strands of it across her breasts as if whipping them, before he made his usual violent entry into her. It was a nice sexy chat-line. She wondered, from what she had later learned, what line he had used on Stuart's wife, and how many times, before they both went to their death.

The sudden unbidden memory made her consider having her hair cut short when she next went into town. In any case, when she was all steamed up with irritation, as she was right now, it seemed to go lank, tangled, and muddy grey rather than silver. She stared into her own grey eyes. Even when she was at her busiest they looked heavy-lidded and drowsy. 'Bedroom eyes,' Peter had called them. But when she was in danger of losing her temper – like right now – her eyebrows lifted, her eyes widened as if drops had been put in them, and the drowsy blue-tinged grey became a steely glare.

At this moment she was glaring at herself. Stupid. Snap out of it.

She washed her hands and face, and groped for the hand towel.

It was blotched with lipstick. She remembered that the brat's mother had used enough to make her mouth look like the slit in a pillar-box. She gathered the towel up along with the others, and headed out to collect kitchen tea-towels, adding them to the basket of things to be cleaned in the usual Saturday routine.

Stuart was waiting, smiling reassuringly. He touched her arm to calm her down. But his fingertips were still sticky. She waved him to take his turn in the bathroom.

The interior of her ageing Volvo retained a lovely clean, crisp smell – the smell of newly planed wood and a hint of varnish, from the last time she had helped Stuart deliver one of his restored bits of furniture to Balmuir Lodge. When she started it up, a faint flurry of sawdust made her sneeze.

Stuart was silent during the drive uphill and over the ridge towards the village. He stared straight ahead, not even glancing at the beautiful plunge of moorland to his left, dappled by the shadows of scudding clouds, or the hills beyond, as insubstantial as the clouds themselves. She sensed that he was mutely driving for her, anticipating each corner and each touch of the brake. Stoical – or taut with frustration? Another three years to go before he would be legally free to drive again.

Brenda was swapping details of some complicated medical histories with a customer almost as broad and red-faced as herself. Anna tried not to catch any of the conversation. People in this village really did have the most nauseating symptoms, yet tended to live well into their nineties. She waved to Brenda and went past her to the laundrette at the back.

When she had got things started, she found Stuart studying the selection of her water-colours along the west wall of the shop.

'How about this one? Looks threatening enough.'

It was one of her favourites, showing a grim, dark Border castle against a shimmering haze of heather. She was almost glad that nobody had so far wanted to buy it. Now she could reclaim it.

She waved at the gap on the wall. 'I'll replace it with a new one next week, Brenda.'

'Another of those rowan tree pictures, Mrs Chisholm? Folk seem to go for that sort of picture.'

8

'It will depend on Mrs Chisholm's artistic mood of the moment,' said Stuart.

Anna could never tell whether remarks like this were genuine or faintly mocking. His long, rather melancholy face remained impassive even when he was obviously making a joke, and she often had the feeling that he had changed his mind about a comment before he was halfway through it.

As she drove back into the stableyard she had to swerve to avoid a bright silver Honda parked beside the old horse trough ablaze with petunias and nemesias.

'Somebody's arrived damned early,' said Stuart.

'Oh, Lor'.' It wasn't just the thought of someone turning up before they were supposed to that wrenched the moan from Anna. It was the sight of another car; a battered little yellow Fiat parked at the end of Stables Cottage. A small dog was leaping up and down on the back seat, yelping and shoving its nose against the window.

The dog was Cocky, so called because it was a cocktail of most of the breeds in the neighbourhood. And with the car and the dog here, she knew who else must be somewhere nearby.

As Anna got out of the station wagon, her mother-in-law made her appearance from round the end of Stables Cottage as if she had been waiting there for her cue, her sleeves flapping as she raised her arms in a gesture that managed to be dramatic and meaningless at the same time. Today, thought Anna resignedly, Queenie was in her mood to personify the scatterbrained, fluttering old relatives seen in so many old Hollywood warm-hearted comedies.

Peter had always called her Mum, and Anna had followed suit; but after his death his mother had insisted that Anna should call her Queenie. It wasn't a name that Anna found easy to use, because it simply didn't seem to fit, especially when she was in one of her tragedienne moods.

Today she was playing a distraught role, laced with puzzled reproaches.

'These poor folk – house with no curtains, nothing ready. Whatever has been going on?'

'They shouldn't be here until four this afternoon,' said Anna, 'and it's not one o'clock yet.'

A couple came out behind Queenie. They looked sullen and dissatisfied.

'Mr and Mrs Robinson?'

'Er . . . oh, yes. Walter Robinson. And this is Sharon. My wife.'

The girl's shoulders twitched under her pink shirt, with the two top buttons revealingly undone. Her thighs moved within her pale grey chinos. She was a fidget, thought Anna; but her twitches were just the kind to fascinate a certain sort of man. Like her husband. If this man was her husband. Anna was used to the signs. But at least they didn't appear to have a marmalade fiend in tow.

As they stood under the hanging basket beside the cottage door, Anna was aware of a flowery smell which didn't come from the fuchsias twitching their silent bells in the faint breeze. Between them, Walter and Sharon had produced a suffocating blend of sweetish perfume and a spicy aftershave. The blend would probably vary according to the direction of the wind.

It suddenly dawned on Anna. 'Just a minute. This is Covenanter's Cottage. You were booked into Stables Cottage.'

'Which is in no state to be occupied,' said Queenie. 'There aren't any curtains. You can't expect people to go into a house with half the curtains missing.'

'Especially in the bedroom,' said Sharon; and giggled.

'Our brochure makes it clear that people aren't expected to arrive until four o'clock,' Anna reminded her. 'And,' she said again, 'it's only just gone one.'

Walter Robinson was beginning to look more and more peevish. 'Now, look. I mean, how can you expect people to know exactly how long it's going to take to get here?'

'You could always have gone for a drive,' said Anna. 'Lots of people do, on their way here. The countryside's rather gorgeous.'

'You can't just send folk away when they've only just got here. I insisted that they made themselves comfy in here.' Queenie favoured the newcomers with her most endearing smile. 'You'll have to forgive Anna. For some time now she's had to cope on her own. Very bravely.' Her gaze did not for even a second flicker in the direction of Stuart, standing beside the car. 'But no harm done. We've fixed it nicely, haven't we?'

Walter Robinson shuffled from one foot to the other. He was a tall, gangling man in his mid-thirties, with a narrow crest of hair aping the latest footballers' fad, and a half-smile, half-scowl, that went awkwardly on and off. 'I reckon we can make do.' Sharon was tugging at his arm, easing him back indoors.

When the door had closed on them, Anna rounded on her mother-in-law. 'You shouldn't have switched them in there. That one's smoking, the other's non-smoking. How do you know that the other people will want the non-smoker?'

'I'm sure they'll manage. Since you weren't around, *somebody* had to cope.'

Stuart edged forward. Queenie still did not even say hello. Without a word he took the painting from the Volvo, and carried it carefully into Stables Cottage. Then he returned for the box of bacon, eggs, bread, butter and milk which were always put in the fridge for newcomers who had not yet explored the village store. Unlike Queenie, he had fitted himself neatly into the programme.

The cleaned curtains were still too damply creased to be put up. Anna went into the Balmuir Mains airing cupboard in search of a spare set, and by four o'clock had finished hanging them, tidying the place up, and replacing the stained brochures and information sheet with clean copies ready for the arrival of the second couple booked in for the week.

At one minute to four, a blue Escort edged into the yard. The woman driver got out and made her way round to open the passenger door. The two made a complete contrast to the couple already installed. The woman had dark hair through which strands of something lighter straggled. She was surely younger than her wispy-bearded husband. As he eased himself out of the car his head was lowered and his shoulders hunched as if bent by some bone disease, or by a reluctance to look anyone in the eye.

Anna went to greet them. 'Mr and Mrs Maxwell? Welcome to Stables Cottage.'

The woman stared at her with alert, bright hazel eyes. 'I

11

thought our booking was for Covenanter's Cottage.'

'They're identical. We had a bit of a mix-up over arrangements this morning, but I'm sure you'll be happy with the result.'

Stuart was standing by the boot of the car, ready to offer a hand with the luggage, but Maxwell thrust himself towards it and took out just one case. He limped towards the cottage door which Anna was holding open.

Inside, she showed them the microwave, the television, and the central heating controls. Then she fanned out the new brochures. 'We do have some very fine gardens in the neighbourhood. One famous one only an hour or so away.'

Mrs Maxwell said: 'We'll only be taking a few short-distance trips, I expect. As I told you when I booked, my husband has had a long illness. Not very long out of hospital. He really needs a nice, quiet place to relax.'

'I don't think you'll find us too rowdy. Only the occasional owl, and maybe a few geese over the loch.'

The woman was staring at the card propped on the window-ledge. 'It says "No Smoking". As I told you when I booked,' she said again, 'we wanted the cottage where smoking is allowed. My husband does rely on his cigarettes.'

If he had been that ill, thought Anna, smoking wouldn't do him much good. But aloud she said: 'I'm sorry. If it's really essential for him, I suppose we can waive the restriction this week.'

And at the end of the week, we'll have to give the place a good airing.

Maxwell gave her a furtive nod as she passed him on the way out.

On her way across the yard to where Stuart had been cleaning out the inside of the Volvo, she noticed that the bedroom curtains of Covenanter's Cottage were closed.

Stuart nodded towards the cottage she had just left.

'Well, what d'you make of them?'

'A bit creepy,' she said. 'I don't know quite how to put it, but . . . there's a sort of smell about him. I mean, he may have spent some time in hospital, but it's not quite—'

'He hasn't been out long.'

'Out of hospital?'

'Out of prison,' said Stuart bleakly. 'That face of his, that's prison pallor. And the smell – like the skin of someone who's been packing mushrooms, right?'

'Yes,' she whispered, not sure whether she ought to look at him.

'I've lost mine by now, haven't I?' said Stuart.

2

The shrill of the phone late that afternoon jarred Anna out of an uneasy doze. She had meant to switch the answering machine on, but had settled down to one of the Saturday supplements and ploughed her way through a feature on single mothers and sex-starved widows before drifting off into a dream too vague to be analysed. She was reluctant to move from the armchair, but the phone went on ringing until at last she had to go and answer it.

Chet Brunner was as peremptory as ever. 'Is Stuart Morgan with you?'

'I'm afraid not.'

'Where the hell is he? I've been ringing his flat and the work-shop, and there's no reply.'

'Sorry, but I've no idea.'

'Bugger it. I've got some urgent work for him. Can't get down to the village myself. Not right in the middle of this game. But I need some bits and pieces for the next one, and I want him to get cracking. Do try to find him, there's a girl.'

Typical of the man. Always expecting you to drop whatever you might be doing, and go running his errands for him.

Shaken into wakefulness now, she abandoned the paper and was making herself a cup of coffee when Stuart came sauntering past the window and tapped at the kitchen door.

'Fancy a walk?' he said. 'Once the new batches have been tucked away in their hutches, everything goes a bit flat, doesn't it? I've been out wandering. Thought you might care for a natter.'

She told him about Brunner's call. His face, always a rueful mask accentuated by the slant of his lazy left eye, puckered into a sour grin of resignation. 'Par for the course. Saturday afternoon.'

'You could always just go on with your walk. I won't tell him that I've seen you.'

'No. Should be used to it by now. Anyway, it settles the question of the post-changeover boredom, doesn't it?'

'I'll run you up there.'

'No, I'll walk. It won't do him any harm to be kept waiting just a little bit longer.'

They went out into the yard. Anna looked across at the two cottages. The curtains of both were drawn tightly shut. 'A right weird batch we've got this week,' she said. 'None of them showing their faces out of doors. Maybe they can't read.'

'You're not running a seaside boarding-house. There's no notice in the cottages saying the occupants have to be off the premises by nine in the morning and not come back until six in the evening.'

'No, what I meant was, what's the use of providing them with all those brochures about the Carrick and Galloway countryside if they don't set foot on it? And on a fine day like this. Not as if it's pouring with rain.'

'Give 'em time. They're probably still unpacking the muesli and the marmalade pots. Or maybe they've got something more interesting to do.'

'I don't see the Maxwells as having a passionate reunion, even if he *has* only just come out of prison. But the Robinsons . . . well, yes. If that's their real name. His, maybe. Hers, I doubt.'

Stuart looked at her for a moment as if he were about to risk some personal question. Then he set off towards the end of the yard and the beginning of the sketchy footpath which led over the brae towards the loch.

Maybe there was a touch of something underlying the gesture of petty defiance in keeping Brunner waiting. Stuart still hated having to be dependent on other people. And hated having to be driven anywhere. Most of all, perhaps, he dreaded having to be driven past that corner of the twisting road between here and the big house where that first accident had taken place. At least the short cut across the estate would keep him away from that memory.

She watched him until he went out of sight behind a cluster of gorse, but in her mind could follow each step of that familiar route, round the loch to the terrace of Balmuir Lodge, and along to the side door and in to face the booming demands of Chet Brunner.

They all owed too much to the unpredictable Brunner, and he was happy to keep them aware of it. Peter had taken it less submissively than the rest of them. His temper snapped more easily and he grew too easily fretful with the day-to-day running of everything.

Stuart, perhaps crushed by that prison sentence and by Peter's treacheries, seemed to have found a way of adjusting. Maybe he would be more comfortable to live with than Peter had ever been.

She tried to stop wondering about him and about herself, and so went on wondering all the more.

He was always there at her side, attentive, helping as if to make up for all the things that had gone wrong in the past. He sometimes kissed her goodnight – a peck of a kiss – before going back to his bed above the workshop. She wondered when his hand on her arm might perhaps tighten, and his lips become more demanding. Really, he was too much a part of the every-day scenery. Yet it would be so neat, so tidy. Neat . . . *tidy*! A makeshift relationship.

She had a sudden searing memory of Peter and their Sunday afternoons in bed before they were married, and sometimes afterwards – before some of his afternoons were occupied by somebody else.

She couldn't decide whether to be envious or cynical about what those two in Covenanter's Cottage must be up to right at this moment.

Sharon sat glumly on the edge of the bed, staring at her reflection in the dressing-table mirror. Walter's hand crept over her shoulder and clawed at her left breast. She shrugged him off. He sank back on to the bed with a groan.

Sharon said: 'I only hope Richard's salmon are a lot heftier than what *I'm* getting.'

Walter heaved himself up again to kiss her shoulder. She jerked away.

'Sharon, my darling. Gorgeous. I'm sorry.'

She jerked away. 'So am I. Flaming sorry I agreed to come away with you.' She stood up, flaunting her naked body at him to make it clear what he was missing. 'I thought it was going to be . . . I mean, Christ, the way you talked. Rogering me to death, this way and that. It made me go all . . . but it was all talk, wasn't it?'

He tried to look resolute, but it was difficult when the rampant organ of which he had promised her so much was drooping so dismally. 'Look, love, it'll be all right later.'

'It had better be.' She groped across the floor for the scarlet and gold tissue lace thong she had bought specially, hiding it away from her husband, and discarding it with such a flourish only ten minutes ago. 'And this room. I mean. Pretty pictures and cute little table-mats. As bad as my Auntie Jessie's.'

'It's all clean enough.'

'Not exactly a luxury hotel, is it? No four-poster bed – for all the good that would be. No gold taps on the bath, or bottles of gorgeous shower gel. And no bottles of champagne cooling in an ice bucket.'

'You know darned well that would have been too risky. We might have bumped into . . . well, *anybody.*'

'Not likely to bump into anybody round here, I'll give you that.'

'That was the whole idea.'

'Was it? I thought the main idea was for you to—'

'It's all that nervous stress. All that business of getting orga-nized, and then worrying if we were being followed here, watching our backs.'

'I thought it was my front you usually had your eyes on.'

'Look, we've only been here a few hours. We need time to relax. And then it'll be marvellous. I'll show you.'

'You've already shown me. Three bloody goes, and so far nothing to make a song about.' As she wriggled the thong up over her ample, creamy thighs, she said: 'Be funny if Richard walked in now, wouldn't it?'

'No, it wouldn't bloody well be funny.'

'Finding he'd got nothing to be jealous of.' She bent to pick up the bra he had gropingly unfastened from her and tossed across the room in an echo of her own flourish with the thong. Dismally she put it back on again. 'Give him a hell of a laugh.'

Anna stood back and stared again at the half-finished painting on the easel. She was tired of rowan berries, bluebells, and clusters of thistles. Sales in the village shop were a welcome addition to her income, especially as Peter had left her nothing but a sprinkling of debts. Tourists couldn't get enough of her watercolours. But Anna was beginning to feel she had done more than enough of them.

Anyway, the light was fading and she would only make a mess of things if she struggled on. She washed her brushes and put them away, and looked out of the window up the long slope to the ridge.

The grass was all in shadow now, but the sky was still smudged yellow from a sun retiring in no great hurry beyond the hill. Clouds were streamers of charcoal grey, stretched out like long shreds of torn fabric across the fading glow. Even in the few moments it took her to move the easel back against the wall and finish the glass of spring water she kept on the old mantelpiece, the light had ebbed away except for a glint in the very top of that infernal mobile phone mast which had been stuck on the edge of the spruce plantation.

She wandered from her makeshift studio into the kitchen, wondered what to have for supper, and aimlessly went on into the sitting-room. She watched the first twenty minutes of a TV wildlife programme about Namibia. Towards the end of it there was an intrusive snuffling and barking which at first she thought must be part of the programme. It stopped; and then, after a few more minutes, there was a rapping on the kitchen door at the side of the house.

The moment she opened it, Cocky sprang in, yelping and wagging his tail.

19

'This dog has been scratching at our door. I thought the only thing to do was to bring it over to you.' The woman from Stables Cottage was already turning away as if she had grudgingly done what had to be done and was in no mood for conversation.

'Mrs . . . er . . . Maxwell, I'm so sorry. I don't know how he came to be running around here. He . . .'

The woman was on her way back into the cottage.

Cocky frisked about, leapt up at Anna, and did several brisk turns around the kitchen and into the sitting-room.

Anna groaned. Either Queenie had taken the dog for a walk – which was unlikely, at this time of the evening – and he had run off; or he had taken advantage of an open door to set out on a walk on his own. She phoned. No reply. Chet Brunner had presumably, as usual, called Alec and Queenie into the big house to listen to him holding forth on one of his crackpot schemes, to look at the bits and pieces he had summoned from Stuart, or to make suitable noises in what he liked to call his brainstorming sessions.

Anna could have got the Volvo out to take Cocky home. But it was not really worth that. She could do with getting out of here and out of herself for a little while. A pleasant evening, with only the faintest breeze. Might as well walk up, just as Stuart had done.

Cocky ought to have been able to find his own way home, but he enjoyed company. He liked showing off, chasing shadows of imaginary rabbits which he could never hope to catch, snuffling about in tufts of heather, and bouncing back for a word of approval. When he reached home, tired out, he would twitch in his sleep, in dreams which would allow him to catch every rabbit or hare that crossed his ken.

They climbed the gentle slope to the ridge, which spread out for their benefit a world of sudden different brightnesses. The moon was up, glinting on an inlet of the Solway Firth far to the south-west. All the windows of Balmuir Lodge on the other side of the ridge were lit up as if it were a luxury hotel at the height of the season. As Anna followed Cocky down the slope to the faint moonlit shimmer of the tiny loch which Brunner had converted into a swimming pool, a keener light in the sky might

20

have been a star or a satellite.

Cocky went rushing ahead as if determined to plunge into the pool, though he was more in the habit of standing on its edge and barking furiously at nothing whatsoever.

Anna whistled. He was going round the wrong way. The ground on the south side was spongy and led on to a tangled thicket. The footpath up to the wing where Peter's mother and father lived made a curve around the northern rim of the pool.

'Oh, for goodness' sake.' Anna hissed it under her breath, and then called more loudly. 'Come back here, Cocky.'

But Cocky was making a beeline for the little shed of changing cubicles at the water's edge. He whimpered, then backed away.

Anna peered into the confusing shimmer of light from the water and the lumpish shadows of the shed and an overhanging rowan tree. There was a dark shape crumpled under the overhang of the shed.

Anna took a cautious step forward, stooped, and tried to control her shuddering breath.

In films and television series, you could always laugh in anticipation of the heroine screaming at the sight of a dead body. Anna didn't laugh. She backed away. And she screamed.

3

The cruise liner slowed round the headland and dawdled even more slowly towards the quayside as if reluctant to return home after the halcyon days at sea. Then she seemed to take a deep breath and, with a sudden furious churning of water as her bows swung a few degrees towards the waterfront, the whole vessel shuddered like a child in a tantrum because the holidays were over. Passengers leaned on the rails and stared down at the men and cables below, waiting for the faint jolt of a nicely calculated contact. When it came, the figures below burst into well-practised activity.

Sir Nicholas Torrance put his arm round his wife. 'Well, back to reality.'

'That last fortnight was pretty real. As honeymoons go, it was quite something.' She kissed him.

'You've got terms of comparison? Previous honeymoons?'

'I've always thought the word was a silly one. Sickly and sentimental. But I've changed my mind.'

Even as messages began booming out through the speakers, they were reluctant to move away from the rail. Clinging to it was like clinging to the last, lingering, salty taste of the fjords and the mountains and the light of northern skies. At last they went down and stood by their luggage, waiting for the gangway to slot into place.

Lesley caught Nick's arm. 'Look! what did I tell you?'

'You've told me a lot of things. It's one of your more endearing habits.'

'That four-wheel drive down there. Thumping great thing. I told you there'd be something like that waiting for our booming fat friend.'

Every cruise ship has its blustering bore who wants to take over every social activity. This one had been no exception. And at that moment the very man came pushing his way through the cluster of passengers to position himself at the rail and start a wild tic-tac to the driver standing beside the car. A dark shape leapt and squirmed in the back.

'See?' said Lesley triumphantly. 'And a Doberman in the back, just the way I told you it'd be.'

'And *I've* told *you* that you're no longer in the fuzz. You're a lady now. And there's no such thing as promotion from Detective Inspector to Lady Chief Inspector.'

'Sorry. I really will have to stop looking at people and sizing them up.'

'Yes. I get a bit worried sometimes, the way you look at me as if you're trying to analyse possible criminal elements in my make-up.'

'Mm. Sexual maniac, perhaps. I can vouch for that. I don't think you've got the time for anything else. Not that I'm complaining.'

They moved forward into the crush of disembarkation.

Nick's Laguna was waiting in the corner of the ferry terminal car park: symbol of their return to normal things and places. They stacked their cases in the boot, took one last look at the hull of the ship glowing in the low, slanting sunlight of early evening, and then he turned the car along the waterfront to join a dual carriageway. Neither of them spoke until they turned off on to a road winding its way into the Ayrshire hills. Then Lesley said:

'I wonder how our conversion's going. Think they'll really be finished by next Friday?'

'Young Kerr didn't envisage any problems.'

'They never do, in the Borders. It's always "nae problem" – meaning that it's no problem to them whether they finish on time

24

or collapse from exhaustion halfway through.'

'All that police training has made you too pessimistic about your fellow human beings.'

'Yes, sir. Sorry, sir.'

Nick caught a last glimpse of the sea in his mirror as he passed a sign warning of a hidden dip. He felt relaxed and happy. All their plans had worked splendidly so far. They were happily married, the cruise had left on time and returned on time, and in between there had been some shore excursions which all went at a leisurely, sensibly timed pace. Back home at Black Knowe, the builders and decorators would be putting the finishing touches to the bedroom and to Lesley's new sitting-room and office. She would never have been content simply to be the laird's wife. She had turned down the offer of a transfer to the police Arts and Antiques section in order to marry him; but there was no way she could bear to let all her forensic expertise go to waste. She would advise all their friends and neighbours on care and main- tenance of their heirlooms and personal treasures; and on how to protect them. And the moment word got round that she was leav- ing her CID post, an alert publisher had commissioned a book from her on art and antique thefts, ways of guarding against burglars, and how the network of thieves, fences, and unscrupu- lous private collectors worked.

In the meantime, to break their return gently and give them time to unwind, there would be five nights in the secluded hotel which Nick had picked out of a glossy brochure.

He glanced at the dashboard clock. Nice timing. Another ten miles to go. Everything going to plan, just the way it should.

After another nine miles, with patches of woodland darkening to either side and then being stripped away again to reveal the shoulders of green-tufted hills, a rift of mist blurred the valley immediately ahead.

'Getting a bit murky,' said Lesley.

'No problem.'

'Nick, darling, please don't say that. It's tempting fate.'

'We're nearly there.'

The mist was tinged with puffs of blackness, and as they descended a shallow slope into it, the smell seeping into the car was that of burning.

They came suddenly into a pocket of clear air. Smoke drifted lazily around the offside of the car and behind it. Immediately ahead, the hotel came into view in its larch-ringed glade, with a burn sparkling its way towards a hump-backed bridge. Water from the burn had probably been used by the fire engine beyond the bridge in an attempt to quench the flames in the hotel. It had not been very successful. The flames were out, but all that remained was a smouldering shell, still puffing out little gusts and streamers like a reflective pipe smoker.

A huddle of people were sheltering under the trees. A man in a dark jacket and kilt was talking into a mobile phone, glancing apprehensively from time to time at the disconsolate guests.

Nick manoeuvred round the fire engine and wound his window down.

'Mr McVicar?'

'Aye.' The man had a black smear across his right cheek, and dark misery in his eyes.

'Nicholas Torrance. I had a booking for myself and my wife, but it looks as if—'

'Sir Nicholas? Lady Torrance?' Nick had to admire McVicar for the way he tried to look efficient and hospitable. 'Aye, sir, we were looking forward to welcoming ye. But ye can be seeing for y'self . . .' He looked over the bonnet of Nick's car, and for a moment appeared almost cheerful. 'Och, at last.'

A coach came bumping down the road, taking the bend towards the bridge cautiously. There was a murmur of relief from the huddle of guests.

McVicar said: 'Heaven be praised. At last. I've booked that coach, Sir Nicholas, to take guests without their own transport to another of our group's hotels in Troon. Splendid cuisine, and golf on your doorstep. Would you be wanting to make your own way there?'

'Wrong direction for us. Quite the opposite direction. But thanks. We'll find somewhere along the way.'

'If I could get my hands on our directory, I'd be phoning ahead on your behalf, Sir Nicholas. Anything I could do. But' – he waved at the gutted building – 'that's all gone up with the rest.'

Nick said: 'I think I remember a nice place somewhere north of Newton Stewart. We'll head in that direction.'

'On behalf of the company,' said McVicar, 'I must offer our apologies. Maybe when we've rebuilt, I could be sending you our new brochure?'

'You've got to hand it to him,' said Nick as he reversed, crept past the coach, and drove uphill towards the junction at the top. 'He does keep up his act no matter what. But now ... well, I'll have to try and remember the route down into Galloway.'

'No problem?' said Lesley slyly.

They had emerged from the thin pall of smoke, but an evening mist was seeping out of the clefts in the hills and along the line of a hidden burn. After fifteen minutes they arrived at a crossroads where the road ahead narrowed, but the roads to either side looked no more inviting. There was no signpost. Nick switched on the courtesy light and spread the road atlas across his and Lesley's knees.

She narrowed her eyes and tried to trace the route they had just come, but none of the names meant anything.

She said: 'We're lost, aren't we?'

'For the moment, yes. But we can't be far from ... well, somewhere.'

He switched on his headlights, and on impulse took the left turning. There were some nasty ruts in the road surface, and for several yards at one stage the offside front wheel was dragged into a long, deep channel. As they jolted free and approached a fork in the road, a signpost loomed out of the gathering dusk. It offered no identification to the left; but to the right its worn finger read: Balmuir.

'Good God,' said Nick. 'We're way off course.'

'You know where that place is – Balmuir?'

'Roughly. And I know who lives there.'

'Another member of the Lowland aristocracy?'

'Hardly. Chet Brunner.'

'Sorry, the name doesn't ring any bells.'

'An old acquaintance from the studio days. He's the one who sent us all those videos as a wedding present.'

Lesley remembered them. A lavishly packaged set of videos

27

of films and television series for which Nick had provided musical arrangements and in some cases conducted the recordings. Brunner's own name, she recalled, had been prominently displayed on the coloured cover of each episode. The name of Nick Torrance had been in a cluster of names of other contributors, all in small type.

'Maybe we could phone from there,' said Nick. 'Even if Chet's not there, someone must know of a hotel and a phone number – or know a road to Newton Stewart.'

'Chet? Weird name.'

'He was probably christened Charlie, but decided that Chet was more cool.'

'Is it wise to go and see him? You've been telling me to forget the years when I was a copper. Are you sure you're not wanting to have a great nostalgic blether about your own past – play it again, Nick, that sort of thing?'

'Nothing of the kind. He was never one of my favourite characters.'

But he was swinging the car down the road, past the signpost.

There had been no mileage given on the sign. Lesley peered into the gloom, trying absurdly to force the road to widen by staring at it, and to coax some sign of habitation from the darkness of the trees. It came almost as a personal triumph when she caught the glimmer of a few lights at the top of a rise, and then they were in a village street, passing a lumpy statue of some forgotten local poet or maybe a swashbuckling fighter of long ago. It was not a very large village, and apart from a scattering of faint lights behind the curtains of a single-storey terrace the main illumination was the moon high in the sky. But a mile or so beyond the end of the street was a splash of brightness from a large building set far back from the road. A pattern of windows flickered through the trees, sparked and dimmed, then blazed again as Nick slowed between two gateposts on to a long, gently curving driveway.

'Looks as if he's turned the place into a hotel,' Nick observed as he steered into the only gap in a long arc of parked cars.

Framed in the front doorway at the top of three broad steps, a small man peered out as Nick got out of the Laguna.

'You're a bit late. They've already started.' Then he came down the steps with his hand outstretched. 'Nick! What on earth . . . I had no idea . . .' Then: 'Oh, dear. Only it's Sir Nicholas now, isn't it?'

'Not to you, it isn't, Alec.'

Lesley got out to join her husband, still trying to come to terms with hearing herself greeted respectfully as Lady Torrance.

The couple who had booked into Stables Cottage had been sitting for an hour in front of the television without taking in anything of what was going on. As he heaved himself out of his chair, squashed yet another cigarette butt into the ashtray young Mrs Chisholm had reluctantly provided, and opened the cupboard to reach for a half empty bottle of whisky, his wife said:

'The way you're going at that, we'll have to go out tomorrow, even if only to the village shop.' When he opened the bottle and poured a large measure into a tumbler without replying, she went on: 'Ronnie, we do have to go out, you know, and size the place up. Isn't that why we came here?'

'It's not that easy. I . . . look, Martine, I haven't sorted it out in my mind yet.'

'But I thought you wanted to get out and get at him, after all that time cooped up. You said you were longing—'

'It'll take some getting used to. I need to weigh things up. Can't just walk up to his front door and say "I've come to shoot you in the guts, Brunner".'

'No, come to think of it, you usually gave the orders for someone else to do the violent bits. Shooting, drowning – or that little incident with the power drill. You *could* have organized someone to do it while you were still inside. Beginning to have doubts about coping on your own?'

'Look' – he tried his old confident growl, the way he had been when he swept her off her feet and took her away from that sod Brunner – 'all I need is time to get my breath back.'

'When it comes to breath, a breath of fresh air right now will do you more good than any more out of that bottle. Look, let's go out now. Just for ten minutes. It's getting good and dark. Even if anybody's out and about, they're not going to recognize us.'

Reluctantly he gulped the last drop from his glass and reached for his coat. Outside he paused, looking as if he might turn back and close the door on the evening air. He took her arm, not so much a gallant escort as a little boy afraid of the dark.

'Sure you don't want to pack up and forget the whole thing?' she said.

'Like hell. I'm going to get him. That's all I've been thinking of these past bloody years.'

'Well, then. Tomorrow we'll have a good walk round and check on the way this place is run, where he goes and when he'll be around. How you can get at him.'

'But if he sees us before I'm ready—'

'With that beard? You don't look anything like the way you used to. And me with this hair and everything?'

They crossed the stableyard and ventured slowly along a path which led past a few stunted bushes to the remains of what must have been a summerhouse, long abandoned. The way ahead was lit by the moon, before disappearing into the outskirts of woodland.

Suddenly a white shape floated out from the trees, swirling for a moment on the path ahead like a dancer wondering which step came next. Ronnie froze. In the moonlight a pale face heavily overlaid with makeup turned towards them.

'Oh, shit. You haven't seen me, right? And I haven't seen you. Spin it out, OK?'

Then she was gone.

Ronnie's grip tightened on Martine's arm. 'What the hell goes on here?'

Somewhere a dog barked. Then, from somewhere in the far shadows, there was a scream.

'What the hell was that?'

'An owl, or something,' said Martine.

'Do owls make noises like that?' He had always been a city lad and then a city hoodlum. The noises of the countryside were beyond him.

They stood very still, waiting for the next sound or apparition.

'There's no point in you bashing on at this time of night,' said Alec Chisholm. 'I know the place you mean near Newton Stewart, but you're way off course. Queenie and I can put you up reasonably well, and tomorrow I'll point you in the right direction.'

'We can't just drop in on you and cause all that bother,' said Lesley.

'It'll be a wonderful break for us. Talking over old times.'

'That's what Lesley's afraid of,' said Nick ruefully. 'She's got a sixth sense: she saw it coming.'

'All right, I'll promise not to reminisce.'

'But you'll bring me up to date with what Chet's up to. That at least I want to know.'

'You can probably get the drift of most of the scenario.'

They were grouped round the coffee table in a small sitting-room in what Nick guessed had once been the servants' wing, with Alec busying himself over filling sherry glasses for Nick and himself, and a tumbler of chilled fruit juice for Lesley.

Nick was shocked how Alec Chisholm had aged. All right, so it was quite a few years since they last met, but surely not enough to wear his features down quite so heavily. All the years of working for Brunner must have bitten their way into his skin and his mind. He had always had a flushed complexion and eyes with a faint droop, and bags under them like an amiable blood-hound. Now there were liverish spots across his forehead and into his receding hair, a few blotches beside his temples like dried scars. His once crisp little moustache looked faded and woolly. It remained an amiable face, but one carrying a weight of disillusion to which he probably never admitted.

Nick prompted him: 'This house, out in the wilds. Not the way one thinks of the Brunner image.'

'Used to be a hunting lodge, belonging to some absentee duke, and then a local bigwig who couldn't cope. Been tarted up since Chet bought it.'

There was a scampering of feet across the floor, and a breath-less greeting. Queenie seized Nick's arms, kissed him

31

extravagantly, and turned to spread her arms wide in front of Lesley as if measuring the width of a picture frame. 'But of course! Just how I guessed she would look. Nick always did have such exquisite taste. How wonderful to see you.'

Unlike her husband, Queenie had hardly aged. The only changes were, as they had always been, in the character she was playing at any given moment. When Alec met her, Queenie had been a small-part actress with an eager, pretty face, star material which never exploded into a nova. She relied for several years on a part in a long-running soap of which Alec had been long-term producer. In real life, depending on circumstances around her, she unselfconsciously slid into the part of Millamant, Mrs Danvers, or Lady Macbeth. You never knew whether you were going to be confronted by a reincarnation of Bette Davis or Betty Hutton. Wariness or unfamiliarity prevented her assuming the persona of any of the modern generation.

This evening, her entrance had suggested Madame Arcati from *Blithe Spirit*; but when Alec told her that the Torrances needed a bed for the night she was at once insistently hospitable, oozing the fussy motherliness of a Spring Byington.

'I'll just run off and make sure the place is decent. Leave you to Alec's tender mercies. Do give them another drink, Alec, and then show them round. Give me time to smarten things up.' She blew them a coy kiss, and fluttered away.

'She's always been wonderful at coping. I'd never have survived without her.' He stood up. 'Ready for a wander round? Or would you sooner stay put and relax?'

'I've always been one for the stately home conducted tour,' said Lesley.

Alec led them down a corridor and through a door opening on to a large hall. Four stags' heads looked down on them from the far wall, incongruously interspersed with huge framed photographs of movie stars and would-be stars, glamorous but all too soon forgotten. Crossing the floor of imitation mosaic, Alec opened a door into what in days gone by would have been called the smoking room, with leather armchairs and a large wine cabinet with a humidor on top. Beyond it was a library, lined with glass cases beyond which gleamed a regiment of leather bindings.

'Not quite Chet's scene, I'd have thought,' said Nick.

'One of his impulses. You know how he is. Decided you don't need to pay high rents to work in London. Nowadays you've got all the technical facilities to work from home – provided the home's big enough.'

'Big enough for his ego?'

Alec laughed with a touch of apprehension. Years of working with Brunner had worn him into a man always about to glance over his shoulder to check whether he was being overheard. He went on: 'Took the place over lock, stock, and barrel. And started making the interior look more like the sort of thing he was used to.' Alec shrugged. 'Won't last, of course. Next year it'll be another attempt to set up in Hollywood, or Bollywood, or trying to buy out Grundy, or something.'

They crossed a corridor and entered a large studio with a familiar paraphernalia of lights and the usual glass panel with, beyond it, what had once been a gun-room and now was a spread of mixing decks and microphones.

'And he still leaves it to you to pull all the threads together?' Nick cupped his palm under Lesley's elbow. 'The best of all trouble-shooters, Alec. Put him in charge of a live transmission, and he'll cut off interviewees when they become boring, then charm them afterwards so that nobody becomes uptight. And if it's a filmed episode, or a difficult bit of cross-cutting between recorded interviews and live interviews, he can juggle like you never saw. And when it comes to props, he knows every costumier and furniture dealer in the business.'

'And every starlet Chet wants to get his hands on,' said Alec dourly.

'Hasn't his wife got that under control yet? Martine, isn't it?'

'Was,' Alec corrected. 'Divorced now. Quite a story there. Got a new one now.' He sighed. 'I don't fancy this one will last, either. Rejoices in the name of Jilly-Jo.'

They moved on into a lounge with several separate tables, each equipped with four chairs and an array of glasses, some of them still half full of drinks of different colours.

'All those cars outside,' Nick ventured. 'But there doesn't seem to be anybody about.'

'Some of them hiding away upstairs, or out in the grounds, playing one of his games.'

'Games?'

'He throws weekend parties. Or longer than that, sometimes. Playing games with guests. Only it costs some of them a packet to get invited.'

'Wife swapping?' said Lesley with distaste.

'Oh, not necessarily. I mean, that may go on sometimes, but it's not on the main agenda. Just lately he's been keen on murder quizzes – runs parties called *Murdermind*. Often uses them as a basis for some television series he's trying to flog – pinches plot ideas without the poor mugs realizing what they're contributing for free. That's where he is right now. Everybody's playing a sort of glorified Whodunit, indoors and outdoors, using a whole range of clues to find the corpse.'

'Definitely not my scene,' said Lesley. 'Not any more.'

4

The corpse sat up. 'You're rather overdoing the screaming, aren't you? Now everybody will know where I am.' She ran a hand over her hair to make sure that it was still smooth and had not suffered from exposure to the night air. 'Still, I must say you're way ahead of the others. How did you figure it out?'

Anna tried to stop herself shaking. She was angry with herself for screaming like a stock character in a B movie; and angry with being put in this situation. She took it out on Cocky, grabbing him as he made a leaping, slithering circle around them, and growling a threat at him.

'Just what's going on?' she demanded.

'Aren't you in on it? I mean, I thought from the way you acted up just then—'

'No, I'm not in on it. But let me guess. One of Mr Brunner's ideas?'

'A game, yes. Called *Murdermind*. Great fun. You know what Chet's like.'

Yes, of course, thought Anna. She knew what Chet was like.

The young woman held out her hand. 'I'm Georgina Campbell. And where do you fit into things, if you're not part of the game?'

'I'm Anna Chisholm. From the home farm down there.'

'Chisholm? Alec's daughter?'

'Daughter-in-law.'

'Sweet man, Alec. Wonderful the way he copes with some of Chet's ideas. All that off-the-cuff stuff, and he never seems fazed.' She peered into Anna's face in the uncertain light. 'And your husband – Alec's son, that is . . . He's a farmer, then?'

'He's dead.'

'Oh, I'm so sorry. I really do make the most awful . . . I mean . . .'

The bright beam of a torch came wavering down the slope, and trapped both of them. Cocky began barking furiously as a hefty, blundering figure lurched towards them.

'So there you are. But Anna, I didn't know you were in on the act. Somebody trying to sabotage my carefully laid plots without me suspecting? Never thought it of you.'

'I'm sorry, Chet. I just seem to have stumbled into the drama without knowing.'

'You've certainly wrapped it up long before everyone had a chance to follow up their theories.'

When he put out his hand to help Georgina up, they leaned against one another for a few seconds longer than was necessary, with Brunner maybe off balance in more ways than one.

Georgina said: 'Couldn't I play possum again? Then you can discover me.'

With the torch beam lurching to and fro across her face like a searchlight scanning the skies, she smiled slyly at Brunner. Anna was familiar with this aspect of Chet Brunner, too. Something was going on between these two. And yet Georgina's carefully made-up but vacant face and the ostentatious thrust of her breasts didn't seem all that different from those of Brunner's current wife. Maybe he was physically or psychologically incapable of reacting to anything other than minor variations on the same theme.

Other voices were chattering in the distance. Members of the party came stumbling down the slope towards the light. One girl, pale as a sylph in the moonlight, cried: 'Somebody nearly spoilt it, but I dashed away before they really had a clue – how *is* it all going?' A middle-aged couple stood with their heads close together, apparently comparing notes.

'Too late to start again.' Brunner grimaced an exaggerated reproach at Anna. 'You know, I really will have to demand a forfeit from you one day, to make up for this.' The grimace became a wolfish grin, all the more sinister in the dithering light, but so automatic and well practised that it provoked no reaction whatsoever – except for a glare from Georgina. 'Come on up and deliver that mongrel back to its owner.' He set off with a masterful stride, marred by his right foot getting trapped in a tuft of grass and nearly bringing him down.

When they reached the house, Brunner took Georgina's arm and led her in through the main door. Anna headed towards the wing, Cocky eagerly bounding ahead of her.

'When you've dumped that fleabag,' Brunner called after her, 'come in and have a drink with this weekend's gaggle of sleuths. And I promise not to tell them all you're really the guilty party.'

Two people were talking to Alec and Queenie, but the moment Cocky came yelping through the door, Queenie broke away and rushed towards him, making glutinous noises over him. 'Where've you been, you *awful* little rascal? Frightening mummy like that.' Pummelling the dog's back, she looked up at Anna. 'I couldn't make out where he'd got to. Must have got out, but he doesn't usually . . . but anyway, I was going to come out after him . . . only then we had visitors, and I've been getting things ready.'

Alec said: 'Anna, an old friend's just showed up. Sir Nicholas Torrance. You must have heard me talk of Nick Torrance. And this is – er – Lady Torrance.'

'Lesley,' Nick Torrance corrected him gently.

Anna had read about Sir Nicholas and his historic tower above Kilstane in the Borders. There had been something about a music festival in one of the brochures she was showered with by tourist offices to leave in her cottages; and something in the papers, earlier this year, about a couple of murders.

Sir Nicholas was tall and had a lean, patrician face, his brow made higher by the way his thick, dark hair was swept back in a long mane. His handshake was firm, yet his whole attitude was relaxed and welcoming, as if he were at ease in his own home. His wife was a few inches shorter, her head coming just above his shoulder. She, too, seemed quite relaxed and self-possessed, yet at the same time trim, almost buttoned-up in a military fashion. It was difficult to imagine her slouching, or casually propping herself against the back of the settle nearby. Her smooth helmet of light brown hair could almost have been another item of austere uniform but for the skittish curls above her ears. She had a creamy complexion touched with an even flush of sunburn, and grey eyes whose disconcerting brightness was flecked with blue, as if reflecting sudden streaks of cloudless sky. When they turned towards her husband they gleamed with deep, confident love for him. Anna felt a pang of envy.

'Well, now.' Queenie had slipped into the role of efficient, bustling housewife. 'If you'd like to come and see your room, freshen up . . .'

There was a resounding thump as Brunner came striding in, bashing the edge of the baize door with his elbow. 'What's this I hear? Nick. Damn it, so it is. Only now it's Sir Nicholas, isn't it? Still making beautiful music, though? Especially with your beautiful bride? What a bloody marvellous surprise.'

Alec started explaining about them staying the night.

'But of course they'll be staying the night.' He boomed even louder. 'More than one night, if you can manage it.'

Queenie tried to cope with Cocky backing away from Brunner and clawing up her leg. 'I've just finished getting our spare room ready, and—'

'No way.' Brunner waved a contemptuous hand. 'Must have a proper suite in the main house. I'm sure Queenie would do her best to make you comfortable, but we'll have to do better than that. Can't have a fellow landowner slumming it in the servants' quarters, eh?' He slapped Queenie on the shoulder, which set Cocky off barking furiously. 'No offence, sweetie, eh? Just nip off and tell the chef there'll be two more hungry mouths for dinner, there's a love.'

Talking of a chef made it sound very grand, thought Anna. In fact the kitchen was run by a tough workaday cook from Glasgow with the help of a general dogsbody, both of them happy to work close to real film and telly people they could talk about to their friends and relations.

She saw the stiffening of Lesley Torrance's neck as Brunner took her arm and squeezed it as he led her away. Odd that in spite of the occasional lecherous wink and grin, he had never touched Anna in a way that would have that effect on her. She wasn't sure whether to be grateful or offended.

Nicholas Torrance's lip curled as he followed. The door swung shut behind them.

Queenie let out an odd little whimper which might almost have come from her dog. She ought to be used to Brunner's brash offensiveness by now. Alec was hardened to it; but Queenie, as Anna knew all too well, reacted to every slight. Her chattering, hospitable mood would soon give way to the brooding gloom of a Russian drama.

Alec squeezed her arm. A quite different squeeze from the sort Brunner inflicted on women. 'Less trouble for you, my dear. Don't have to worry about making up the bed now.' He had always been protective towards her, always the antidote to the spites and insults of life – even more so since her beloved Peter had died.

'I'd much rather they stayed with us than with him. Always taking over, shooting off his mouth without giving a thought to other people's feelings.'

'Yes, I know. We all know. But that's just the way he is.'

'One day,' Queenie intoned, staring straight ahead. 'One day . . .'

Lesley made polite noises as she was introduced to the crowd in what Brunner had already described with a flourish of his left arm as the banqueting hall, but she still could not entirely dismiss that inner self which had been Detective Inspector Gunn. She could not help sizing up the assembled characters, not making snap judgments yet instinctively slotting them into categories with which experience had made her familiar.

Voices ebbed and flowed, waves overlapping so that half-finished sentences were dragged away and then overlaid by ripples from a different direction.

'A pity it had to be cut off just as I was getting to grips with the clues . . .'

'Just what *did* that bit about the locked door and the icicle have to do with the poison cupboard?'

A middle-aged couple showed each other slips of card on

which they had scribbled notes, smiling and agreeing, then shaking their heads.

Abrupt and loud, a young man who had been standing alone nursing a tumbler of whisky said to nobody in particular: 'Maybe tomorrow we could try a whole new game. Of fraud.'

Brunner turned and glared. 'Too complicated. Ask any lawyer. No way you can simplify it dramatically.'

'You haven't usually found it too complicated.'

There was a shocked hush.

Brunner's face had gone very red. Then he uttered a booming laugh. 'Come off it, Harry. We don't like bad losers. In these games or any other.'

Hastily he drew a heavy-breasted girl in a low-cut silver gown towards Lesley and made a big show of introducing her as Georgina Campbell— 'One of the most promising of my protégées.' Georgina said 'Lady Torrance' and made a slight curtsey, accompanied by a supposedly roguish smirk to show she wasn't *that* impressed. Lesley categorized her as basically a tawdry but expensive tart on the make.

A pair of willowy young men were not as queer as they tried to make out, thinking this was the in thing. One woman with an afro hairdo that threatened to sag down one side of her brow headed for Lesley and gushed: 'But surely it was your husband who wrote that terrific backing track for dear Liam and Susie?' Others were putting on a big countryside act, yet failed to look authentic in their Barbours and tweeds, conflicting with two men who had opted for dinner jackets and one woman who must recently have been to an Edinburgh fashion show.

'We all looked smarter last night, didn't we?' Brunner made a booming apology. 'Had a Highland Ball. And games. No, not those sort of Highland Games. No caber tossing on my premises – don't want the china and glassware wrecked. This evening we'd started on a murder game. Clues galore. Unfortunately it was cut short by an intruder wrecking the plan.'

'But isn't that how most murder investigations turn out?' said Lesley. 'Thrown off course by the unexpected?'

'Aha! There speaks the expert. Still not shaken off the old uniform? No, sorry. Of course, CID – always slinking around in ordinary clothes, taking unsuspecting villains by surprise.' He spread his arms towards the gaggle of guests. 'Now, *there's* an idea. We have a real live detective, only recently retired, on the premises. Maybe tomorrow we can concoct another mystery, really authenticated by an expert?'

'You mean we have to sing for our supper?' said Nick.

'I can promise a good supper, don't worry. And maybe something else, if you're interested. You couldn't have shown up at a better time.' He put a stop to further introductions or general conversation by steering Nick away towards the huge baronial fireplace, far too big for what had once been only a hunting lodge. He did not invite Lesley to join them; but his inability to keep his voice down to a confidential level meant that she heard nearly every word. 'Don't want to let your talents rust just because you've acquired an ivory tower, eh? And it must cost a bit to keep places like that heated. Don't I know! I could put some work your way if you're interested.'

'What kind of work?'

'I've signed up a fabulous new group on a long recording contract. Don't really have time to concentrate on them as much as I ought to. Remember "Play Bach"?'

'Jacques Loussier?'

'That was the guy, yes. Well, these kids have got something way ahead of that. Right in the mood of the moment. Swinging Symphony Babes – you know, classical stuff but shaped to appeal to the kids. Smart kids, not just the punk brigade. Bach Blues, Fugueing the Beat, we'll dream up some titles. But although they're good, these kids don't know how to mix to get the right balance. They need someone who can tell them where to position themselves, where to point the fiddle, and everything, to make the mixing easier. Somebody at the control desk who knows good music and good sound from bad.'

'I haven't been in on that scene for a few years now.'

'Look, Nick, there's no way a musician like you could forget. And,' he intimated heavily again, 'you must need regular injections of cash to keep that castle of yours going. Come on, you don't have to feel embarrassed with me, old partner. We Lowland lairds have to stick together, haven't we?' In that

rumbling undertone which failed to be an undertone, he added:
'You inherited in a roundabout family way, old son. Me, I had to
work in a devious way for mine. But here we are, fellow quaf-
fers of the quaich.'

Lesley wished they had passed that turn-off and driven on
through the night to any other destination.

Anna kept to the path on the way down, with only the fitful
moon to guide her. But on the lower level were the reassuring
lights in both cottages. Two cars neatly parked in the slots at the
far end of the stableyard, exactly as specified in the brochure,
with the rear pointing outwards in order not to blast exhaust
fumes into the neat little flowerbeds. She wondered about the
couple in Stables Cottage, and what Maxwell had been in prison
for. If Stuart had been right about that. And the other two . . .
well, Covenanter's Cottage had a very comfortable bed. She
could only hope they wouldn't make too much of a mess in it.

Stop fretting! She had to keep telling herself that. Stuart, easygoing Stuart, was right when he accused her of twitching too
much over details and unfounded apprehensions. There were
times when she almost invited minor panics – created them,
went looking for trouble because that gave her something to
cope with, something to keep her from looking back, something
tangible to cope with instead of brooding over things which
could never now be altered.

There had been the occasional silly flicker of anticipation.
That young forestry researcher who had taken Stables Cottage
for two weeks, a few months ago, and been so easygoing and
chatty. Sharing a few meals with her and laughing and making
her laugh. Promising he would come back for a real holiday
instead of just working here. A bit of a daydream, like in some
dreadful woman's magazine. Wiping out Peter's betrayals, the
gruelling, repetitive work, the seedy atmosphere created by Chet
Brunner and his schemes. Wiping the whole slate clean so that
she could fall in love and head straight for a happy ending.

So corny. So pathetic, so utterly ridiculous.

On her own doorstep she had a sudden vision of Peter slam-
ming the car door and striding towards her. Just as she

sometimes remembered him on the corner by the village pub, both of them laughing about something ridiculous. Only there had also been corners where she remembered them quarrelling about money, about some sharp practice he had been up to, though the real reason behind it was her growing awareness of the situation with Stuart's wife.

Yet it was lonely without him. Better, maybe, to have some-one to quarrel with than have nobody around at all?

Of course there was Stuart around now, if she needed him.

She opened the front door and looked back across the yard. All as it ought to be. Both the present couples seemed to be in favour of peace and quiet and being left alone. Nothing to concern her. Quiet occupants. A pleasantly warm, tranquil evening. No problems.

Apart from the odd make-believe corpse. She must be careful not to trip over any more of those.

5

For two weeks they had been accustomed to the soothing sway of the ship, rocking them to sleep after Nick had rocked Lesley to ecstasy, and reflections from sea or fjord had sent a hypnotic rhythm across the ceiling. Now the sheer steadiness was unnatural, disturbing. Lesley had spent a restless night. Nick had woken in the small hours to realize that, although she was lying still in order not to disturb him, she was tensely wide awake.

'You all right?' he murmured.

'After all those nights at sea, I'm not used to a bed that stays still.'

'Shall I make it move, then?' He edged his left arm around her shoulders, and his right hand began to stroke her in a soothing rhythm. After a few minutes she was not soothed, but hungry. They made love, and she sighed, and murmured, 'Is it really going to keep getting better and better?' and turned over and went off to sleep. But around dawn he woke again, and she was staring at the ceiling as if willing it to rock and glow and lull her to sleep.

Unexpectedly, drowsily, she said: 'I like your friend Alec.'

'He was always a first-rate bloke to work with. Utterly reliable. And patient, no matter what happened.'

'He'd need to be, working for that slob.'

'You didn't take to Chet?'

'Did you expect me to? I know a crook when I see one.'

'Not exactly a crook. Just a smart operator. Came into his own when television franchises were fiddled about with in Thatcher's time and there were openings for little independent companies.

And cheapo films for the sex cinemas. Then all he had to do was talk bigger, and make the smut glossy instead of just tatty, Suddenly you're a cult figure. Begin to take yourself seriously. And get other people to take you seriously – and put up the money.'

'You mean you went along with him? Let him use you?'

'Never had to work with him when it didn't suit me.'

'I still say he's a crook.'

'Police intuition? Prejudice? Determined to secure a conviction at all costs? Poor old Chet – he doesn't stand a chance now.'

'You always want to believe the best of people, don't you?'

'While it's been your full-time job to believe the worst of them.'

Lesley propped herself up on one elbow. Nick looked up at her and marvelled at the smoothness of her bare shoulder in the light of dawn, the grace with which she invested even the awkward act of pushing herself up and then swinging her legs off the bed. She pulled the curtains back. Early morning sunshine fingered those shoulders and her hair.

'The sooner we get out of this place, the better.'

The room had some pseudo-Georgian panelling which suited its generous dimensions. Things which had been added did not suit at all: a print of a stag that Landseer would have been quick to disown, and a blown-up still from a costume drama with Vikings dashing up a beach towards a line of men in kilts.

'Not in the best of taste,' Nick agreed. 'And rather rich in anachronisms.'

She came back to bed and lay in his arms.

She yawned, contented. 'We can phone that hotel you mentioned, and be on our way.'

An hour later there were noises of people moving about downstairs, and the hiss of wheels on gravel as a delivery van came up the drive and went round the side of the house. Reluctantly they got up and dressed.

Breakfast was served in buffet fashion, from a long mahogany sideboard. There was a babble of argument from tables under the lights of a massive chandelier which Nick was sure he had seen in one of Chet Brunner's more extravagant costume dramas.

46

With its garishly coloured drops it had not clashed with the equally brash costumes in the film; but here it looked well out of place.

A voice rose from the far side of the room, taking up a theme that had been almost done to death at dinner the previous evening. 'If it hadn't been cut short by that young woman, whoever she was, I swear I'd have been there in no time at all. Cracked it before we'd even left the room. The heavy hints on the housekeeper's recipe from that magazine—'

'It was the bad grammar and handwriting in that phoney letter. I told you, didn't I. . . ?'

Nick and Lesley helped themselves from the array of chafing dishes, lifting lids to expose bacon, kidneys, tomatoes, and black pudding, quite different from the Scandinavian layout they had grown accustomed to. After filling their plates they looked round for an unoccupied table. The moment they found one, they were joined by the middle-aged couple they had seen fussing over their notes that previous evening.

'Of course you only arrived last night, didn't you?' The woman was plump and friendly, eager to make them feel at home but not pushy. 'We've been here from the beginning. A bit disappointing, here and there. My husband – oh, I'm Felicity and this is Edwin – he saw several flaws in the reasoning of the first game. He's a writer of detective stories himself. Edwin Godolphin, you know.'

They didn't know, but Lesley said: 'How interesting.'

'You know, of course, that Dorothy Sayers wrote one of her novels about the countryside not far from here?'

Nick nodded and finished a mouthful. 'Yes. *Five Red Herrings*, wasn't it?'

'They don't write stories like that any more.'

'They'd have difficulty. The whole plot depended on the trains running to time. When did that last happen?'

'Quite apart from the fact that most of that particular line was torn up long ago,' said Edwin, 'by order of the blessed Beeching.'

'Who is now,' contributed Lesley, 'busy stoking the fireboxes of Hell.'

Chet Brunner made his entrance. Nick would not have been surprised if some minion had been placed by the door to sound a fanfare. As it was, Brunner roared a 'Good morning, one and all,' and spread his arms as if to embrace the whole gathering. His hip jarred against the sideboard and set two dishes vibrating against each other as he helped himself to fruit juice and drew attention to his helping of corn flakes and prunes by booming, 'Got to keep the system moving, eh?' He turned his attention to Nick and Lesley. 'Newlyweds up so early?'

'Coming from you, that's rich.' The arch squeal came from Georgina Campbell, impatient to attract his attention. She was sprawled at a table for two, her hair artistically tousled and drooping a few blonde strands into the very open neck of her cerise pyjama suit, all suggesting she was still too drowsy to grope for its buttons. Nick did not need his wife's analytical expertise to assess the girl as the sort of blonde whose artless giggle and look of shy inability to deal with the hostile world around her would inevitably draw men eager to simplify things for her. In the end the men were probably more naïve than she, and incapable of realizing just how finely her sweet gaucheness was calculated. Even so, it was a calculation that might not always provide a rewarding total.

Brunner stooped to kiss her noisily, but scraped the spare chair away along the floor to insert it between Lesley and Nick.

'Sorry the wife's not here to say hello. Off on a jaunt to Glasgow, but she'll be back soon. Don't think you met her, did you, Nick?'

'I met Martine, but—'

'Oh, that's an old episode. Written out of the script, you might say.'

Trying to keep tabs on Chet Brunner's ex-wives and discarded mistresses was like trying to recite the exact chronological order of Elizabeth Taylor's husbands. Nick ventured: 'Things didn't work out that time?'

Brunner's fleshy face darkened. 'No, they didn't.' He forced a loud laugh. 'Don't think *you'll* be having any problems, though – you'll see to that, eh, Lady Torrance?' He put his hand on Lesley's arm. She slid it away on the pretext of reach-

48

ing for the water jug.

Nick said: 'You've got a phone directory, Chet?'

'A whole set of them in the library. Want to check that the ancestral establishment hasn't burnt down in your absence?'

'Actually we're having a lot of work done on the place while we're away. Converting a few rooms and bringing some ancient heating systems up to date.'

'I'm with you there, old lad. Can't burn disrespectful peasants over a slow fire any longer, right?'

'We were going to stay at a hotel back in Ayrshire last night, but that one was burnt down. I'd like to book ahead for a few nights before we see what they've done to Black Knowe.'

Brunner protested. 'Make yourself at home here for as long as you like. We've got a lot to talk about.' His smile at Lesley was one that Nick recognized from the past – radiating a friendly appeal, flattering, oozing calculated sincerity. 'You *could* spare him for an hour or two?'

'I do think we ought to move on.'

'Now, don't let him bully you. There's no hotel where you'll be able to relax as easily as you can here. And if I take up too much time twisting his arm into helping me out with a couple of new deals, then perhaps I can persuade you to have a share. You could help me plan a more authentic *Murdermind* session. Great to have a real sleuth laying down the law.'

Nick saw the distaste behind Lesley's polite smile. He got up. 'Chet, I really do need to make a few calls. I can probably do them from the car, but—'

'Like hell. If you insist on making them, you'll do it in comfort. I could get my trainee runner to put the call in and then bring the phone to you, if you like. All part of our room service.'

'I'm not quite too decrepit to handle a phone call myself, Chet.'

'Obviously not. Pretty obviously not, eh, Lady Torrance ... Lesley?' Brunner looked round and snapped his fingers. 'Jamie, show Sir Nicholas to the library. And point him towards the phone and the directories.'

Jamie was too obviously a village boy who did his best to keep the chafing dishes topped up, mop up any spillages, and run errands for guests who might all be famous TV stars – and if they weren't, that wouldn't affect the inflated tales he told to his awe-struck pals in the village.

Nick had not wanted to admit in front of Brunner that he had forgotten the name of the Galloway hotel he had in mind. It took him several minutes rooting through the business directory of the region before he tracked it down.

Only to find that it was fully booked for the next two nights. A major golf tournament was reaching a crucial point.

Sharon heaved herself dismally out of bed and reached for her bra and pants. Wally watched her as if the mere sight of them might tempt him into insisting that she take them off again. But the sight hadn't worked under the bedside lamp, and it wasn't showing signs of being any better in daylight.

He groped for words. 'Look, I'm sure that if we—'

'Oh, for heaven's sake, let's have breakfast and drive into the village or something. You suppose there's some wild swinging life there? Maybe there's a shop where they sell do-it-yourself books – like sex manuals.'

'It's Sunday.'

'Oh, Christ. A Scottish Sunday. D'you suppose we're allowed out without going to church or chapel or whatever? Let's risk it. Let's be daring and go for a walk. The scenery out there's got to be a whole lot more interesting than it is in here.'

They worked their way through Weetabix and then bacon and egg without exchanging a word except for Walter's faint moan over the fact that the yoke of his fried egg had broken and run over the plate instead of waiting for him to lever it into position over the fried bread. When they went out to the Honda and set off, Walter was silent again, driving grimly out of the yard and turning at random up a narrowing road into the woods. On one corner he had to swerve and bump on to the verge as a timber lorry came thundering out of a clearing.

'That's the most dramatic thing that's happened so far.' It was the first time Sharon had spoken since they set off.

'At any rate somebody's working. So much for the Scottish Sabbath.'

A mile further on, he had to stop while a tractor dragged felled logs across the road, stirring up a cloud of dust and fragments of bark. Larch and pine grew increasingly thick and dark along either side of the road, pressing in more and more closely. The break in the regiment of trees, when it came, was a shock. In the distance the sky was charcoal grey, sullen and threatening. But here, light streamed down from a blue sky, hazy yet dazzling on the curved end of a loch. Bright green grass on the fringes of the water became a shadowy green under a cluster of oak trees.

Walter stopped the car. When he opened the door, there was utter stillness outside. Not the faintest whisper of a breeze. Just a piny tang in the air.

'This is super. Let's get out for a few minutes.' He hurried round to open the passenger door, and watched Sharon's legs as she eased herself out.

They walked down to the water's edge. There was a damp warmth in the air, and the hills beyond the loch were swimming in faint smears of mauve and deep purple, shading gradually into that distant, ominous darkness.

'I didn't bring my suntan lotion out with me,' Sharon grumbled, heading back into the shade.

He came behind her, watching the swing of her bottom and the glint of sunlight on her calves.

'Sharon,' he said urgently. 'Sharon – stay right there.'

'What for?'

He pulled her round and dragged at her blouse, and she gasped at the speed with which he tackled her skirt. When he had dropped his own clothes on the grass as fast as he could manage, she stared down at him. 'Ooh, Wally, that's more like it.'

He advanced on her, and his hands wandered over her. They had done this several times since yesterday, without result. Now the greedy clutches of his fingers were the accompaniment to what he had promised and she had been waiting for. He kissed her, and their mouths opened. She tottered back a step, and as he forced himself closer she stumbled and fell over backwards on to the grass, half her body shadowed by the edge of the trees, one breast pale and cool and one glowing pink until he came down upon her and obscured them both.

51

Then she screamed. Not the way he had wanted her to scream. He reared up to look past her head, wondering if some hikers had come out of the forest. She wailed, and dragged herself free of him.

Then Walter screamed as well, loud enough to set a couple of crows flapping up from the depths of a larch.

What had come out into the open were not ramblers but midges from the rim of the loch, attacking, swirling and attacking again in their blood lust. Wally's briefly resurgent manhood shrank in pain and terror as he struggled into the protection of his trousers.

'Well,' said Chet Brunner, 'that settles it, doesn't it? Fate has decreed that you stay here and organize a few spectacular puzzles for us.'

He had led them into the studio and went on at length about the banks of equipment which Alec Chisholm had already summed up more succinctly. Brunner was fawningly seeking Nick's approval, promising to phone up a few musical friends who could get here at short notice and let Nick try his hand at a recording, just for the hell of it.

He winked at Lesley. 'Just to get him back in the fold, you know.'

And what kind of musicians would come running into this remote place so swiftly at Brunner's command? They'd hardly be rewarding types to work with, thought Nick. He remembered those young hopefuls or fading not-so-hopefuls who had come crawling to Brunner with their demo tapes and pathetic promises. One thing Chet Brunner was good at, though: sussing out any glimmer of a good idea in their amateurish material, dismissing them with a patronizing wave, and later adapting the one useful bit for his own ends.

There was a sudden ear-splitting howl above the roof, dragged out into a fading whine. Lesley had instinctively ducked, and somewhere along the corridor somebody dropped a tray.

'Bloody things,' Brunner snarled.

'Low-flying aircraft?'

'Always at it. Frightens every bloody animal and old lady for

52

miles around. And no warning. Had to call off shooting on a film I was hoping to set up. Every time we were ready for a take, two of the damned things would come scorching overhead.'

'A film?'

'Scotland's been all the rage in the States, you know. I was doing some trial shots for a big feature. Was going to call it *The Wolf of Badenoch*. Of course those ignorant bastards out west were lukewarm. How could they pronounce "Badenoch"? How would it play in Peoria?'

'Mm. I can see you'd have to change the title.'

'Might as well call it *The Wolf of Loch Ness* and turn it into a monster movie.'

There was a tap at the door. Alec Chisholm came in, waiting for Brunner's sentence to finish before delivering his message.

'There's been a call in the office. From the police.'

'Ah, the splendid Kyle and Carrick Constabulary. Wanting us to do another charity weekend for their funds? Or has somebody forgotten to renew my road fund tax for me?'

'Just to let you know,' said Alec levelly, 'that Waterman is out. They thought you ought to be warned.'

'Waterman?'

'Ronnie Waterman. The one you got put away on that true crime programme of yours in Birmingham. Five years ago, wasn't it?'

'Oh, him. I wouldn't have thought he was due out yet.'

'He wasn't. They'd shifted him into a resettlement prison where he could wait for some sort of board interview.'

'Resettlement board,' said Lesley. 'If they assess him favourably, they can pass a prisoner for supervised work in the community. If he behaves himself for four or five months, he can be passed for unsupervised work. Provided there's no breach of licence conditions.'

'Summing-up by an expert,' said Brunner. 'Fascinating.'

'But it seems he did breach the conditions,' said Alec, 'and scarpered. Couldn't wait to work out his time.'

'So now what?'

'The police can't offer you full-time surveillance—'

'Too busy nicking kids trying their first joint round the back of the bicycle shed. If they still have bicycle sheds nowadays.'

'But,' Alec went on, 'they'll be keeping an eye out for him.'

'Very public-spirited of 'em.'

'And they think you ought to do the same, after what he said when he got sent down.'

Lesley looked at Brunner. 'One of your games went wrong?'

'Not a game. A documentary about a crime syndicate in Brum. Very violent crowd. Time they got their comeuppance. A first-rate exposé.' Brunner smiled approval of his own brilliance. 'Fixed him. He'd been asking for it.'

'You make it sound almost personal.'

'It got that way in the end. After he thought he could walk off with my wife.' Brunner's face developed that dark, unhealthy flush again. 'That's what happened to Martine,' he said to Nick.

'When he was sentenced and taken away,' Alec explained very quietly, 'he yelled at Chet in court. Said he'd get him.'

'So he did.' Brunner seemed to be relishing the drama, as if it were a scene he had carefully shaped and placed in a crime series episode. 'I seem to remember the exact words were, "I'll get you, you bastard." Right?'

Lesley said: 'They all say something like that. Well, a lot of them do.'

'Thank you, Lady Torrance. More expert stuff.'

'Maybe,' said Alec even more quietly, 'some of them mean it.'

6

Opening the cupboard door produced a squeak and a rattle of glasses which echoed right through the cottage. Martine came hurrying in from the bathroom. Ronnie set the bottle down with a guilty thud on the tiny coffee table.

'It's empty,' he said.

'Not surprising, the way you've been at it. Now we'll have to go out. See what the village has to offer.'

'On a Sunday? Probably everything's shut.'

'We won't know if we don't go and check.' Martine went into the bedroom and began tidying her hair, pushing strands of its real colouring under the dyed ones. It was a declaration that she had every intention of going out right away.

Ronnie checked for the tenth time since they had arrived that the case in the bottom of the wardrobe was securely locked and the three-symbol code had not been jolted out of sequence. He fidgeted while Martine continued brushing her hair; and after a moment opened the case, unwrapped the handgun from the shirt which concealed it, wrapped it up again, closed the case. and set the lock again.

They both wore sunglasses as they got into the Escort – a bit of a comedown after the great days of Ronnie's cherished Jag.

A few cars were parked outside the squat brick church at the west end of the street. In England, the village inn and the church usually stood side by side. Here, The Carrick Arms was at the far end of the village from the granite church. Between them,

55

terraces of single-storey cottages on both sides of the road were broken in two places by two-storey buildings. One of them, a craft and souvenir shop, was closed but had a notice in the window saying OPEN SUNDAY 2 p.m. TO 5 p.m. Twenty yards down on the far side was a general store and post office with two metal advertisements on the pavement for ice cream and the lottery. The post office counter was closed, but three young women, each with a small child in tow, were edging between the cramped shelves of wrapped bread, tins of baked beans and spaghetti, and a cold cabinet.

Beside the narrow counter with its till were shelves tightly packed with canned beer, a few wines, and spirits.

Ronnie reached for a bottle of Bell's.

The middle-aged woman behind the counter tugged her blue overall straight as if to turn it into an official uniform, and said: 'I'm sorry, sir, but we can no' sell spirits on the Sabbath before twelve o'clock.'

'What time d'you close?'

'One o'clock. Open till six, weekdays.'

'And I suppose the pub's closed all day?'

'Och, no. Opens at twelve today. Eleven, weekdays.' Ronnie tried not to flinch as she peered at them. 'Ye'd no' be from these parts?' It was hardly a question.

'We're on holiday,' said Martine. 'Staying at one of the cottages down the road.'

'Och, that'd be Mrs Chisholm's wee place?'

'I suppose you see quite a lot of her.'

'She's often in the craft shop over yon. Got some interest in it, and in the workshop. Does come shopping here. But not always.' A note of accusation whined into the woman's voice. 'A lot of things she'd be getting from the supermarket in town. Just like them up at the Lodge.'

Ronnie drew a sharp breath, but let Martine do the talking. 'That'd be the big house, above the cottages?'

'Aye. Some of the parties they have there . . . too grand for us to do the supplying, ye ken. Gey queer goings-on there sometimes.'

'Queer?'

'Stupid treasure hunts, or something. Trampling all over the place. Playing hide and seek like a lot of squalling weans.'

An elderly man hobbled in, picked up a copy of *The Mail on Sunday*, and muttered, 'An' the usual, Vera.' She reached under the counter and produced a small twist of plastic round a knob of tobacco. 'There's a fine day it is.'

'It is that, Jamie.'

The ritual was quiet and obviously much practised.

The three mothers all decided at the same moment to head for the counter with their wire baskets. Each child made a grab for the bars of chocolate in a rack beside the till, and each was automatically slapped by the mother.

When they had racketed out into the Sunday somnolence of the street, Martine bought a loaf, a packet of crackers, a tinned steak-and-kidney pudding, and a jar of honey. As she was paying, Ronnie edged himself into a position from which he could see the main headlines and front-page stories of the newspapers spread out on their shelf. Any temptation to buy several and frisk through them to see if there was anything about a convict on the run was checked by the fear that gathering up a whole wad would somehow focus attention on him and lead to suspicious examination of those inner pages.

Martine was saying: 'In a place like this, the big house must be very important. The centre of local activity?'

'Och, no. Not the way it used to be when the Pitcairns had it. Then there was work at the Mains for a lot of the locals—'

'The Mains?'

'The home farm. Of course, that's still providing work, but only for the Chisholms. No more sheep or cattle on the estate any more.' There was nobody else in the shop. The woman seemed glad to talk to outsiders. Her locals would be as taciturn as the old man buying his paper and tobacco, or would simply swap local chat whose every syllable they knew by heart anyway. 'And that Mr Brunner, who took Balmuir Lodge over, he's a great one for inviting folk down for weekends and driving around too fast, but he takes no part in the village, the way the old colonel used to.'

Ronnie could restrain himself no longer. 'You don't see much

57

of him, then? He doesn't have much of a . . . well, a sort of routine?'

'That he doesnae.'

The rattle of the door opening cut the talk short. A woman and a younger man came in. Martine took a quick glance, and just as quickly turned away, scanning the shelves as if for something she had forgotten. Then she jerked her head towards the door, urging Ronnie to leave with her – and quickly. But the church clock struck noon, and his eyes turned towards the whisky on the shelf.

'Morning, Queenie,' the woman at the till was saying. 'Morning, Mr Morgan.'

'We're under orders,' said Queenie. 'Last minute flaps, as usual. His lordship wants a photograph of one of his bimbos framed and ready by this afternoon. Dragging poor Stuart out yet again.' She glanced at the young man with a malicious pretence of sympathy. Then she looked puzzled. 'Oh, dear. But what did we come in *here* for? I've forgotten.'

'He wants two *Sunday Telegraph*s.'

'Of course. Two *Sunday Telegraph*s, if you please, Vera.'

'We delivered him three not an hour ago.'

'And he moaned about them being late.'

'Late? And why d'ye think they were late? The wholesalers don't give a damn about us, way out here. Well, I know he got his *Telegraph*s and all of them wi' their supplements, because I folded them myself and our Andy delivered them along wi' the rest.'

'I know. But he wants two more.'

'Well, I'm sorry, dear, but we've no' got two more.'

Queenie Chisholm fussed down the narrow aisle with her head bobbing forward like an agitated hen. 'There's one here, anyway.'

'That's for Mr Greig. He'll be in for it any minute.'

'I could take it, and you could tell him you'd had a short delivery.'

'No, dear, I couldn't.'

'Queenie,' said her companion, 'let's forget it. I'll tell Chet he can have mine. We'll pick it up on the way. And that'll have to do him.'

'Always crawl to him, won't you?' Emerging from the parallel aisle, she came face to face with Martine, who hastily pretended to be reading the label on a pot of pickles. 'Oh . . . aren't you from one of my daughter-in-law's cottages? I didn't actually see you moving in, but when I was helping her move a few things I . . . er . . . no, I don't think we met.'

Ronnie said: 'Spot on. Maxwells, that's us. Robert and Mary Maxwell.'

'I'm sure we'll bump into one another while you're here. I'm often down there, helping poor dear Anna.' Abruptly, triggered by some random thought, she said: 'Really, you know, Mr Brunner's been good to all of us. I shouldn't really say what . . . I mean, I do owe him a lot. Wouldn't want anyone to think otherwise.'

Then she and her companion were gone.

The shopkeeper crumpled up a few receipts discarded on the counter. 'Puir thing. The way she gets pushed about. Anything that man wants from us – and that's rare enough, and never anything but trifles – he sends poor Mr Chisholm or his wife. As if they were servants. Can be difficult, sometimes, when she's in one of her scatty moods. You have to feel sorry for the twa o' them. Treats them shamefully. If it weren't for their daughter and her cottages, I wouldn't be surprised if they . . .' She broke off as a young man came in and picked up a *Sunday Herald*.

Ronnie took a bottle of Bell's from the shelf and set it down on the counter. She swiftly wrapped it into a plastic bag as if to make sure it didn't flaunt itself in the street, and said: 'If you're here for the week, mind how you drive. That Mr Brunner doesnae give a thought for anybody else on the road. Especially when he's coming back from fishing the Grey Loch. One day . . .' She was interrupted by another customer, but smiled as the new visitors turned towards the door. 'Enjoy your wee holiday, then. If there's anything ye need, ye ken where to come.'

They crossed the street to look idly in the craft shop window. Martine said: 'Christ. I hadn't thought about Queenie.'

'What about her?'

'I knew her, of course. From when I was married to bloody Chet. She and Alec being shoved around then, and it doesn't

59

sound as if much has altered.'

'She didn't recognize you?'

'I don't think so. She'd have said something. The way I look now' – she tried to catch her reflection in the shop window – 'no, I'm sure she didn't.'

Ronnie was glad to shrug it off. 'The pub'll be open.'

'You don't want to risk going in there, do you?'

'Like you said, if we're going to get anywhere, we have to get out and about. Find out that bastard's movements. And what people think of him. And there's no place like a pub.'

She took his arm. As they strolled along the narrow pavement, stumbling over a few cracked flags and gaps unevenly stuffed with gravel and tarmac, they could have been any affectionate middle-aged couple heading for their regular Sunday lunchtime glass.

At the door of The Carrick Arms Martine laughed. 'You never could stay out of a pub, could you?'

'I've done more useful business in pubs than . . .' He led the way into the public bar.

They were followed almost immediately by the young man who had accompanied Queenie into the shop. The landlord greeted him with a 'Morning, Stuart' while at the same time lifting a pint tankard from under the counter and beginning to pour.

'That bloody man.' Stuart reached gratefully for the beer. 'Anna, poor girl, mucked up one of his games last night, and now he's going to insist on rejigging it today. Wants me to frame a picture in ten minutes flat *and* cart up some extra props for this afternoon.'

'So they'll be wandering about the countryside again? A treasure hunt in their BMWs, this time?'

'God knows.'

Cautiously Ronnie leaned on the counter and tried to present himself as a flippant incomer. It might be riskier to attract attention by staying silent and unfriendly than to join in pub conversation the way he'd always done. 'Does that mean we'd better not go out for a quiet drive this afternoon?'

The landlord grinned. 'If you don't know the roads round here and take a wrong turning, you won't know just where and when he's likely to come bombing round a corner on the wrong side of the road.'

'Save excursions till the end of the week, then?'

'Maybe not that long,' said Stuart. 'This little lot's supposed to wrap up on Wednesday.'

'Beating the bounds to impress his cronies?' The landlord was happy to explain, with a cynical growl, to his new customers. 'Inventing what's called an ancient tradition, of riding out and beating the bounds. Only you don't have to do it every few months – except to put on an act before your paying guests.'

Martine was tugging at Ronnie's elbow, afraid that the pub atmosphere might be restoring his old pushy self-confidence too swiftly.

Stuart and the landlord edged towards the far end of the bar. 'Anyway,' Stuart was saying, 'at the very least he'll put on his lumberjack shirt and wellies, and go clomping his way round his estate to see if they've left any litter. Sort of beating the bounds, only without any entourage – the one thing he seems to enjoy doing for himself instead of letting anyone else do it. Always the same route.'

'Like taking the dog for a walk.'

'Only he's never had the patience to train a dog.'

On their drive back, Martine said: 'We don't seem to have found anything useful.'

'I wouldn't say that. We're beginning to get the hang of his movements.'

'Most of those are indoors, except for him doing a wander when he's got rid of his guests.'

'Yeah. After playing his stupid bloody murder games. Making a joke of it. After what I went through because of his other silly games on the telly.'

'Maybe,' said Martine, 'he'd appreciate the irony of being a real murder victim himself?'

The bell over the door of the craft shop jangled as Anna pushed it open, to find Brenda leafing through a catalogue of Christmas cards.

'A bit early in the year, isn't it?'

'If I don't do it now, there'll be all sorts of excuses for non-availability and all that sort of talk.'

The bell jangled again. Stuart said: 'Oh, great. Saw the old wagon outside. Queenie seems to have walked out on me, and I was wondering how I was going to get things up to Cecil B. de Mille. Any chance of a lift?'

'I'll be going back in a few minutes. Drop you off.'

'I'll go round and bring the bits out.'

When he had gone, Brenda said: 'And what are *you* intending to carry off?'

'Nothing special. Just that I want to borrow your Local Craft Trail Directory. I want to check we've got the up-to-date autumn opening times and phone numbers in the information folder we leave in the cottages.'

Brenda fished the book out from under the counter, and reached for a ballpoint. She flipped over a few pages and struck out an entry. 'The potter up the glen has just packed it in.'

'Not enough passing trade?'

'Some of it went past too quickly. One customer took the puir wee man's wife awa' with him. Maybe he's gone after them. Anyway, he's shut up shop.'

Anna put the directory under her arm and went out to the car. Stuart was only a couple of minutes behind her, with a framed picture wrapped in sacking under his left arm and a large leather bag in his right hand.

'A painting?' said Anna, curious. 'Something olde-worlde to embellish the walls of the Lodge?'

'Don't worry. No competition with your rural scenes. Just a framed photograph of Georgina whatsername.'

'Oh, *that* one. I wonder what Jilly-Jo will have to say when she gets back?'

As she drove out of the village, Anna was aware of Stuart glancing at her, as if wondering whether to make some advance, say something that would lead somewhere. She began to talk quickly. 'He's got a nerve, our friend Brunner, dragging you out yesterday and now again today, just on some whim.'

'That's the way he is.'

'You give in too easily.'

'And what about you? When did you last put your foot down and threaten to walk out? Leaving poor old Alec and Queenie to his tender mercies?'

'They're not really my concern. I mean, I've got good reason to be fond of Alec, but they *have* been working for him all these years. Long before I came on the scene and married into the family. They know what the score is.'

'Do they? And do you? Wouldn't it affect all of you if Brunner decided to pack it in here? Without bothering to let anyone know until the last minute?'

The Volvo swerved and sent up a flurry of grit from the road-side. Anna corrected it and stared firmly at the road ahead. 'You've heard something?'

'Through my own little grapevine, which may be warped. Just a hint that he's been talking of putting the Balmuir estate – including the lease of your cottages – on the market. Just to see what price he might get from some entrepreneur interested in laying out a golf course and a luxury hotel, getting his hands on fishing rights on the loch, and all the rest of it. And a lot of the stuff I've made for him recently hasn't been for use on the premises. It's all gone direct to a production company back in London.'

'I see. Moving on again?'

'It's only hearsay, but there's a fair old whiff of it about. Might be an idea if *we* moved on ahead of him. The two of us. If we—'

'No, Stuart. Let's not get into any complications. No need to panic yet.'

'But when we do decide to panic?'

'In spite of everything, we all owe the old bastard quite a lot. I don't know what would have happened if he hadn't ... I mean ...' She floundered. Perhaps if Brunner hadn't been there behind Alec, and Alec hadn't been there behind Peter and herself, might things have been better in the long run? Might two people now dead still have been alive?

*

63

Stuart Morgan and Peter Chisholm had supported one another through the chilly rigours of school life at Gordonstoun, and could never entirely break away from each other afterwards. They would not have dreamt of attending school reunions or subscribing towards appeals or old boys' newsletters; but somehow they found excuses for meeting in Edinburgh, displaying a succession of girl friends for approval or otherwise, and exchanging letters about business projects.

Stuart's flair was for the painstaking restoration of antique furniture and small, delicate *objets d'art*. He worked, adequately paid but in an uninspiring groove, for a firm specializing in reproduction furniture, sold through major stores in Scotland and northern England. Even in routine jobs he was a dedicated craftsman – fussy, even.

Peter, as Anna discovered within a short time of being married to him, was by nature a dabbler. He had been a glib, charming courier in a holiday tours firm; public relations officer for a small hotel chain; and finally a supplier of props to the film and television production company for which his father worked.

From time to time the two friends had talked vaguely of getting together on a permanent basis one day and setting up a high quality workshop of their own, with Stuart concentrating on the creative side and Peter handling the commercial and promotional end. A lot of talk, and all of it tapering off when Peter found some other brief obsession.

After the two of them married – Peter first, Stuart three months later – the Chisholms moved out of Edinburgh and into the grey-green fells and glens of Carrick. Still the friendship was not broken. The Chisholms spent long weekends in Edinburgh with the Morgans, and the Morgans were given free holidays in one of the cottages at Balmuir Mains.

It was largely because of Peter's father that Anna found herself running the self-catering cottages and craft shop, at first with Peter, and now on her own. Alec Chisholm had used his influence with his employer in the big house to get them possession of what had been the Mains – the old home farm house and outbuildings. He helped out with a loan towards the cost of turning the stable block and barn into self-catering cottages.

Sometimes she let herself wonder whether the whole idea had been a bad one from the start. They all, at one remove or other, owed too much to the unpredictable Chet Brunner, and he was happy to keep them aware of it. And there were too many awkward people to deal with, soothe, pander to, sweep up after . . . and, in the end, too many personal problems. Peter's temper snapped more easily than her own; and he grew too easily bored with the day-to-day running of anything.

One autumn evening while the Morgans were staying with them, Stuart ran over a cyclist, who lost one arm as a result and suffered severe brain damage from the impact. The police breathalyser and urine test showed him to be more than twice over the limit. Stuart pleaded guilty to driving dangerously while under the influence of drink. The only mitigation he offered, apart from that admission, was that he and his wife had been arguing and that he had allowed himself to take his eyes off the road. Carol Morgan confirmed this, though neither of them wished to go into any detail about the argument. Stuart expressed deep regret about the injuries to the young cyclist. He was sentenced to two years in prison, a fine of two thousand pounds, and banned from driving for five years.

He was released from prison after eighteen months. In his absence from the furniture company he had been replaced, and it was made clear that he would not be welcome back.

His old friend Peter insisted that of course he and Anna must come to the rescue.

There was a workshop behind the craft shop in Balmuir village, and a flat above it. Peter had used the workshop mainly as a store-room for sorting out things for the shop and doing odd little deals to round up props for Balmuir Productions, based in the big house above its one-time farm. Now he was insistent that his old mate Stuart and Stuart's wife should leave Edinburgh and move into the flat, and Stuart should have the use of the workshop.

Through Peter's father, Stuart was fed enough commissions for film and television set design and construction to support his own creative work. And Peter was only too glad to handle the business side of all this on his friend's behalf.

It was only later that Anna cringed at her own gullibility. Wasn't Peter's eagerness not just part of the old pals' act but also had an element of guilt feeling? Guilt because in Stuart's enforced absence, Peter had been going frequently to Edinburgh and having it off with poor, lonely Carol Morgan. Had it in fact all begun before that, and could that have been what Stuart and Carol were arguing about, the evening of the accident?

And with Stuart temporarily out of the way, how tempting it had been to have her on her own in Edinburgh, needing sympathy.

After Stuart's release and their move into the workshop flat, Carol was conveniently even closer. Then came the second crash. Again Carol was involved, this time not in the car with her husband but with Peter. And this time there were no court appearances save for witnesses at the coroner's inquest. Both had been killed outright when Peter's Astra came off the road on the way back from Girvan.

And what had they been doing in Girvan? In which sleazy hotel?

The past was suddenly so vivid and immediate that Anna had to blink away the pictures that blurred her view of the road, and slow down while she dragged herself back into the present and headed for the solid reality of Balmuir Lodge.

If Brunner really was going to leave, he was bound to take the indispensable Alec with him. But what about the rest of them?

'If we're going to get chucked out in the cold,' Stuart was saying in the seat beside her, 'we may as well keep each other warm.'

Anna swung in behind the wing allocated to Alec and Queenie. 'Tradesmen's entrance,' she said, getting quickly out of the car and opening the side door of the house so that Stuart could lug his bits and pieces in.

Lesley Torrance was in the small side lobby, chatting to Alec. She nodded politely and glanced at the items Stuart was taking out of his bag and lining up on the shelf just inside the door. Suddenly something caught her eye. She leaned over the small box with elaborate marquetry in its lid.

'That's a nice piece. It's one of those trick cigarette boxes, isn't it? Russian, beginning of the century?'

'A copy,' said Stuart. 'All my own work,' he added, his voice unusually shrill and would-be facetious.

Anna wondered if he was sensitive about the quality of his craftsmanship, and sensing some sneer from an expert like Lesley Torrance, which she had surely never intended.

'A copy? There aren't many originals left.'

'Chet saw one in an exhibition somewhere, and of course it was just what he wanted for some gimmick in one of his murder games. Fortunately I had a print of it from somewhere.'

He snatched up the box and another small wooden carving, and hurried off through the connecting door into the hall. Anna followed, with Lesley on her heels. As if he had been waiting for an audience to appreciate his thunderous entrance, Chet Brunner stormed in on his way from the phone. He was wearing bright blue slacks and a gaudy Hawaiian shirt, one hairy brown arm displaying a gold torc, the other a Rolex watch.

'Stupid bloody woman. She's done it again. Pranged it again.'

They waited, silent, for him to deliver his next line. 'Jilly-Jo. Stupid bitch. Pranged the Merc again. But this time I've no intention of driving all the way to Glasgow to fetch her. I've told her to find her way to the station and catch a train.' He looked past the two women, and bellowed over their shoulders. 'Alec, you there? Look, take the Alfa and pick her up at Brawhill, there's a good fellow.'

'A train?' said Anna. 'On a Sunday?'

Alec came through the door. 'There are only the two now, I think.'

'All right, check on it before you go. She's got plenty of time to catch that one that gets to Brawhill around five o'clock. We've picked guests up there before now.'

'But—'

Brunner cut him short, and when Stuart came through to say he had brought the things required, Brunner waved him aside, too. 'Oh, dump them somewhere, I'll get round to them later.'

There was a small knot of guests in the far corner of the hall, two of them sitting down and making desultory stabs at a Sunday crossword. A few others looked at a loose end, vaguely resentful. Georgina and an awkwardly worshipful middle-aged man were drinking after-lunch coffee which must be thoroughly chilled by now.

Mr and Mrs Godolphin crossed the floor arm in arm, like partners about to embark on some old-time dancing the moment the music started.

Felicity Godolphin said plaintively: 'Mr Brunner, we did think you'd have another little mystery for us by now.'

'What? Oh, of course. Look, let me have a look at a few props, and we'll get down to another session just as soon as . . . well, let's say half an hour from now.'

Anna wondered how anyone could fail to see that he had completely lost interest in this particular line, and was now thrown off course by other ideas rolling across his mind. Had Stuart's rumours been well founded?

Suddenly it began to grow darker outside – a darkness that came seeping into the room like a black flood under and around the window frames. There was a distant roll of thunder, then a loud clap much closer. After a long moment's gap of stillness there came a faint hiss which exploded into a wild lashing of rain against the window.

'Oh, hell, that does it.' Brunner looked almost cheerful. This was a perfect excuse for him to drop any idea of outdoor activities. 'That really messes up what I had in mind. Quite impossible in this weather.' Another great drum-roll of thunder hammered into the room. 'That's the trouble with Scotland, you know. Can't rely on the weather. Mucked up more than one of my film projects.'

'It's a wonder you don't pack up and leave.' It was the dry resentful voice of young Harry Jardine, whose willingness to attend these games had baffled Anna from the start.

'Love to see me out of the way, Harry?' Brunner spread his arms as if to draw all his guests into a jolly embrace. 'Well, this settles it. I tell you what we'll do. I'll show you a true crime story. The real thing. The video of one of my most successful campaigns. And I'd appreciate your comments afterwards.'

Anna and Lesley Torrance exchanged glances. Anna was sure that the same thought had occurred to both of them. Having been told that Ronnie Waterman was on the loose, Brunner wanted to defy him, re-live his old triumph, reassure himself and a captive audience that he was still top dog.

'Lesley, you've never seen the sort of thing Nick and I used to produce together, have you?' He spread his arms again to encompass the rest of the party. 'Such distinguished guests to add to the distinguished guests I've already assembled, hey? I think they should have the privilege of sharing the memories of our collaboration, eh, Nick?'

'If it's the Waterman tape you're going to show,' said Nick Torrance, 'I didn't provide the backing music for that.'

'Didn't you? Oh, hell, so you didn't. But anyway it gives a pretty good idea of the general shape of things we sewed together, between us.'

Before anyone could object, he began shepherding them into the viewing room beyond the library.

The video was one of a series. It reminded Anna of a success-ful TV real crime series which had run for years. But then, that was Brunner's forte – like his *Murdermind* series on the screen and his adaptation of the format here for his paying guests, and a brief series he had recently produced about restoring antiques and faking them. Taking somebody else's existing success and twisting it to his own ends. Never too close to risk any action for copyright infringement. There had been his Financial Boom and Bust series, spin-offs from which had been a big success in the States and in Germany. Alec had wearily told her of so many shabby operations of this kind.

'Poor little Waterman,' Brunner was booming. 'Thought he was such a big shot in his day. Reckoned without me, though.' As the room lights dimmed, he added: 'I don't think the poor little shit carries any clout any more.'

Letters swirling on to the screen formed themselves into a name filling the entire space: BRUNNER PRODUCTIONS INTERNATIONAL. Another roll of thunder outside was over-powered by thundering drumbeats, and then a tattoo of gunshots.

Chet Brunner looked proudly along the row of faces in his audience, silently exhorting them to be impressed by what they saw and heard.

7

Nick was aware of a faint sniffle of contempt every few minutes from Lesley, beside him. He would not have been surprised if she had interrupted the screening with a complaint about unethical procedures or downright implausibilities. He could sense every twitch of her professional outrage at trivial errors in Brunner's behaviour and presentation. She would probably have been outraged even more if he had explained to her that the medium of television was designed not for presenting complex facts but for dramatic simplification and distortion to hammer home points the producer wanted to make.

Not that there ought to have been any need for distortion in the Ronnie Waterman story. It was sensational enough in itself to satisfy the most bloodthirsty viewer.

Ronnie Waterman had started out as a small-time crook in Birmingham but expanded his activities through contacts in Newcastle and Edinburgh. For a while he specialized in dodgy motor cars, and then took a step up in the world by providing getaway vehicles for bank and post office robbers, and heftier material for ram-raiders. In his programme, one of a series called *Villains Versus Victims*, whose concept owed a lot to a more soberly researched and presented BBC series, Brunner alternated dramatized, souped-up episodes with newsreel and specially filmed shots of Waterman and his cronies captured on film in different settings – some innocent on the surface, some as he was on his way towards a police court or emerging from one, grinning.

It became clear that Waterman had a taste for violence. Footage of a warehouse blaze in Birmingham was linked with a battle with another rival. No accusations had stuck at the time, but evidence at Waterman's later trial confirmed it as the work of two of his henchmen.

A number of beatings up and two murders, heavily over-done in Brunner's programme, were never pinned on Ronnie himself. But Brunner, sharing a Box-and-Cox commentary with a supposed detective, unravelled some threads and pulled others together. Suggestive vignettes of Ronnie in a notorious casino faded into a 'talking head' of Ronnie in a boastful interview, superimposed upon the scene of two battered corpses in a back alley. Without praising himself too crudely, Brunner's slant on events made clear to the audience his courage and determination in following the crook, at grave risk to his own life, until the villain could be finally brought to justice.

'And wait for this next shot.' It was Brunner, live, in the room here and now, overriding his own voice from the screen. 'Really hammers it home.'

There was an interview with a woman whose face had been smashed in because her husband had set up as one of Ronnie's rivals. The close-up gloated over the hideous injuries.

'Caused a hell of a fuss, that shot. The station wanted it cut out. Scared of letters of complaint from the public. But I held my ground. By this time I was going to show him for what he was, and damn the consequences.'

There was a swift montage of newsreel material about prosti-tutes in Leith, car chases up the M1, and a mocked-up gunfight in a back alley, with close-ups of blood splashes up the wall. 'But the net was closing in,' intoned the actor playing a detec-tive. Background music exploded through a swift crescendo to a blaring brass discord.

At this halfway point, where there was obviously a break for a commercial, Brunner switched off and called out across the room: 'Any questions?'

There were a few self-conscious rustling and mutterings. At last Mrs Godolphin piped up: 'What kept you going, taking all those risks? Weren't you ever afraid you might be the next victim?'

It was just the sort of question Brunner could have written into the script. He coughed modestly, and pretended to be reluctant to answer.

'When you get your teeth into a story,' he said at last, 'you just have to keep going. You can think only of working it all out, getting at the truth, and the hell with any risks you may be taking.'

No mention of Martine as the trigger, thought Nick.

Beside him, his wife said: 'The music. It's far too intrusive. Far too loud.'

It was only now that the sound track had stopped that Nick realized the steady background roar of the rain had also slackened, dwindling to a whispering trickle from the gutters, down the windows.

'It's that sort of thing that kept your husband in wine and caviare, Lady Torrance, before he became landed gentry.'

'Not that sort of thing,' said Nick. 'And certainly not my handiwork in that programme. That was well after my time.'

'So it was.'

'And I never let my stuff be chopped up and recycled in over-amplified chunks like that.'

Brunner laughed too loudly and was about to set the video off again when Queenie came in, bustling nervously towards him.

'There's word from Alec, Chet. At Brawhill. Says Mrs Brunner wasn't on the train.'

'Managed to miss *that*, as well as pranging the . . . oh, what the hell. Tell him to wait for the next one.'

'Alec says he's decided to do that anyway.'

'No problem, then.'

In the semi-darkness Georgina Campbell was heard laughing breathlessly for no apparent reason.

Queenie had turned back towards the door when Brunner said: 'Hold it, Queenie, love. I've just remembered, this next scene has you eating your heart out. Remember? Don't go – sit yourself down. And everybody' – he had put on the frenetic voice of a game show compère – 'just watch this. Queenie at her most characteristic. What I always think of as one of her soubrette rôles. Such a lovely old-fashioned word, isn't it?'

Reluctantly, looking apprehensive, Queenie sat on the edge of a chair at the end of the nearest row.

One of the dramatized sections, with a subtitle identifying it as a *Reconstruction*, included two young actors and Queenie as a bed-and-breakfast house proprietor in Stranraer whose son had fallen in with one of the Northern Irish lorry drivers. She was suspicious of the driver's attempts to get the young man to give him some help with storing a fragile consignment he had been lumbered with at the last minute. Delivering it meant going miles off his usual route, but one of his mates would be along next day, heading that way, and could pick it up for him. Perhaps the lad could collect it and keep it in, maybe, Mrs Black's little storeroom.

'We'd make it worth your while. Save us a lot of trouble.'

Queenie played the dithering, suspicious yet susceptible mother. She fluttered across the screen, wept at one stage, and then laughed archly at the Irishman's leg-pulling. And Brunner, off screen, laughed. 'Nicely done, Queenie. See what I mean by a soubrette? Expecting you to do a song and dance any minute. One of your most characteristic performances. All that twitching and twittering. Type casting, eh?'

The scene was unconvincing, mainly because it was so neatly acted and rounded off. Real life, shown in fits and starts, snippets from handheld news cameras and truncated interviews, was erratic and unrehearsed.

'They say all roads lead to Rome,' came the sonorous declamation on the sound track, 'but it gradually became clear that these roads were leading towards Stranraer.'

There was a display of graphics tilted at various angles, as supposedly seen from the cab of a lorry belting along the A66, falling in alongside one heading north on the M6, passing Carlisle and then heading for the A75 and the port of Stranraer.

At the same time two lorries were coming off the boat for which the others were heading. The audience was left in the dark as to which movements were more relevant to the plot.

Waterman, it turned out, was in personal charge of this operation. In the early stages he was tracked by one of Brunner's hirelings with a concealed camera – one who really took risks, thought Nick. It was a protracted scam involving shipments of drugs to finance the Northern Irish gangs and fanatical religious cliques operating via Stranraer. Two Irish trucks coming off the ferry and heading for Newcastle were turned down a diversion swiftly set up off the A75. One of the truck drivers was in on the hijacking. The other and his mate weren't, and put up a fight.

Nick wondered uneasily whether the whole set-up had been planned more by Chet Brunner, fired by a rage for revenge over Waterman's theft of Martine, than by Ronnie Waterman himself. The speed with which Brunner's team got to the scene and did their own photography, ready for dramatic reconstruction later, was suspicious.

As if reading his thoughts, Brunner said above the heads of the audience: 'The police got quite peevish about us being so quick off the mark. But if we hadn't been regularly supplying them with our findings about Waterman, they might never have been able to pounce on him.'

And how long had Brunner had to wait, Nick wondered, and what risks did he expose his team to, until he could be sure Waterman himself was in on this heist and in violent mood?

In court, all those involved tried to switch blame to the others. But whichever of the hijackers shot one of the drivers through the head, there was no question that Waterman was in charge and had given the orders to kill.

An out-of-focus face swam up out of a grey smear on the screen. It was a hazy close-up of Ronnie Waterman with his head down, defeated but twisted with rage. Shadows across the lower half of his face darkened the expression and, as he moved, seemed to add a wispy beard to his chin.

Queenie gasped suddenly. As the credits rolled, again with Chet Brunner's name in large lettering, she slid from her seat and grabbed his arm.

'Oh, dear. How could I . . . oh, I ought to have realized. How could I have been so silly?'

The lights went up. Some of the audience were making polite complimentary remarks to Brunner. Others looked peevish. They had not come here to sit through a self-congratulatory film show.

Georgina Campbell moved in and brushed against Brunner. 'Sorry your wife's been delayed. And in such awful weather, too.'

Nick, standing up, saw Queenie almost thrust the girl out of the way and edge Brunner to one side. The fluttering was gone. She looked frightened and intense. 'You've got to listen to me.'

'I was only joking about you, back there. Come on, old girl, you know me by now.'

'It's serious. There's something you've got to know. Before it's too late.'

'What the hell. . . ?'

The general buzz of conversation drowned them out. Nick heard no more as Queenie took Brunner's arm, almost dragging him towards the door through to her own quarters. Georgina watched, not sure whether to laugh or protest. But Queenie was surely not a serious rival.

Young Harry Pitcairn's voice rose above the general buzz of conversation. 'Isn't that just typical? Leaves us high and dry. Doesn't even follow up that next precious idea of his.'

'Another game?'

'The nerve of it. A ghost story. Had the nerve to ask if I'd let you all into our home – the old chunk of a castle where we live now. And I'd be there to let you in and play stupid tricks on you, one at a time. Only he's never got round even to that. Just a way of insulting me, I suppose.'

'If you find Mr Brunner so disagreeable,' said Mrs Godolphin, 'why did you accept his hospitality?'

'Because I thought I might find a chink in his armour.'

'And have you found it?'

'No, but there's time yet.'

There was a sway of embarrassment across the group.

Lesley took Nick's arm. 'That film of his. It ought never to have been shown. All right, so he did make some pretty cunning points about the sleaze that lets people like Waterman and his thugs get away with things. But that's not the way the law should be shoved around.'

'In the world of television, my love, everything out there is up for grabs. Knockabout drama beats plodding facts every time.'

'He'll contaminate you if we stay here any longer. Darling, we do have to get out of this dreadful place.'

'It's too late to go tonight. And tomorrow night the hotel is still full.'

'We could find *somewhere*. Some pub. Anywhere. This place gives me the creeps.'

'Let's help ourselves to one of Chet's drinks, and go to bed early.'

'I don't need the drink. But the other bit sounds promising.'

There was a sudden eruption. A woman in a long grey coat with a jaunty fur hood came in, shaking a few drops of moisture from her shoulders and tossing the hood back to reveal a long mane of blonde hair which she fingered into a carefully practised informality. She was flanked by a man in a grey striped suit with wide lapels, squeezed around a large body with improbably broad shoulders and a head too small to be in proportion.

'Well, at last,' Georgina piped up. 'If it isn't Jilly-Jo.'

'Hope I haven't interrupted anything.'

'Alec found you all right, then.'

'Alec?'

'Waiting for you at the station.'

'Oh, the hell with the station. You don't catch me queueing for trains. My friend Mr Hagan here was kind enough to give me a lift. Tam Hagan. A real gentleman. Brought me all the way.'

Nick appraised the newcomer as another hoodlum. Just as one crook, Waterman, had walked off with Brunner's wife Martine, so there was a whiff in the air of Tam Hagan in line for the present one.

'So Alec's still waiting at the station?' said Georgina.

77

'More fool him.' Jilly-Jo looked around. 'All right, where is he? Where's Chet? We have some things to talk about. Like a divorce. And the sooner the better.'

Most of the guests looked away or drifted into twos and threes in corners of the room. Georgina twitched so ecstatically that her breasts threatened to escape their flimsy containers.

'And I see you're all set to move in.' Jilly-Jo looked her up and down. 'Got your picture hung in the entrance hall already. A bit impatient, aren't we?'

'I don't know what you're talking about.'

'Fancy taking my place and being treated the same way? Been taking any other very special pictures of you, has he?'

Georgina went scarlet. 'I don't know what you're talking about,' she repeated.

'For your own very personal, private collection, eh? Only you'll find he goes for cash rather than confidentiality. Thanks to my friend here, I find that he's been flogging all my so special, so private, so intimate pictures to porn dealers in Glasgow.'

Georgina tried to look haughty. She was not very well equipped for it. 'At least *I've* never posed for anything you could call porn.'

'You'll be amazed what he knows about trick photography.'

Another disgruntled guest began muttering about starting a game. If the host was neglecting them, that was no reason why they shouldn't enjoy themselves. Nick had a feeling that he had come prepared with some bright idea of his own, and Chet had probably not let him get a word in. Ruefully you had to admit that the old rogue was a good organizer. A bully and a braggart, but good at shoving people around and keeping them on the move. Once he had lost interest, everyone else was at a loose end.

'Until he gets back, then . . .'

'Well?' screeched Jilly-Jo like a garish, hoarse parrot, 'where *is* he?'

As if her screech had triggered it off, the rain came back in a thudding, drumming downpour.

*

Anna was in a hurry to make her escape. She had had more than enough of the atmosphere in this place. She looked around for Stuart, to drive him back. He was nowhere to be seen. She checked in the side lobby. Only a few of the pieces he had brought up with him were still on the shelf. He must have shifted the others to where Chet wanted them – or where he thought Chet would want them.

Irritated, she crossed the path of the awkward but reliable lad from the village whose job it was to carry drinks and canapés around at stated intervals.

'Mr Morgan? I think he said something about going out for a stroll.'

'In this downpour?'

'Och, no. That'd be before it came on again.'

It seemed an odd, impetuous gesture. The village was a good distance, and would seem more so in the dark. But then, she had been stand-offish with him, choking him off. He was a febrile, temperamental sort. She hadn't realized, though, that he had been peeved with her.

Looking up at the gaudy portraits in the hall, she saw what Jilly-Jo had meant. A huge colour photograph of Georgina Campbell, widening her eyes coyly over her bare left arm, curved along a chair back, had been hung between one of a leading lady of doubtful reputation and a beautiful older woman whose reputation was too fine to be jostled by these companions.

Anna turned into the wing to say goodnight to Queenie, but was met only by Cocky, yelping ecstatically and throwing himself up on his hind legs in imploring little leaps. He was determined to go wherever she went, whining an appeal, playing the poor abandoned little pooch with overwhelming sincerity. Queenie was nowhere to be found, and Alec was obviously not back yet. Anna picked Cocky up, gave him a reassuring squeeze, refilled his water bowl, and shut him in the kitchen.

As she braced herself in the doorway, poised to dash through

79

the rain to the Volvo, Stuart appeared out of the shadows, bringing a smell of damp cloth with him.

'Wherever did you get to?' she demanded.

'I wasn't in the mood for hanging around through all that show-off crap.'

'So you flounced off and got wet.'

'Yes, I got wet.' He edged into the doorway and shook himself the way Cocky would have done, spraying moisture in every direction.

'You'd better go in and dry yourself off. I'll wait for you.'

'No, thanks. Not in the mood for going back in there. I just want to get back to my own pad. Be it ever so humble, and all that.'

'And make a sodden mess all over my car?'

'It's gone through worse than that.'

'True. All right, brace yourself. Let me get the doors open, and then make a sprint for it.'

She drove slowly out on to the drive, then through a succession of puddles to the main road. The surface here was not much better. Ruts had filled up with water, spurting up under the wheels. Even with the wipers on full, it was hard to see anything but a shimmering curtain of rain distorting the road ahead.

She said: 'I suppose it was you who put that picture of Georgina up?'

'Yes. I assumed that was where he wanted it to hang, along with all the others.'

'You're sure of that?'

'He'd said something about it.'

'But right away? Didn't he say something about leaving all the bits and pieces until later?'

'I thought I might as well get rid of that piece while I was there. Nothing much else to do.'

The headlights picked out a tree trunk with branches dangling dangerously close. Anna swung the car into the middle of the road, hoping nobody else would be out tonight, coming towards them.

'Quite a smack in the face for Jilly-Jo,' she said, 'when she got back.'

80

'Oh, I'm sure she could cope.'

'And Chet?'

'Oh, I've had a bellyful of Chet Brunner.' It came out in a furious gust through the hiss and swish of the downpour. 'I don't know how much more he expects me to take.'

They crawled into the village street. There was not a soul about. A few lights glowed from behind heavy curtains and were repeated in the sheen of water along the pavement.

At the side door behind the craft shop, Stuart said: 'Thanks. Coming in for a warming night-cap?'

'Thanks, but I think I'll be glad to get to bed.'

Another man might have been flippant enough or pushy enough to take her up on that. Stuart merely hesitated a moment as if debating this, then said: 'Any chance of a lift into Ayr tomorrow morning? I do need to get some more paints and oddments from the craft shop there.'

'How early?'

'Half eight?'

'Suits me. And I want to go into Ayr, anyway, to have words with that infernal agent.'

'About marmalade?'

'And a little matter of theft. And some other things.'

'Right. Half eight then.' He made a move as if to kiss her on the cheek, then dug into his pocket for his keys, opened the car door, and flattened himself against his own door, fumbling to get in.

There were other subdued lights in the cottages when Anna got back and made her slow turn into the stableyard. Her head-lights picked out something lumpy on the slope beside Covenanter's Cottage. It might have been a shadow distorted by the rain, or a sack of something dumped on the slope beside the clothes-drying carousel. But she knew every shadow here at any hour of the day or night; what tubs and flowerpots there were in front of the cottages; and exactly where the wheelie-bins were positioned behind them.

Parking the car, she took a few steps towards the indistinct gap between the cottage and the remaining stump of a drys-tone wall. Surely there was somebody crouching, or lying on the small lip of ground?

But the guests in Balmuir Lodge could hardly have contrived a hasty substitute of a game and started it up in weather like this. She wasn't going to investigate any further in these conditions. Facetiously, she said aloud: 'All right, I haven't seen you. I'll clear off and leave somebody else to discover you.'

As she went into the house, taking her usual backward glance, she saw the door of Covenanter's Cottage open. A shape that must have been Mr Maxwell looked out. Hastily she went in and shut her door behind her.

In the morning, Lesley awoke to noise under the window. Drowsily she turned over to focus on the orange figures of the bedside clock.

'Good God, look at the time!'

Nick turned over and mumbled an incoherent question.

Outside, a loud conversation was going on, voices lurch ing over one another, one of them a woman's rising in disbelief.

Lesley shrugged her dressing-gown on and pulled back the window curtain. The sun was shining, and the air was sparklingly clear. All she could see was the post van parked beside the house. Then the postman stepped back into view as he leaned into his van and reached for a mobile phone on the seat, impeded by Cocky scurrying and yelping round him. Feet were running along a corridor somewhere. Voices rose again, then were cut off as a door slammed.

Behind Lesley, Nick sat up. 'What's going on? Not starting some damfool charade at this time of the morning?'

Along the landing somebody was shouting over the banisters, also asking what the hell was going on and was this some sort of joke?

Lesley turned away from the window and opened the door on to the landing. 'Are we having a fire drill, or something?'

On the turn of the stairs Georgina Campbell in a short see-through nightie was crying and waving her right arm as if desperate for something or someone to grab and hold on to.

'They've found him,' she howled.
'Found who?'
'Chet. He's been murdered.'

8

Detective Chief Inspector June McAdam arrived at the blue and white tent on the grassy slope to find the police surgeon fidgeting, impatient for her appearance. As she ducked under the phosphorescent tape, each step made a sucking, plopping noise underfoot. The ground was sodden from last night's rain, and they would all have been better equipped with gumboots.

Her sergeant held the tent flap open for her.

'Chief Inspector McAdam, doctor.'

'How d'ye do. Ian Fairlie.'

The corpse, a heavily built man with a heavy jaw, was sprawled face upwards on the grass, its head twisted awkwardly to the left.

'Cause of death?'

'A blow to the temple for starters.' Dr Fairlie indicated a deep gash above the nose, with a smear of dried blood down into the right eye. 'Some force behind it. Deep enough to crack the skull. And twist the head and break the neck. No doubt when he's on the slab it'll be possible to establish the angle of impact, and how much force would have been necessary.'

'Time of death?'

'I'd say within the last twelve hours. There again, should be able to narrow it down when we've got him on the slab. And folk in the house should be able to pin down when he was last seen.'

'Identification?'

Detective Sergeant Brodie said: 'The postie who found him says it's the owner of the place. A Mr Chet Brunner. Knew him

85

well. And I get the impression he didn't much like him.'

'Lining the postman up as our first suspect?'

'Good Lor', no, chief. I didn't mean it that way.'

'Next of kin?'

'His present wife should be on the premises.'

'He's had more than one?'

'Fairly well known in these parts,' the surgeon contributed, 'as a womanizer. One of those telly people who moves in and thinks his neighbours are only fit for what I believe are called bit parts.'

There were voices outside. The SOCO team of the Kyle and Carrick Constabulary had arrived in a white Transit. Easing themselves into their sterile overalls and overshoes, two made a preliminary circuit of the body while the photographer took shots from every angle, using a zoom lens for close-ups of the surrounding grass so that he wouldn't need to trample over evidence which might escape the naked eye. Not that there was much to be seen other than a tangle of sodden grass and mud which even the most cautious steps would churn up into a mess worthy of a farmyard.

DCI McAdam backed out of their way and stood outside the tent with her sergeant. They looked down the slope at the old farmhouse and cottages tucked away within a windbreak of larches, and then at the big house to the west. A few men and women came out of the house and went back in again; came out again, stared, looked as if they were going to come closer, and then went back in once more.

'Once we've got some bodies from Ayr, we'll have to comb that ground between here and the house. Looking for a weapon isn't going to be easy, unless it was dropped in a hurry to get away. Something simple, like a heavy piece of wood?'

'Or a metal bar?'

'Depending on who carries what or works with what around here.' She glanced back at the tent. 'One odd thing. If he was struck down and his neck broken so that it got wrenched the way we've just seen it, oughtn't the blood to have run towards the left eye rather than the right?'

'Might have . . . well, sort of lolled over when he went down.'

'I'd have thought that once he was down, he was well and truly down and done for.'

Cool morning sunlight slanting across the hillside glinted on soaked grass, showing up ridges and puddles which might be the indentations of recent footprints made by whoever discovered the body – or by the killer? Or they might simply be natural dips in the ground between exposed hummocks of grit and heather. The whole hillside would have to be thoroughly combed, and everyone except the investigatory team kept well away.

McAdam and Calum Brodie made their way up to the house. She knew that some of the sergeant's superiors, including the DIs in her group, called him Calum. She preferred to stick to Brodie, just as she preferred to be McAdam to her senior colleagues and to herself, though she knew that behind her back the lads made jokes about it being too appropriate – a stony surface and a heart of stone. A few colleagues had tried to call her Jane as she made her way up the promotion ladder, but she had always preferred impersonality. In recent years she had come to think of herself simply by her rank or as McAdam, and early on she had made it clear that from her subordinates she preferred 'guv' or 'chief' to the 'ma'am' they all ventured at first. The name of Jane was slotted away into a rarely used recess at the back of her mind.

She was thirty-two and already showing strands of silver-grey in the dark charcoal grey of her hair, drawn back severely from her forehead and finishing in a small, tight knob like a sailor's quid of tobacco. Her lips were thin, largely because of her habit of sucking them in and clamping them tightly together. Looking in the mirror as she did her hair each morning, she was some-times taken aback by the cold severity of her appearance; but she didn't mind using it to advantage when questioning a suspect.

It was obvious that everyone in Balmuir Lodge had been wait-ing for them, half apprehensive, half thrilled by what had happened. There were a middle-aged man and woman in the hall, and what looked like a sizeable cluster of folk in a large room beyond. While the DCI was trying to get her bearings, the man stepped towards her.

'You're the police?'

Automatically she produced her warrant card. 'Detective Chief Inspector McAdam. And this is Detective Sergeant Brodie. And you are. . . ?'

'Alec Chisholm. Chet's . . . Mr Brunner's assistant. This is a dreadful business. Dreadful.'

'Unbelievable.' The woman beside him came dramatically to life. Shivering, she clasped her hands to her face and her eyes widened as if to add emphasis to every syllable she uttered. 'Quite, quite unbelievable.' But in spite of her eyes being so restless, they never turned fully in McAdam's direction.

'My wife,' said Chisholm. 'Queenie.'

'I gather it was the postman who found the body?'

'That's right.' Chisholm shook his head. 'Poor Jimmy. A bit of a shock for him. Taking a cut across the edge of the glen to old Mrs McIntyre. Still looking after herself in one of the old estate cottages, and he finds himself nearly falling over *that*.'

'Where is he now?'

'Jimmy? Finishing off his rounds.'

'Surely he'd know that he ought to have stayed here until the police had spoken to him?'

'Said he had his job to do, and anyone could tell you where to find him.'

'Damn. Now it'll be all over the district, and we'll get the usual horde of ghouls trampling over the ground.'

She moved on into the reception room beyond. Standing by the window, a commanding man in young middle age was tall enough to be seen over the heads of the others. The woman beside him was a few inches shorter, and McAdam glimpsed her only when a few of the group between them moved fretfully. She was sure she had seen that face before – somewhere, way back, in quite a different context.

'Look.' An epicene young man with a cluster of gold rings in his left ear fussed up to her. 'If you have to question us, can you make it quick? I think we've all had enough of this place. A pretty badly organized weekend, absolutely *not* up to the standards we'd been promised. And now *this*. I really do have better things to do.'

'I'm sorry, sir, but nobody must leave these premises until we have elicited every relevant detail.'

A blonde girl in a low-cut dress which clung to her as if plastered on with the tears she was shedding let out a howl of despair.

DS Brodie approached her sympathetically. 'Would you be Mrs Brunner?'

'No, she bloody well wouldn't.' The young woman who snapped this out at a pitch uncomfortable to the human ear was, thought McAdam, almost a carbon copy of the other woman. '*I'm* Jilly-Jo Brunner. *Mrs* Brunner, whatever ambitions that slut may have had.'

'Mrs Brunner.' McAdam kept it polite and level. 'As next of kin, you realize we'll need you to make formal identification of the body.'

'Oh, how awful. Does he look too ghastly?' But her eyes were shining. 'You want me to go and do it now?'

'If you'd prefer to wait until the . . . until Mr Brunner has been shifted to the morgue—'

'Oh, what a frightful word. No' – she held her head high – 'let's get it over with.'

'Good, if you think you're up to it. Sergeant, I think the surgeon will still be there. Take Mrs Brunner down there, and give her any help she needs.'

Jilly-Jo looked at the detective sergeant and managed a courageous smile. McAdam would not have been surprised if she had immediately taken his arm and blinked endearingly up at him through her long eyelashes.

'I'll come wi' yer.' It was a sudden growl from a thick-set, heavy shouldered man with a dark line down his left cheek which McAdam suspected was the memento of a razor attack.

'Whoever you are, sir—'

'Tam Hagan, that's who.'

'A very good friend of mine.' Jilly-Jo's smile switched easily from one man to the other. 'He was kind enough to bring me back from Glasgow last night.'

'I think, Mrs Brunner, it would be better to let my sergeant look after you.'

On her way out, Jilly-Jo turned and jabbed a thumb

venomously at Georgina Campbell. 'Maybe you ought to ask *her* where Chet was last night. He wasn't here when I got back, and there's been other times when the two of them went missing.'

'*I* was here when you got back. Right in this room.'

'But what happened afterwards? A special arrangement? And what happened to him when you'd finished?'

'Why, you—'

'In due course,' McAdam assured them both, 'I shall be asking everybody where they were and what they were doing.'

Suddenly she remembered who the woman near the window was.

'It's DC Gunn, isn't it? We bumped into one another two years ago, over the robbery of some family silver from that place outside Selkirk.'

The tall man said: 'I'm Nicholas Torrance. This is my wife.'

'Of course.' McAdam managed a cool smile. 'I did hear something about you quitting the Force and going up in the world.'

Behind her, Alec Chisholm said with a hint of reproof: 'Sir Nicholas Torrance, and Lady Torrance.'

'Quite so. You're enjoying the change, Lady Torrance?'

'I haven't had much of a chance to assess it yet. We've . . . been away.'

On honeymoon, thought McAdam. All too ready to go soft and give up trying to be a tough enough police officer. Not good enough for promotion, so instead of catching criminals she had caught herself a baronet. Calculatingly – or just letting it happen? McAdam could see how any man could fall for Lesley Gunn. She assured herself she felt no resentment, although no man had ever fallen that way for herself; perhaps because she had never invited the attempt.

'I certainly never expected,' said Lady Torrance, 'to be at this end of an investigation so soon.'

McAdam did not bother to offer a sympathetic smile. 'You were here last night?'

'We were,' said Sir Nicholas, 'unfortunately.'

'You were a friend of the deceased?'

'We used to work together. It was just chance that we realized

90

we were close to his place, and came here. We had a bit of trouble over accommodation, and only intended to spend one night here and then be on our way.'

'I'm sure that with her past experience Lady Torrance will be the first to understand that I have to ask you to stay and give your version of the events leading up to Mr Brunner's death, so we can complete our PDFs.'

He looked blank.

'Personal Discipline Forms,' his wife explained. 'Details of friends, business associates, social habits.'

'As far as we're concerned, you could hardly call it a discipline. Social, I suppose. We spent some time yesterday watching an old video and discussing the background. Had something to eat, and went to bed. It was only this morning we heard of this business.'

Some of the house guests were sitting down in nervous little huddles, chattering spasmodically. Alec Chisholm stood almost in the middle of the room, as if waiting to be helpful in identifying each person present. Once or twice he touched his wife's shoulder reassuringly.

McAdam joined them in the centre of the room.

'Ladies and gentlemen, I realize this is a distressing time for you. We have a serious crime to investigate, but I promise you that we'll be as quick as we can, though you'll understand we have to be thorough. I shall need to speak to each of you individually, and wherever possible I would hope you can then leave, provided you let us have an address where you can be contacted. And now' – she turned to Alec Chisholm – 'as you seem to be in charge of this place, can you tell me where we might establish an incident room?'

'Incident? I thought we'd already had enough in the way of—'

'We do need one specific room in which to collate all matters arising from this murder. Privacy for interviews, but facilities for contacting Forensic and the team out there.'

'I reckon the studio should provide you with anything you need.'

It was clear that Chet Brunner hadn't believed in doing

anything by halves. There were enough computer terminals to provide a virtual reality James Bond movie or connect the police with Interpol or the FBI if they had any such thing in mind.

Which DCI McAdam hadn't.

She said: 'Since you're here, Mr Chisholm, perhaps I could start with you. As assistant to the late Mr Brunner, you'll be able to give us a full background.'

Behind them Chisholm's wife came scurrying in. Queenie Chisholm: it was the sort of unreal Christian name which some-how belonged ideally to such a fluttery, dithering type. Quite unable to keep still or to refrain from interrupting, she would be a distraction during any questioning of her husband.

McAdam said: 'I think it would be better if I spoke to you alone, Mr Chisholm. At first, anyway. Shorten the procedures.'

He got the message. 'Queenie, darling, those folk out there are tetchy enough as it is. Do rustle up some snacks and drinks to keep them quiet.'

His wife seemed glad of the excuse to scuttle away.

'Right,' said Chisholm. 'What can I do to help?'

'You can fill me in about the deceased and his background. Who he was, what he did, and what all these people are doing here.'

Chisholm was obviously a good organizer, with a methodical mind. His metal-rimmed glasses and wilting little moustache reminded her of the storeman in the Armoury at HQ – an ex-Army NCO whose moustache was more aggressive in width than Chisholm's and most lovingly waxed, but whose meticulous attention to detail was similar.

Without wasting a word or vaguely skirting awkward topics, Chisholm produced a neat biography of Chet Brunner and his career. Starting in the fleapits of the East End and then more expensive but even seedier establishments in Soho, he had shouldered his brash way into cutting rooms and commercial promotions, scraped acquaintance with a leading cameraman to whom, Chisholm bluntly reported, he had supplied a number of rent boys; and through sheer persistence had raised the money for a number of cheap horror films and then more pretentious films – 'Which were still pretty horrific but more slickly made.' He had worked for a while in Hollywood, but made too many enemies and didn't have enough talent to overcome that endemic Hollywood disease. So he vowed to show the Americans how much better it could be done over here. And cheaper.

The Scottish phase was a late venture. Romantic fantasies set against a background of hills and heather appealed more to an international market, especially the American one, than psychological marital dramas in smart London or drab realism in northern English cities. Also Brunner himself was captivated by the surroundings. He moved all his operations, apart from final editing and production, to the Lowland hills.

'And it worked out?' McAdam asked. 'He could produce enough and make enough profit to continue living here and working from home?'

From what Chisholm was telling her, the surface glamour was becoming more important than the job itself. Like a tatty film, the glitter and hype were more important than the content. But the man still had a knack of gathering useful people around him, by payment or flattery, or both, and keeping them at his mercy by the same methods plus brazen bullying. You could work for him, she calculated, while admiring him enough to sweat your guts out in a desire to please him, and at the same time hating Brunner's own guts.

'But things were going off. Chet still liked the big act, the laird of all he surveyed. And then the house party idea – "themed weekends" was a term he had picked up somewhere. People were prepared to spend good money on playing murder games in surroundings like these. But I don't think it was going to last much longer. I've known Chet a long time, and I know the symptoms when he's getting cheesed off and ready to move on to a new patch.'

'Which brings us to our latest drama. Tell me what you can remember about last night. What time was Mr Brunner last seen?'

'I'm afraid I can't tell you that. He wasn't here when I got back.'

'Got back? From where?'

93

'From Brawhill station. Mrs Brunner had rung through to say she had crashed Chet's Mercedes and would have to come back by train. Chet sent me to meet her. But she wasn't on the first train, so I waited for the next one. The last one, actually.'

'At Brawhill station, you said?'

'Not a very cheery place. I went down into the village and had a pie in the pub. By the time I started back, the skies had opened. Windscreen wipers top speed, and still weren't coping. I nearly came off the road at one corner. Water running down the hillside and flooding the road. Some nasty bends. I pulled over, listened to the radio. When it slackened off, I set off again. Still pretty treacherous. And then it all started again. I made it eventually.'

'And what time would it be when you got back?'

'Around ten-thirty, I think. Didn't look at the clock. All I wanted was a dram. And then another one.'

'You didn't see anything as you came up the drive?'

'Only the lights of the house. And mighty glad to see those, believe me.'

'Nothing on the grass that ought not to have been there?'

'I wasn't looking for anything. Anyway, wasn't the body found on the slope round the other side?'

'You knew that?' said McAdam sharply.

'It's what the postie told us.'

'Of course, yes.' Her lips tightened. 'You had no reason to dislike Mr Brunner?'

'He paid me my salary, kept me in work, let us have accommodation here.'

'That wasn't the question, Mr Chisholm. Did you have reasons to dislike him? Hate him, even? It can happen even in the best paid working relationship, and you've been pretty frank about your own view on your employer's character.'

'He could be a bastard at times. Could fly off the handle, charge at a thing in a rage – and charge at *you*, yourself, if there was nobody else about to shout at. But I was used to him.'

'You have any views on the other people here?'

'You mean suspicions?'

'Just any judgement that might be useful.'

Alec Chisholm shrugged. 'We've had one lot of eccentrics

and exhibitionists after another. Nothing especially unusual this time round. Except . . .'

'Yes?'

'Well, I was a bit surprised that Chet had invited Harry Pitcairn. And even more surprised that Pitcairn had accepted.'

'Why would that be?'

Chisholm looked uncomfortable. 'I don't like to stir up any false impressions. The lad's had enough grief as it is.'

'Grief?'

'His family used to own all this land. Harry's dad was Lord Lieutenant of the shire, until he got into some financial trouble. Just neglect, nothing criminal – spending too much time in ceremonials instead of keeping the books straight. Had to resign, and then had to sell up, and hated doing both. And the two of them, father and son, hated Chet for having cheated them, as they saw it, over the sale of the estate.'

'And did he cheat them?'

'Chet always drove a hard bargain. Never happy with a deal unless he felt he had scored somehow. And once he'd pulled this one off, he did get a bit bossy. Put up a fence to spoil part of their view. Closed what they claimed had always been a right of way across the top of the estate to the bluebell woods.'

'And had it been a right of way?'

'Apparently not. The Pitcairns had simply let people use it. Chet wouldn't. But the Pitcairn family had been here so long that they felt all their ways ought to be preserved, even when they had been banished, you might say.'

'Yes, I see. And yet the young man is invited to join this house party here, and he comes. Must have known what to expect.'

'Bit of bravado on both sides, maybe.'

McAdam thought for a few minutes before deciding whether to continue this interview or to switch to another witness. Chisholm's story seemed straightforward. She wondered whether she ought to have asked him what was on the radio during the time he was in the car. It was the sort of trick question that could trip people up. But she couldn't see that, even if he had forgotten or didn't get it right, it would give much of a lead in any significant direction.

Sergeant Brodie came into the room. 'Yes, the widow's identified the body. Made a big scene.'

'But?'

'I think she rather enjoyed it.'

Alec Chisholm smiled wryly. 'Jilly-Jo's an actress. Of sorts.
They do know exactly how to react to any dramatic challenge.'

'The body has now been removed,' said Brodie formally, 'for
detailed forensic examination.' Meaning that Brunner's corpse
had been zipped up into a bag and carted off.

McAdam glanced at her watch. 'I think we'd better see Mrs
Chisholm next. And then maybe that resentful young man. Or
Mrs Brunner, when she's recovered.'

'I don't think that'll take her long.'

'Mr Chisholm, will you ask your wife to come in?'

'You won't be too tough on her? She's very nervy, I wouldn't
want her to be subjected to—'

'We're not the KGB, Mr Chisholm.'

As Queenie Chisholm swept into the room, she looked even
more distraught than before. Obviously she, too, had been in
the acting profession and was now busily conveying distress at
the thought of a grisly murder together with the demanding
chores of providing food and making soothing noises to the
guests.

'Do sit down, Mrs Chisholm.' McAdam indicated the chair
vacated by Queenie's husband, and pulled her own chair a few
inches closer. 'Think carefully, and I'm sure you'll be able to
sort out all my questions in no time.'

'I don't know. It's all so confusing. I simply can't take it in.'
Her gaze wandered round a room that must have been perfectly
familiar to her but which she seemed to be seeing as a strange,
unaccountable place. Her glances became more and more apprehensive as they went to and fro across the tall, solid figure of
Sergeant Brodie, perched on the end of the table beside a VDU.
'And I wish I'd never . . . we'd never . . .'

'Never what, Mrs Chisholm?'

'Oh, just that . . . I mean, that we'd never got involved with all
this murder game nonsense. And let the wrong people into the
. . . on to the premises.'

'Let's take it step by step. You were here all yesterday evening?'

'Yes.'

'In the main rooms with the guests, taking part in whatever was going on at the time? Or just supervising the food and drinks?'

'Well, not much *was* going on. There was that awful thunderstorm, and no way of going out. And he . . . Chet . . . Mr Brunner . . . he seemed to have lost interest. And then there was the business of Jilly-Jo wrecking the car, and Alec having to go to the station to meet her, and being kept waiting. So after a while I went back to our quarters to wait for Alec to come home. Watched the telly.' Unexpectedly she smiled a broad, eager smile. 'Came in on the middle of the drama programme. It was the . . .' She paused, and smiled roguishly. 'What we have to call "the *Scottish* play", you know. Bad luck to give it its real title. I've always wished I could have played Lady Macbeth, but it wasn't my forte. Once you've been type-cast, you know, they never give you a chance to—'

'Mrs Chisholm,' said McAdam, 'what time did your husband get back?'

'Mm? Oh, I suppose it must have been about half ten.'

'A bit late, wasn't it?'

'Yes, it was.' Queenie switched to indignation. 'Having to hang about there, just because of that stupid woman. Not even as if Chet really cared twopence about her any more. I've learned to know the signs. Ready to ditch her and go on to the next one. If you ask me—'

A phone rang. Sergeant Brodie looked round in search of the source, and finally found it a few yards away. The two women were silent until he nodded, said 'Will do', and put the phone back into its slot.

McAdam raised an eyebrow and waited.

'A little technical matter,' he said, using his own right eyebrow as a means of communication. 'We can fit it in later.'

She turned back to Queenie Chisholm. 'How long would it have taken your husband to get back from the station?'

'You'd have to ask him what time the last train went. But it

97

must have been an awful drive in that weather. You can go over the edge on some of those roads, the way they twist. He did say that he'd pulled in for a while and listened to the radio until the rain slackened off.'

McAdam tried an abrupt new tack. 'How did Mr Brunner come to go out into the grounds on a night like that?'

'Goodness knows. Oh, I couldn't say.'

'What time was he last seen?'

'I don't know. I mean, not by me. I must have been talking to him about nine o'clock, but—'

'About what?'

'I ... er ... oh, it must have been about the video he'd insisted on showing earlier.'

'Insisted? What was so important about it?'

'Oh, it was of those true crime investigations. Did a lot of those programmes for telly, way back. You know the sort of thing.'

Yes, thought McAdam sourly, she did know that sort of thing. Amateur meddling.

'You can't think why he should have gone out into the grounds on a night like that?'

'I must have been back in our sitting-room when he did it. Whatever.' She looked at Brodie again, then looked away, but did not look back at McAdam. 'Poor Anna,' she rushed on. 'It won't be good for trade, will it?'

'Trade?'

'My daughter-in-law runs those two holiday lets down by the Mains. This sort of publicity's bound to put people off.'

'She might be surprised,' said Brodie. 'Some people have gruesome tastes. Might even be a selling point.'

'Oh, how dreadful. How could anybody. . . ?'

McAdam said: 'You can't think of anything else, Mrs Chisholm? About Mr Brunner's movements, his general demeanour – anything that would give us a clue to his murder? Or anybody else behaving oddly, or going missing at the same time as Mr Brunner?'

She expected Queenie to remind her that she had already said she had gone back to her own quarters before Brunner disappeared. Instead, Queenie's eyes widened and she looked like an eager bird about to pounce. 'Oh, there was Stuart. He did go off somewhere. I mean, after he'd come up with Anna he somehow drifted away again, and . . . but no, I really oughtn't to make trouble when I can't be sure.'

'Please, Mrs Chisholm. Who is Stuart?'

'He was a friend of my son. My late son. Or made out he was a friend. And now he's hanging round Peter's wife. His widow, that is. I never did trust him. Never believed he was ever a *real* friend. And he did do a spell in prison, and then heaped blame on my poor Peter for something between him and his wife.'

'Please, Mrs Chisholm. Could we take it just a bit more slowly? Your son's wife – Anna that would be. . . ?'

'No, I was talking about Stuart Morgan's wife. And him telling such lies about her and my Peter. But I don't see that it's got anything to do with Chet and his death.'

'No,' sighed McAdam. 'Neither do I. Not offhand, anyway.' She was about to ask whether Queenie had any other suspicious movements to report, but restrained herself. It could take up more time than was justified. 'Very well. Thanks for your help, Mrs Chisholm.' When Queenie had gone, the rustle of her loose flowered dress sounding almost like a gasp of relief, she turned to Brodie. 'Now, what was that phone call about?'

'The search of the ground has shown up something interesting.'

'OK, let's have it?'

'Footprints. Two lots of them.'

'Brunner and his killer?'

'No, guv. Two extra, according to SOCO. Pretty heavily dug in, and blurred by that damn downpour. But the signs are that one lot comes from a woman's shoes. What's more, they could have come from part way down the hill.'

'*Could* have?'

'There are too many other marks around the place. Some of them muddled by the rain. But this pair – a man and a woman, if that's the way it was – could have come up together and taken the victim by surprise.'

'Pretty exposed setting for a surprise, isn't it?'

99

'True. And anyway, it's difficult to decide whether they were made at the same time, or whether they could have been part of these cockeyed murder games they seem to have been playing.'

'Mm. Murder games and one murder for real – somehow those have to be separated.' She stood up. 'I think we'd better go and have a look for ourselves. And then maybe some words with this prickly Mr Pitcairn. Unless we can think of a man and woman who worked together to dispose of this charming Mr Brunner.'

9

After the rain, the sky was cloudless and innocent, but runnels of water still made patterns like erratic snail tracks across the road. They had left just before eight-thirty, and even when approaching Ayr there was still a feeling of freshness, a grateful awakening of a new, cleansed day after a tempestuous night.

Stuart had hardly said a word on the drive over the hills. He looked either tired or sullen, or both. It was only as they came over the final crest and the town was spread out ahead, with a shimmer of the sea beyond, that he said: 'I've had about enough, dancing attendance on that lout. If I have to do weird things for him, why not do them for myself and pocket the whole profit?'

'What weird things?'

'Oh, all that reproduction stuff, copying things that take his fancy, cutting corners fine.'

'What else did you have in mind?'

'Like I said, the two of us. And maybe your pa-in-law will find himself at a loose end soon. Get him to come up with some capital—'

'He did that way back. Setting us up with the cottages, and then you and Peter.'

'Right. Maybe now's the time for him to play a more active part. He's a good organizer. Let him run the business side of it, give him a cut, and give me scope to produce the goods. With you in the team as well. A lot better than having that thumping great shadow looming over us all the time. I've made quite a few contacts of my own this last year.'

The note of peevishness jarred on her. She dodged answering by making a show of concentrating on the traffic at road junctions in the town.

'All right if I drop you on the corner of Sandgate?'

'Fine. And where shall we meet? That café in the arcade, at ... what's the time now?'

'Meet you there at eleven?'

'Make it eleven-thirty.'

Anna wondered why he needed so much time just to pick up some art materials; but it suited her to have enough leeway to thrash things out with Mr Ritchie and then do some casual shopping.

Below the florid, gilded names of Haining & Ritchie, Solicitors & Estate Agents, wide windows were filled with colour photographs of desirable properties, with one side section devoted to self-catering holiday cottages. Anna noticed that the Balmuir Mains picture was fading in the sunlight, and needed updating. The outer office was staffed by one middle-aged lady with steel-rimmed glasses and a younger woman who would probably be here for no more than six months before finding herself a job with some livelier organization such as a travel and holiday firm.

Mr Ritchie came out to meet Anna, looked warily between the two women as if afraid they might overhear something he had no wish for them to hear, and hastily ushered her into a dark little side room. He was not a tall man, yet he had the stoop of one who was continually trying to avoid banging his head on a low lintel, so that his eyes were always peering upwards from his lowered head.

'Guid of ye to come all this way, Mrs Chisholm.' He fussed her towards a small armchair which creaked as she sat down. 'It's a gey long time since we last had the pleasure of a wee talk, aye?'

'And high time for one.'

'Och, aye, indeed. Now, we've been thinking that maybe it's time to consider adjusting our commission right across the board.' He had a reedy, constricted voice combining a frog in the throat with pinched vowel sounds. 'There's a rather unfortunate matter concerning a recent booking which I'll have to be having out with ye, and some adjustment—'

'Before we go into anything of that kind,' Anna interrupted forcefully, 'there are one or two matters concerning the recent let of Stables Cottage. The outgoing tenants caused a certain amount of damage.'

'I'm sorry to hear that. What was the extent of it?'

'There was marmalade smeared everywhere. I had to have the curtains cleaned, and I'll need to have new copies of the policies leaflet. And two pages of the visitors' book are stuck permanently together.'

'Och, marmalade. Is that all?'

'Is that *all*? Do you know the mess it can make? We shall have to consider whether to accept small children at all.'

'We canna be expected to vet every tenant, Mrs Chisholm.'

'And,' said Anna, 'they stole a painting. Took it down from the wall and took it away with them.'

'Now that's serious, I'll grant you.'

'Good. You must have their address. So chase them up.'

'It may be difficult to prove that they actually stole it. Very difficult to find a way of searching their home and—'

'Find it. Or else sort out the insurance. We do have insurance cover from you, don't we?'

'Och, aye. Of course. I'll look into it.' He sounded reluctant, and switched abruptly into something which might counter the need to consider action on her complaint. 'But now there's an awkward matter ye'll need to deal with. Your present tenants – name of Maxwell.'

'What about them?'

'I fear they have misled us. I have just this very morning had a call from a credit card protection agency. The card the Maxwells used to make the booking was a stolen card. The real owner has only just realized it was missing and reported it.'

Anna thought of the shifty, cowering appearance of the man and his evasive wife. And what Stuart had said about the prison aura.

'They may not be called Maxwell at all?'

'Indeed not.'

'I'm afraid that's another headache for you, Mr Ritchie.'

'Well, now, I'd be thinking you might face them with this yourself.'

'Me? I'd have thought it was up to you. You're the agent who makes the bookings. You're the one to sort out any problems.'

'But then, I – that is, our firm, Mr Haining being very particular about balancing our books – I'd have to take time off from here and charge accordingly, and with you on the spot, it would be easier for you to put the matter to them.'

'Mr Ritchie, this is outrageous.'

'After all, I'm thinking that if you went along with your Mr Brunner, they'd not be inclined to argue, Mr Brunner being . . . would ye not be saying impressive?'

Anna kept her voice down. This hushed room was not suited to loud argument. 'I'll certainly put it to them when I get back,' she said. 'But I think it's up to you to back me up quickly with some legal restraints. And I shall expect you to find some way of paying me what you owe me. As well as taking action against the thieving marmalade spreaders.'

Five minutes after leaving the office, she was angry with herself. Of course it was not up to her to confront guests who had cheated on their payments. She was tempted to turn back and tell Mr Ritchie that the whole point of paying commission to an agent was to have somebody carrying all the financial problems and coping with upsets.

Instead, she went into a large store set back from the river and bought herself a crisp daffodil-coloured blouse. At half-past eleven she found Stuart waiting for her in the arcade café. Propped against the wall was a large plastic bag bulging with his purchases.

'Got everything you needed?' she said.

'Pretty well.'

He bought her a coffee and a pastry, and she poured out her exasperation about Mr Ritchie and his choice of tenants for the cottages.

Stuart whistled faintly. 'Well, well. Better be extra careful about fixtures and fittings when that couple leave. And maybe we ought to warn the big house. They may be planning a little bit of burglary.'

There was a sudden blast of pop music from a speaker pointing towards them from the end of the counter. Anna winced. The girl by the till turned the noise down slightly, but had no intention of switching it off altogether. Her dangling strands of red-tinted hair twitched to the nodding of her head.

As they finished their snack and Stuart was getting up to pay, the moaning vocal faded and a short news bulletin began. There was a hurried summary of a speech by a local MP about essential road improvements which he was urging upon the government, and then a more excited announcement blurted out news just coming in of a sudden death in the Carrick region. 'The police have been called to Balmuir Lodge, where the dead body of well-known film producer and landowner, Mr Chet Brunner, has been discovered. Mr Brunner has been a colourful personality who brought many well-known screen personalities to the region for a number of his film and television projects. No reason has yet been advanced for his death. A statement will be issued later in the day when the police have concluded a preliminary investigation. And now, back to Jason Jarvie for a round-up of the latest sizzling singles . . .'

Anna stared at Stuart. He stood frozen by the cash desk, his wallet half open, a note halfway out between his fingers.

'What the hell?'

'We'd better get back.' Anna forced herself to stand up, clinging to the edge of the table. It was all unreal. Impossible to believe what she had just heard in this ordinary little café with its harsh little radio burbling away. 'When . . . how on earth. . . ?'

When they were on the road up to the bypass, she turned the car radio on, but it was not the time for a news bulletin on any of the channels. Anna tried to force some sort of coherence on to the impossible ideas.

'Who'd have wanted to kill him?'

'Lots of people.'

'Oh, I know lots of them would talk that way. But who'd actually get round to it?'

'No doubt the police are asking that very question right at this minute. And they'll be including us in their enquiries.'

She turned off the main road on to the twisting road over the hills, climbing and falling like a badly proportioned roller-coaster, and accelerated.

'But just a minute. They didn't *say* it was murder. They just said his body's been found. Might have died in his sleep.'

'But they did say it was a police matter.'

'But when d'you suppose it happened? After we'd left this morning? Or during the night?'

'We'll find out soon enough.'

Over a blind summit she plunged the car down into a pool enclosed in the dip, and emerged with the wheels fighting to escape from her control. Slowing and ordering herself to take things easy, she said nothing for a few miles. But then something floated up through her memory. At the time, the shock of the radio announcement had blotted out everything else. But now it came back to her. Even in that moment of shock, she had noticed that Stuart's wallet was well stuffed with twenty-pound notes. He had gone out to buy a few small items for the workshop, supposedly spending money rather than acquiring it.

Without thinking, she said: 'Just where did you get to last night?'

'I was in the house. And then I left. And turned back because I was getting wet. You were there.' He grunted a laugh. 'You can vouch for me, right?'

'Not all the time. I mean, you didn't join the general gathering.'

'Like I told you, I was fed up with all that crap. I just put one or two things in place. Like that picture of the Campbell girl.'

'You didn't see anything while you were wandering about the house last night?'

'I wasn't wandering. Just putting things where Chet wanted them.'

'Or see anything while you were outside?'

He wasn't laughing now. 'Look, if you're going to set up as a detective, I'd rather wait until I'm grilled by a real one. For crying out loud, you're not trying to pin something on me when

106

we don't even know what happened or when and where?'

'It's just struck me. That shape I thought I saw, behind Stables Cottage. Maybe I really did see it. It wasn't just part of a game, or a trick of the light. Was that where it happened?'

'What the hell are you on about?'

Safer not to say anything. Wait until they were put properly in the picture. Anna concentrated on getting safely home.

There were two cars in the yard. Neither of them belonged to the couple who called themselves Maxwell. One was the Robinsons' Honda. The other, to her dismay, was Queenie's yellow peril.

Anna was only halfway out of the Volvo when the farmhouse door was flung open and Queenie erupted.

'Wherever have you been? This dreadful news, and I couldn't find you anywhere. Surely you couldn't—'

'We went into Ayr quite early,' said Anna. 'We only heard the news on a radio there.'

'It's dreadful. And it's my fault. All my fault.'

'What happened? Some accident?'

'Oh, no. He's been murdered. And it's my fault. If I hadn't told him, he'd still be alive. I should never have told him.'

The footprints and ruts, filled with water and mud, had been distorted almost beyond recognition into a quagmire, but the two Scenes Of Crime Officers had been right. Enough remained to suggest that Brunner's body had been dragged some distance uphill before being left in the position where he was found.

'It's a bit of a mess down there, but he could have been clobbered not far behind that cottage on the left.'

McAdam turned to Sergeant Brodie. 'Do we know who's staying there?'

'Mrs Chisholm – the younger one – can probably tell us. She lets them out and looks after the places.'

'Better go and check with her. But take it easy. We don't want a couple of innocent holidaymakers complaining of police harassment.' She turned back to the two white-coated men stooping over the sodden grass, delicately poised as if to make sure that not a trace of their breath should disturb whatever

107

evidence might lie there waiting for them. 'Let me know what else you come up with. I'll be in the house interviewing a certain Mr Pitcairn.'

This proved to be an optimistic statement. Harry Pitcairn had apparently left and gone home.

'Left?' She glared at Alec Chisholm. 'But I told everybody to stay put until I'd questioned them.'

'He went last night, late on. I thought I'd mentioned that.'

'No, you didn't.'

'Said he'd had enough of being insulted. I told you his attitude about that. And surprised he ever came in the first place. Anyway, he'd had enough and he was going to walk home.'

'Was he, indeed. Before or after Mr Brunner went off and left them to it?'

'Afterwards, I think.'

So young Mr Pitcairn could have met the man he hated most out in the open, with nobody else nearby?

She said: 'You've got his home address?'

'Glengorm Castle. Just over the brae there, to the east. Along the old cart-track. But if you're thinking of driving over there—'

'That's exactly what I'm thinking of doing.'

'It's a quarter of a mile along the village road, and then there's a single-track road with passing places on your left. Another half mile or so, and you'll see the gates of the drive. One of them's a bit dicey – likely to fall down any day now. Best not to scrape it.'

His description was all too accurate. The gateposts might once have born heraldic beasts, but now only one of them retained a lump of stone which had been decapitated at some time. The other one was cracked all the way down, and threatened to split open down the middle like a tree struck by lightning.

The house, at the end of a short gravelly drive, was little better. Despite being called a castle, it was little more than a decayed stone house with three pepperpot towers, probably added by some Victorian trying to keep up with the baronial fancies of the time.

The front door had a rusted iron knocker in the shape of what might have been a coil of rope, a serpent, or a conger eel. When McAdam hammered on it, the door was opened by a young man with close-cropped brown hair and a square, stubborn jaw.

'Mr Pitcairn? Mr Harry Pitcairn?'

'Yes.'

She slipped out her warrant card. 'Detective Chief Inspector McAdam.'

'Police? What can I do for you?'

'May I come in?'

'Well . . . look, what's this about? We don't have any double yellow lines to park on round here. And I certainly haven't been exceeding the speed limit. Not on these roads.'

But he stood back and let her in. The interior was in keeping with the exterior. The entrance lobby was squashed into the dimensions of a suburban semi-detached. Beyond, what in any real castle would have been the grand hall was shrivelled here into a cramped drawing-room. The long oaken table in the centre emphasized the smaller scale.

Harry Pitcairn grudgingly indicated an armchair beside an empty fireplace, and propped himself against the end of the table.

'Now, what's all this about?'

McAdam was sorry she had accepted the armchair. She had to look up at him, in a commanding position in his own household. She made a point of speaking with clipped authority. 'It's about Mr Brunner. You were at his house last night.'

'I was.' His eyes had a puppyish melancholy in them, but his mouth went hard, and when he spoke he jarred his teeth together in a grating, unsteady rhythm. 'What about the bastard? Getting mad because I walked out on his scruffy charades?'

'You mean you haven't heard the news?'

'What news? Poisoned by his own lousy food – or his own bile?'

'He has been murdered.'

Pitcairn's hands tightened on the rim of the table. He leaned towards McAdam until she was afraid he was going to topple over into her lap. 'Murdered? Who by?'

'That's what I'm attempting to establish.'

109

'Good God.' He began rocking to and fro. 'Just fancy that! Give him my regards when you find him. Or her. If I had any spare cash, I'd gladly contribute towards the defence fund.'

'You really hadn't heard, Mr Pitcairn? You don't listen to the radio?'

'At this time of day?' He made it sound like the habit of a pervert.

'Can you tell me your movements yesterday evening? And why you left, when I gather the charades, as you call them, were by no means over? Hadn't you paid for the full course, if that's what you call it?'

'That's not what I'd call it. A con is what I call it.'

'But you paid to attend?'

'I wanted to see if there was any way I could get at him. See just what he was up to, what sort of scam he had in mind, what way there might be of showing him up. Oh, hell, I don't know why I thought I stood any chance of skewering a wheeler-dealer like Brunner.'

'So you left in disgust. And how did you get home?'

'I walked. Took the route that that spiteful bastard's been trying to close off.'

'What time would this be?'

'Damned if I remember. Oh, one thing – it was just before the rain started. I got home just before it started tippling down.'

'May I ask you what your profession is, Mr Pitcairn?'

'I work for Forest Enterprise. And Brunner would like us to cut down on that. Forever complaining about the noise of saws, and encroaching on his land. Which isn't so.'

'You do feel very bitter about the whole situation.'

'It's difficult not to. Wouldn't have been so bad if the estate had gone into the hands of someone who knew the traditions hereabouts. Someone who belonged, and would keep things going in the accepted way of these things. But of course every-thing had to be twisted into his own pattern. Even when he'd driven us out and taken over Balmuir, he couldn't leave it at that. Kept pestering us, sneering at us. When he found that we'd had to move into this dump – more of a stump than a castle – he made a big thing about offering to film a series here, with us dressed up as clan chieftains, going through mock skirmishes.'

A door at the far end of the room creaked open. An elderly man leaning on a gnarled stick hobbled in, slow but stiffly upright.

'Thought I heard the door.'

'Father, this is Detective Chief Inspector . . . er, sorry, I . . .'

'McAdam. Sorry to be troubling you, Mr Pitcairn, but—'

'Colonel Pitcairn,' the young man corrected her.

The older man had the same chin as his son's, but fat, self-indulgent lips which made him look permanently supercilious. There was no pretence of being a courteous host. 'And what might a police officer be wanting from this household?'

'She's investigating a murder, father. Of Chet Brunner.'

Colonel Pitcairn stamped his stick on the floor. 'That's the best news of the season. But why would you be bringing us the glad tidings in person, officer?'

'Your son may have been a witness to some crucial aspects of the case.'

'Hmph. He should never have gone there. Can't imagine what he was up to.'

'I told you, father. I was hoping I might somehow catch him on the wrong foot. Show him up for what he was, in front of his friends.'

McAdam risked a ranging shot. 'Or find some way of disposing of him?'

Colonel Pitcairn stamped his stick against the floor again, this time aggressively. 'If you're going to throw accusations like that about, young woman, you'd better give me time to call our family solicitor.' He accentuated the word 'family' with smug hauteur.

McAdam turned back to Harry. 'Can you give me exact details of where you were during the evening?'

'Hanging about most of the time. Our host had chosen to wander off and leave us to our own devices. Typical. No manners. Clears off and doesn't come back.'

'No explanation at all?'

'None. Mrs Chisholm came in with some message for him, and he upped and went. And the next we know about him is here and now, with what my father just called the glad tidings.' There was a tart relish in Harry Pitcairn's voice. 'Murdered. And not before time.'

'You didn't follow Mr Brunner when he left the room?. Or catch up with him later?'

'No, I didn't. Ask some of the others. They'll vouch for me saying what I thought about the whole disgraceful set-up, and then leaving before he came back.'

But when you left, thought McAdam, did you go off in pursuit of Brunner? And catch up with him?

He looked a fit enough, sturdy enough young man to tackle an enemy head on. Brunner might have been a large, heavy man; but he was flabby, and no match for someone who probably took plenty of healthy exercise.

Aloud she said: 'It was Mrs Chisholm, you say, who brought him a message? A telephone message from her husband at the railway station, maybe?'

'I've no idea. But he certainly went off with her fast enough.'

Did he, indeed? Queenie Chisholm hadn't mentioned this when questioned. But she was such a twitterer that it was quite possibly just one of many things during the course of that evening that had been muddled with others. And yet, if she had been the last one to see Brunner alive . . .

'I didn't kill Brunner, you know. I'm sorry I didn't. I'd love to have done it. But I didn't.'

As she drove back, McAdam noticed serried piles of trimmed, sharpened stakes which had been assembled in pyramids beside the road. As she passed the phalanxes of jabbing points, she remembered that terrific gash in Chet Brunner's forehead.

Jilly-Jo was sprawled tragically on the couch in the sitting-room beside the main hall. As the DCI appeared, she began dabbing her eyes, and produced a few ready-made tears. Yes, she was eager to agree that she had not taken the train but had been driven down by this dear friend of hers, who had been so helpful in her time of distress.

Tam Hagan shifted his bulk on the incongruously delicate Rennie Mackintosh design chair, eyeing her like an adoring dog quite capable of turning into a snarling beast if his mistress was disturbed in any way.

'And what time would it have been when you last saw your husband?'

'Oh, he wasn't around when we got here.'

'And you weren't worried?

'I thought he must have been hatching another game, keeping everyone in suspense. He was like that.' She dabbed at her eyes again. 'Such a man! So full of ideas. Our wedding – who else would have thought of anything so romantic? Miles up in the Highlands, in the ruins of an ancient monastery – just him and me, and a few close friends in the business. Oh, and that lovely old priest, of course. Just like someone out of . . . oh, you know, that historical novelist. And a lonely old wayside inn, and a housekeeper who just wept and wept. It was so beautiful.'

Georgina Campbell swept in like an actress impatient for her cue. 'You really can turn on the tap, can't you? Screeching about a divorce one minute, and then getting all lovey-dovey. Talk about putting on an act.'

'You common little bitch. At a time like this, all you can think of is making a scene. And when it comes to scenes, what about that stuff we found in Glasgow? If it hadn't been for my friend here, checking on one of the shops in his security services contract, would I ever have had the evidence? Filthy pictures, that's what. Pictures of you.'

Georgina went a shade of pink which might have been pretty but was not. 'I may have done a few artistic poses early in my career, but there was never anything filthy about them.'

McAdam said: 'Please, ladies, I do have some questions to ask.'

'And taken,' Jilly-Jo was raging on, 'in *my* dressing-room. Here, upstairs, in my room. Over my own dressing-table chair. Disgusting.' She turned to McAdam. 'That's probably where he was when I got back. With that floozy. Only they scuttled off when they heard me coming.'

'I'd got nothing to be afraid of,' crowed Georgina. 'You wouldn't catch me scuttling away. And any pictures you might have come across – well, your friend here probably has experts at touching up photographs for sale in his shop. Not the only thing he fancies touching up, either.'

Hagan stirred threateningly. Before he could say anything, the two Chisholm women came into the room.

McAdam was about to ask them to wait until she had finished questioning Jilly-Jo, who had changed from a grieving widow into a battling virago, when Anna Chisholm almost pushed her mother-in-law forward and said:

'All right. Go ahead. Tell her.'

10

The view from the farmhouse window was tranquil enough. The windows on the other side of the yard gave no sign of life – or death. The only movement was a glimpse of the hem of a blouse fluttering behind Covenanter's Cottage. Each cottage had its own concrete base about three feet square with a carousel for drying the tenants' washing. Nothing moved behind Stables Cottage.

McAdam had phoned for armed back-up. She was beginning to wonder if they needed to wait. The Watermans' car had gone, and most likely would not be coming back. Huddled here in the kitchen, they were letting valuable time go by.

Suddenly Queenie was at it again. 'I'm so sorry. I ought to have said something before, but I thought I was imagining things, only after what's happened it looks as if I wasn't. I mean, I saw her in the village, and somehow I got that queer feeling, but I had so many other things on my mind that I—'

'Do hush, Mum,' said Anna. 'It can't be helped now.'

'Of course it had a lot to do with you, dear.' Queenie turned and gripped McAdam's arm. 'I didn't want to get Anna into any trouble over letting that cottage, you see. So I told myself I must be mistaken. Only I wasn't, and it *was* Martine, only she must have dyed her hair, so I couldn't really be sure at first sight. Dyed it a sort of dark bronze. Used to be blonde. Chet always went for blondes.'

McAdam said: 'But you did get round to telling Mr Brunner

115

your suspicions. Warning him.'

'Oh, if only I hadn't. He wouldn't have gone marching off like that and . . . and . . .'

'You think he just went off, on his own, knowing that Waterman wanted to kill him?'

'He was quite capable of that,' said Anna. 'Or maybe to do a bit of snooping first. Looking in through the side window to check on what was going on. Seeing if he could recognize them both. And then just going in bald-headed, hoping to take Waterman by surprise and beat him up. That's the more likely idea. Too conceited to be frightened.'

McAdam fidgeted. 'I don't think there's anybody there. We're just wasting time. Mrs Chisholm, do you have a spare key for the door?'

'I don't carry keys around with me,' Queenie objected. 'I only collect them when I'm helping Anna out. And I don't know it'd be right to—'

McAdam turned to Anna. 'I meant you, Mrs Chisholm.'

'Yes, of course.' Anna took a ring with two keys on it from one of the hooks along a shelf of the kitchen dresser.

Sergeant Brodie said: 'I'll go, chief.'

'We'll both go. From opposite sides.'

The front door was not even locked. Inside, the keys lay on the coffee table. An empty whisky bottle jutted from the kitchen bin. There were two unwashed plates, cups and saucers, and half a loaf, on the draining board. In the bedroom, the bed had been left unmade. McAdam looked around, disappointed. She could hardly have expected to find the murder weapon here – they had probably taken it with them – but there ought somehow to have been something significant, some trace of the occupants which would spark recognition.

Brodie came in from the back. Yes, the hummock behind the carousel had a few lumpish ridges up it which could have been made by somebody dragging a corpse away from the place where it had been killed. Quite a struggle, getting it the rest of the way up the slope to where it was found. But the footprints already detected of two people could probably be traced from here upwards.

'I think we'll check with the people in Stables Cottage.'

'I've already done that. That's what you sent me down to do,' Brodie reminded her. 'They didn't hear a thing.'

'I'd still like a word with them, just in case.'

The door was answered by a youngish middle-aged man who, even as she was holding out her warrant card, said: 'Oh, not again?'

'I gather from my sergeant that you didn't hear anything suspicious last night?'

'I've already told him that.'

'And this morning? Or even during the night? Any little thing you might just remember. For example, you couldn't tell us what time the occupants of that other cottage drove off?'

'Sorry, no. Didn't hear a thing.'

'Except that damned rain.' A young woman in a striped blouse and white slacks edged out beside him. 'Couldn't get a wink of sleep, with that rain pissing down on the roof.' From the way she was scowling in his direction, she seemed almost to be blaming her companion for the Scottish weather.

There was nothing else to do but put out a call giving a description of Ronnie and Martine Waterman and their car, and alerting Stranraer and Cairnryan ferry terminals and Prestwick airport. It was barely completed when a van arrived, disgorging two police officers bulging with protective armour and guns. They looked mildly peeved at being deprived of their target practice.

After Walter had closed the door, Sharon said: 'Look, we'd better get out of here. If there's going to be police swarming around—'

'We're not doing anything illegal.'

'We're not doing anything much at all.'

'Think of it! Last night, someone gets bumped off, right close to us, and we never heard a thing. And they haven't told us exactly how he got done in.' He was hoarse with a mounting excitement. 'Bloody murder, right on our own doorstep.'

'It wasn't on the doorstep. And we don't know if it was bloody.'

'From what that sergeant said, it was pretty nasty.'

She stared at him. 'You're getting all worked up about it, aren't you?' As he moved towards her, she took a step back. 'Honest, that's disgusting. How you could think, after hearing . . . I mean, thinking about it . . . I mean, kinky, that's what you are.'

But when he began tugging at her blouse and she was saying, 'No,' and 'a pervert, that's what,' she stopped backing away, and her own hand reached for the zip on his trousers.

His first thrust drove her against the brass handles of the sideboard drawers. She howled, and tried to push herself away, but he held her with a firm pressure which surprised and delighted him – good, great, *this'll* show her – and then put his hands round her neck. 'Like to die in a passionate embrace, eh? Rape and then murder – how does that grab you?'

'Kinky,' she gasped. 'Kinky, that's what.'

But she wailed with dismay when it ended, and he slowly sagged away from her. Now her hands reached for his neck, and she forced him down to the floor and climbed on to him and her fingers moved down from his neck and tried desperately to force him back to life.

There was a banging on the door.

'Oh, for Christ's sake. What do they want this time?'

Wally groped for his trousers, but one leg had been pulled inside out when Sharon wrenched them off, and he was still struggling when she grabbed her green silk dressing-gown from the hook behind the door and clutched it loosely around her as she opened the door.

The man outside was saying over his shoulder: 'Maybe it's the other cottage.' Behind him, in the middle of the yard, a television camera was lining up on the front of the building. There was an appreciative whistle as Sharon appeared. The man at the door looked back at her, and eyed her up and down. 'Sorry to interrupt, but I wonder if you could tell us anything about the dramatic events of last night? The police statement says something about the folk in one of these cottages. Obviously not yours, I suppose?'

The camera was zooming in on her. Sharon could not help smiling back at it. She had always wondered what it would be

118

like to be on the telly.

'You out of your mind?' Wally's hand was on her shoulder. The dressing-gown slithered under his fingers, and her bare shoulder glowed in the late afternoon sunlight. There was a faint groan of disappointment outside as he dragged her in and slammed the door.

DCI McAdam had finished giving instructions for wrapping up in the incident room and was gathering the guests for a statement when the TV crew arrived at Balmuir Lodge itself and started asking for a statement for viewers as well. Anxious to be done with the whole thing, she decided to let them watch and take whatever shots they needed while she told the guests they were now free to go.

'And about time, too.'

The interviewer said: 'Might we say these good people have been suspects until now?'

'No, you may not. They have simply been helping the police with their enquiries.'

'While you let the murderer slip away under your nose?'

'He won't get far, believe me.' She raised her voice and continued. 'Ladies and gentlemen, we already have your names and addresses in case we need to call you as witnesses. If you haven't already given them, please have a word with Sergeant Brodie before leaving.'

Several of them looked incapable of making up their minds. Everybody felt let down, yet at the same time tingling with the leftovers of excitement.

'What a day!' gasped Felicity Godolphin. 'Edwin and I, we're quite exhausted.' She ogled the camera. 'But we do prefer activity holidays, you know. We've been on so many literary and cultural cruises. But nothing like this. So dreadful. So absolutely ghastly.'

'But we did come here for a murder game,' said her husband, 'and it has to be admitted that we got our money's worth.'

His wife gave him an arch nudge in the ribs. 'What an awful thing to say. You ought to be ashamed of yourself. But it's true.' She returned to her moment of stardom on camera. 'It really has been a remarkable experience. It just has to give my husband an idea for his next book. He's Edwin Godolphin, you know.'

They would have so much to tell their friends when they got home, thought McAdam.

'And you don't have to worry about me.' Jilly-Jo was not going to stay out of the limelight. She half turned towards the camera, as if caught unawares while talking frankly to somebody nearby, knowing which half-profile showed her at her best. Her eyes were bright with sincerity, attentive to whoever she was supposed to be speaking to at the time. When attention was off her, they would go completely dead. 'I belong here, and here I stay.'

Sir Nicholas and Lady Torrance were more subdued, but suggested that for many of them it was too late to get anywhere tonight. There were murmurs of agreement. They would all leave first thing in the morning.

Alec organized a supper, under orders from Jilly-Jo, playing the grande dame, bravely bearing her sorrows and giving the orders now. One of the first of them to be ordered out was Georgina Campbell.

'I'm staying.' Georgina, too, was playing to the camera. she would be only too glad to create some viewable drama.

'This is my home,' said Jilly-Jo, 'and I don't want a slut like you in it.'

'No way is it your home. Chet wanted *me* in it.'

'Wait till we find out about his will. Whatever you've been trying to squeeze out of him, he won't have had time to alter it yet – unless you've been a sight sharper than I think.'

Tam Hagan, who had been standing well back in order not to interfere with her act, came to life. 'I don't know,' he mumbled. 'You can't, really.'

'Can't what?'

'Yer can't throw the lassie out at this time of night. She's not doing any harm.'

Jilly-Jo glared at him suspiciously. Georgina simpered.

McAdam became aware that Sergeant Brodie was whispering in her ear. 'Quite an act, isn't it? I remember her in that horror film a couple of years back. *The Bride of the Monster*. Only a remake of an old film with Elsa Lanchester in it, and of course there was no comparison between them, but she was still pretty creepy.'

'When you've finished doing your film critic's column, sergeant, perhaps you'd be good enough to check you've got all those addresses. And see that that girl at the VDU has been told she can get back to HQ. Then we'll get out of here.'

Watching the crowd of them shuffling to and fro, some swapping reminiscences of things they had guessed about Brunner right from the start, and some complaining about the collapse of the whole programme, McAdam felt drained. She ought to be glad that the investigation had been wrapped up so quickly and neatly. All the thought she had given to the possible suspects, all the theories she had juggled with, all of it meaningless now. So many of those present had behaved so oddly and suspiciously, yet in the end there were no subtleties. Whatever silly complicated murder games Brunner and his hangers-on might have played, real-life murders were usually straightforward, brutish killings with a gun, a knife, or a blunt instrument.

Ronnie Waterman had done time because of what Chet Brunner had revealed about him, and after years inside brooding about it had come here to murder Brunner. And he had succeeded, the job was done, and he had cleared off.

As simple as that.

11

Nick felt the front wheels of the car slither to the left, and coaxed them back carefully. The sky ahead looked brighter, but with a sullen sheen rather than any promise of sunshine out of a blue heaven.

'Thank heavens we're on the move,' said Lesley. 'I can still feel the atmosphere of that place. It clings. Like the smell of bad drains.'

'Exaggerating a bit, aren't we?'

'No, we're not. Even before the murder, there was something about the house that gave me the creeps. Your friend Brunner most of all.'

'Well, now he's gone, maybe somebody will fumigate the place.'

They went over a ridge and on a winding course down towards an overflowing burn. Clinging moisture in the shallow gully was breathing a thin steam, from which you almost expected ghosts and elves of the glen to appear. Instead, a local bus with a mud-coated number-plate came lumbering out of the cloud wraiths. It proclaimed itself SCHOOL BUS, but there were no children in it. Presumably they had been dumped somewhere over a hill, in a village hidden from what could hardly be called a main road.

After a while Lesley said: 'It's a pretty nauseating concept, isn't it, when you come to think of it?'

'What concept do we have in mind this time?'

She laughed, inviting them both to ease off and enjoy their release from Balmuir Lodge. 'All those women he seems to have had. What sort of lover do you suppose he would have been?'

'A heavyweight one, most likely.'

'Yes, that's just about what I mean. How could even a greedy little tart like that awful Jilly-Jo—'

'And the equally awful carbon copy, Georgina—'

'Exactly. How could even those two put up with that great fat slob crushing down on them?'

'The weight of money and influence is quite tolerable when the casting couch is padded well enough.'

'You speak from personal experience?'

He glanced at her with a mock scowl, then braked for a sign indicating twists and turns ahead. Why should they have bothered to put it here, when all the rest of the road had already been like a snake in intricate contortions?

'Never,' he said.

Now that she had raised the subject, he couldn't help letting his mind wander over the disgusting picture. Subtle foreplay would never have been something you'd associate with Chet Brunner. Bang, bang, and that was it. One could only hope that for the women the expensive trimmings were worth it.

Lesley broke into his thoughts. 'So there was quite a cast of convincing suspects.'

'Just a minute. Hold it. We know who had the strongest motive of the lot, and the whole script points to him doing it and then making a run for it.'

'It's too neat.'

'Are some things too straightforward for an ex-copper? You prefer some complexities and an intellectual challenge? Your speciality, as I recall, was stolen artworks and fakes. Subtle, complicated stuff. In cases of violent crime, isn't it usually something pretty crude and straightforward?'

'Mm, yes. Not playing contrived games like Brunner and his hangers-on. Blunt and brutally obvious.' But still she was uneasy. 'Most of the time.'

'So what's different here?'

'I can't put my finger on it. Just that I've got this weird feel-ing it's all too pat.'

'For heavens' sake, how many times do I have to remind you you're not in the job any more? You don't have to spin cases out in order to clock up the overtime. Straightforward this time. Brutal murder, killer immediately identified, case solved. And it's somebody else's job to catch the killer. Which shouldn't be all that difficult.'

'No. Not even for that snotty DCI.'

'Jealousy? Wishing you could be in her shoes?'

'I'd have been a lot more thorough in questioning some of those folk. About those games they were playing, for a start. How can we be sure that Brunner's own murder might not have been part of a game gone wrong – or cleverly contrived?'

'But there wasn't any game going on at the time he got killed. We were there, remember? And everyone was at a bit of a loose end, and grumbling about it.'

'Couldn't that have been part of it? Brunner and someone else devising a cunning ploy? Only for Brunner it went wrong. Became the real thing. Which he wasn't expecting.'

'And who did you have in mind as the guilty party?'

'You want me to run through them?'

'Be my guest. Show me how the mind of a sleuth works.'

'Quite a few people in that house had good reason for detest-ing Brunner. Whoever it was, they might not have been planning a murder, but then the opportunity suddenly presented itself. Remember that phone call? Everybody in the place was informed that Ronnie Waterman was on the loose.'

'Not everybody. Brunner's wife, Jilly-Jo, hadn't got back.'

'True. But any one of the others might all at once have seen Waterman on the prowl as being a perfect cover for a killing. Who else *was* in the room at the time?'

Nick thought for a moment. 'I think that gushing couple, the Godolphins, were there. And that young man with a chip on his shoulder about Brunner in his old family home. Oh, and the chap who seems to wander about with Alec and Queenie's daughter-in-law.'

'And what about your friend Alec himself? He was the one

125

who brought the glad tidings. He and his wife were maybe reaching the end of their tether. And Alec knew more about Brunner's goings-on than anybody else. Faithful house dog finally turns on its owner.'

'Oh, come off it. Alec and Queenie wouldn't have it in them to smash someone in the face and break his neck.'

'You never know what people will do when they're pushed. I'd guess Brunner had given them a hard time of it over the years. And Queenie did realize it was Waterman in that cottage, and kept quiet about it until after the deed was done.'

'Leaving the corpse outside the cottage in the hope it'd be found in the morning and suspicion would be thrown on Waterman? Didn't their daughter-in-law, Anna, say she thought she'd seen something down there, only she hadn't been sure right away. And later it was shifted. By whom?'

'How should I know? Maybe you're right, and none of it was carefully planned. Everything was rushed through on the spur of the moment.'

Nick shook his head in time with the twists in the road. 'Just for the hell of it, let me contradict myself. Waterman *had* been planning it. Only the exact opportunity took him by surprise. But then why shift the corpse afterwards – drag it all the way up the hill?'

'To divert attention from their own proximity.'

'Could be.'

'I still think it's too crude. Suppose, just for the hell of it, that your friend Alec had got back from the station before he admitted, and Queenie told him where Brunner had gone – where she had sent him after she had remembered Martine – and Alec took the chance he'd been waiting for, after years of being pushed around. And then they hauled him out of the way.'

'Why would they bother to do that?'

'Well, er . . . not to embarrass Anna, who made her living from those cottages.'

'Sorry, but I can't wear that. Poor old Alec. Or Queenie. Don't see them having the strength. Let alone the strength to bash Chet in the head in the first place.'

'It's often poor old this, that or the other that finally turns and bites the hand that feeds it. Or that's been beating it.'

'I still think the simple explanation is the right one. Pretty clear who did it. Why complicate matters just because you can't bear to let go of your old job?'

'We wouldn't have been in that ghastly place if you hadn't had a hankering to see *your* old playmates again and maybe get a chance of doing some work at a mixing deck.'

Nick laughed. If this was their first marital row, it was good fun. Especially as Lesley was laughing, too; yet was still frowning slightly, turning things over in her mind.

She unfolded the map on her knee. 'You said Eskdalemuir? And then Langholm?'

'That's right.'

'It looks like a long way round.'

'From where we've just started,' said Nick, 'everywhere is a long way round.'

Whatever their criminal behaviour might have been in other settings, at least the Maxwells – or Watermans – had left Stables Cottage reasonably tidy. Apart from the unmade bed and the bits and pieces in the kitchen, they might never have been on the premises. And even if he had been a crook, at least Ronnie Waterman hadn't nicked any of her paintings.

After hauling the vacuum cleaner out of the cupboard and running it over the carpets, Anna turned the television on just to make sure it was working. It was part of her automatic routine. It had been left set by the Watermans to the news channel, and began reporting on a suicide bomber somewhere in the Middle East. That sort of news was becoming almost as routine as reports of pile-ups on the M8 between Glasgow and Edinburgh.

She was tipping the few scraps from the wastepaper basket and the kitchen bin into a plastic sack when the picture on the screen switched suddenly to a local announcer warning the public that police had followed up last night's news about the disappearance of a suspected murderer from Balmuir district with a warning that he was still at large. He could be dangerous and should not be approached. Any sightings should at once be reported to a number flashed across the bottom of the screen or to a local police station.

Just as she was about to switch off, the picture changed again, and she found herself looking at the outside of the building she was in. It was a weird sensation, watching a camera advancing on Stables Cottage as if to keep going until it was in the room with her. Then it veered away and followed an interviewer towards Covenanter's Cottage.

The door opened, and Mrs Robinson – if that was really her name – stood in the opening, dishevelled and clad in the skimpiest dressing-gown Anna had ever seen, even in the most provocative magazine advertisements.

The voice over was trying to find an excuse for lingering on the sexy image: 'And it has come as quite a shock to holiday-makers to learn that a murderer has been staying in the neighbouring cottage. Not the sort of excitement you expect during a relaxing break!' Behind the girl, Robinson's face appeared for a moment, contorted with anger, and his hand on her shoulder dragged her back indoors. The voice continued without any apparent break: 'And up the hill, close to the big house . . .' The camera was panning up towards the swimming-pool, pausing for a moment by the small tent and the corral of police tape, and then heading for Balmuir Lodge.

Anna had seen enough of those faces and heard enough of those clamouring voices to last her a lifetime. She reached for the remote control to reduce Jilly-Jo's shrewdly distraught features to a brief blotch of light across the screen, and turned her attention to stripping the bed. She had just piled sheets and pillow-cases on the end of the couch, ready to go to the laun-drette, when there was a screech of brakes in the yard outside.

Alec and Queenie had arrived in the battered yellow Fiat. Cocky leapt out and dashed around the stableyard to check that nothing new, fascinating and smelly had happened in his absence.

'I just knew you'd need some help, dear.' Queenie bobbed her head jerkily at Anna and started talking at a high pitch, churning out a wild gabble. 'Such a time! Such a mess to be cleared up, one way and another.'

Anna was not really in the mood for Queenie blundering and

fussing all over the place. 'I'd have thought there was much more pandemonium up at the house,' she ventured.

'Oh, you have no idea. We simply had to get away for a breather. Nothing to be done up there. Just let them pack up and go home, and then we can get some peace. Only they're not all going, of course. Jilly-Jo's acting as if she owns the whole place already. And shameless about that dreadful man she brought along. I can't help feeling that if we didn't know the killer was that old enemy of Chet's, there'd be good reason to wonder about—'

'The police are dealing with it,' Alec interrupted gently. He put his arm round her shoulders, but she was still quivering like a taut string about to snap. 'It doesn't concern us any more.'

'Doesn't it? When we might be thrown out tomorrow. Just the way she's told Georgina Campbell to get the hell out. Her own words: "Get the hell out of here, right now." Only that awful man, he's taking the poor little trollop's side, and that's not helping. All that pouting and tossing their heads about.' A wistful note crept into Queenie's voice. 'A real Bette Davis scene.'

Anna looked past her, out of the window. On the ridge she saw two cars heading away from Balmuir. There would be others to follow. Maybe, very soon, one with herself in it. Would it be an escape – or a banishment?

Nick realized that he had taken a wrong turning. That wrong turning which had taken them to Balmuir Lodge had also taken them into trouble. He did not fancy a repeat performance.

'Let's have a look at that map.'

'Sorry, I wasn't concentrating. I was thinking of—'

'Thinking of another false trail?' he grinned.

The road had been narrow enough already, but this one was even tighter, twisting up and over hummocks in convolutions making it difficult to get out of second and third gear. The light, too, was deceptive. Above a black shroud of forestry plantation, glimpses of hills with white caps made one think there was still snow on the peaks, but they were only outcrops of bare rock, still sparkling with moisture in the sunlight.

It looked as though nobody had been along this road since the rain, and even before that it had not been much used. Tufts of grass grew along the centre of the road. A couple of triangular signs said 'Passing Place'; but there were other bare poles whose triangles had long since rusted and fallen off.

'I hereby swear to concentrate on the map and not let my mind wander,' said Lesley.

They had gone another tortuous mile when, on a steep hundred yards with a stream feeding into a culvert under the road, and a perilous dip in the camber, Nick saw below them a smear of blue which did not belong to the natural scenery. He stopped, and wound down his window. Way down the slope there was a car on its side. It must have come off the wet road and careered down the grass before being stopped and tossed on its side by a tree trunk. Had it been there long? One might have expected to see a 'Police Aware' notice stuck in the window.

Lesley, leaning across him, said: 'There's somebody inside. In the front seat. I can see a head, propped against the window.'

Nick bumped the Laguna warily on to the verge, fearful it might be trapped in a waiting quagmire. They got out, and edged step by step down the slope, the earth sucking greedily at their feet. Beside them, all the way down, tyre tracks wove a giddy, rambling pattern.

What Lesley had seen was a woman with her shoulder in an awkward, unnatural position. Her face was white and twisted with pain, her eyes half closed. She became aware of them peering in, and mouthed something inaudible. As Nick straightened up to look around, a man came up behind him. A gun jabbed into Nick's ribs.

'You're going to give us a lift.'

Nick said: 'Your name wouldn't chance to be Waterman, would it?'

12

Ronnie Waterman grinned. He looked almost proud to have been recognized. Setting his back against the buckled wing of the tilted Escort, he licked his lips and swung the gun between Nick and Lesley.

'Spot on,' he said. 'Can't say I know you two, though. Tourists?'

'The name's Torrance. And we've been staying at Balmuir Lodge.'

The woman in the car gave a faint whimper through the half-open window. It was impossible to tell whether it was a gasp of pain or of apprehension.

Waterman said: 'Have you, now. Then you'd know what's happened there.'

'Yes. And we know that the police are out looking for you. I fancy it won't take them too long to find you.' Nick leaned over the windscreen to look more closely inside. Waterman at once jabbed the gun towards him, gesturing him away.

'Your wife needs help,' said Lesley.

'Yeah. But not as much as I do. And I reckon that's where you come in.' Waterman glanced up the slope to the shape of the Laguna at the roadside. 'One of you's going to get me out of here.'

'It's your wife we're talking about.'

'Martine'll be all right there until I'm good and clear. Then someone can do something about phoning for an ambulance. But not till then.'

'Selfish bastard,' groaned his wife. 'But then, you always were.'

Nick sensed that Lesley was poising herself for a leap upon Waterman. He tried to frown a warning, mutely imploring her to suppress her old professional instincts. This scrawny little man looked too stooped and shrunken to be a serious menace. But he had killed once already, and he was desperate. Nothing more to lose. Perfectly capable of living up to that threat.

'Right.' Waterman seemed to have sized them up, and was gaining confidence. 'Do you have a mobile on you?'

'It's in the car,' said Lesley quickly.

Waterman smirked. 'I wonder if it really is? Maybe in hubby's pocket, eh? But let me make one thing clear. If you try to use it to raise the fuzz, mister, your little lady is going to get hurt. Seriously hurt.'

'If you've got any sense,' said Nick, 'you'll give yourself up now. And get an ambulance here for *your* little lady.'

'What we are going to do,' Waterman rasped, 'is this. You, Mr Torrance, are going to stay right here. Since you're so concerned about my wife, you can keep her company and tell her a few fairy stories. While your missus here drives your car away with me in it.'

'If you think for a moment—'

'Shut up and listen. Your missus comes back up there with me, and she drives me until I'm ready to ditch her. Once I'm sure I'm in the clear, and can fix things the way I want 'em, her time's her own. *Then* she can ring for an ambulance. Or' – he grinned slyly – 'she can ring you on your mobile, if you've got it in your pocket after all, and let you know she's all right, and you can do the ambulance calling. But get this straight. Any attempt to get the police moving before I'm well on my way – any jumping the gun – and this little gun here will go off. Make no mistake about that.'

His eyes were yellow. The knuckles of his right hand, clutching the gun, were a deathly grey through the skin.

'You won't get away with this.' As soon as he had uttered it,

Nick thought what a pathetic cliché it was.

Lesley said: 'I'll be all right, Nick. Really I will.'

Waterman looked at her suspiciously. He was taut and on edge – and all the more dangerous for that. By contrast, her calmness worried him.

'Right, then,' he said. 'We'll be on our way.'

He indicated that Lesley should start back up the slope. Nick judged the distance between them as Waterman himself began the short climb. If he made a spring now, hurled himself forward . . .

Waterman glanced briefly over his shoulder. 'Any funny business, and she's the first to go. Understood?'

Nick clenched his fists until the nails bit into the palms of his hands.

Standing still and helpless wasn't in his nature. The sight of Lesley being herded towards the Laguna with Waterman jabbing the gun at her like a cattle prod made him sick inside. He took a step away from the car.

Martine said: 'Worried about your precious car?'

'I'm worried about my wife. I can't just stand here and—'

'Don't risk it. The state he's in, he might just fire that thing. Just out of panic.'

Her head lolled against the window. There was already a large blue and purple bruise on her left cheek, where maybe she had hit it against the fascia board or the window itself.

Nick bent carefully towards her. 'How bad is it? What actually happened?' He reached for the door handle, but she let out a groan to stop him. 'No, please. Something's broken. I can just . . . keep it in . . . propped up like this. Don't make me fall out. Please, leave it.'

'You haven't got a car-phone? Or a mobile? We do need that ambulance.'

'He's got a mobile. With him. And anyway, you heard what he said. Better wait.'

Nick tried to force the tension in his muscles to ease off. He told himself that Lesley would be fine. She still had all that training to rely on. She would choose the right moment; she would know exactly what to do. She'd be fine. He kept telling himself that. She'd be fine.

'Where do you suppose he's heading?'

Somewhere a bird began singing. The smell of damp grass and damp leaves must have been there all along, but was suddenly intensified by a breeze rustling through the branches above. Leaves in the sycamore tree against which the Escort had finished up began shedding a fine shower of raindrops on to the roof of the car.

Martine sighed. Her eyes were bleared with exhaustion. Her mouth drooped at the corners. 'I've no idea. And I don't suppose he has. There's nobody likely to offer a helping hand.'

'Not much loyalty when one of your old cronies has committed a murder?'

'Oh, he hasn't committed a murder. Not this time. He wanted to, but all the wind's gone out of him. He didn't have the guts to go through with it.'

'But just a minute. Chet Brunner was murdered. And you two made a run for it.'

'I'm telling you,' said Martine in little more than a whisper. 'Ronnie didn't kill Chet.'

'I can tell you one thing, anyway,' said Ronnie Waterman. 'I didn't kill Chet Brunner.'

Lesley swung the car around a ragged hole in the road. 'Then why are you making a run for it and waving that gun at me?'

'Because I'm not stupid enough to think they'd believe me. They'd just love fitting me up. And don't try chucking the car about like that again. I'm not going to lose control of this shooter.'

She could not risk taking her eyes off the road, but tried to work out from his voice inflections and breathing what state of mind he was in.

'You really don't have any idea where we're going, do you?' she said as lightly as possible.

'Just keep driving. I'll tell you when to stop.'

They were approaching a small crossroads with a very outdated signpost, its lettering sprouting a green mould. 'Right now,' she said, 'maybe you can tell me which turning to take.'

'Turn right. That should take us back towards the Stranraer road.'

'Thinking of emigrating to Ireland?'

'I've told you' – the words came out slurred and shaky – 'just keep going.'

Maybe killing Brunner had used up his last resources. It was finished, and now he was drained. If she could keep her head, he would sag and give up of his own accord.

Keep him talking. 'You can't seriously expect me to believe that you didn't kill the man you hated so much? You'd sworn to get him. That seems to have been common knowledge. And why else would you have moved into that cottage and bided your time? And when exactly did the opportunity present itself?'

'It didn't. I had no hand in it.' As if it were some valid excuse, he added: 'He wasn't shot, you know.'

'No, I know. So why don't you put that gun away and let us ring for an ambulance for your wife, and—'

'Just because I didn't shoot that time, doesn't mean I won't do it this time.'

'How *did* you do it? Some pretty hefty blunt instrument, judging by the mess on his forehead. And that broken neck.'

'I'm telling you, I had no part in it. That's how we found him. Outside our cottage. We'd been into Ayr to the pictures, just to pass the time. Came back in that rain, and there he was, planted right outside our cottage. We weren't going to have that dumped on us. We lugged him as far up the hill as we could.'

'But who would have known you were there? I mean, known who you were? If someone else was going to commit a murder, knowing all along that you'd be likely to get the blame, how did they *know* you were sitting there so conveniently?'

'Hell, don't you think I'd like to know? But that Queenie suspected something. And that Mrs Chisholm who runs the cottages came back from somewhere and gave us a funny look when we opened our door to look out.' He wriggled in his seat. 'Look, you'll have to stop for a minute.'

135

'Thinking of listening to what I say, and turning back?'

'Not sodding likely. I'm bursting for a pee.'

Lesley laughed as she slowed on to the ragged verge of the road.

'Nice little cluster of bushes over there.'

'Don't get smart. I'm doing it right here where I can keep an eye on you. Don't try anything funny.'

She felt oddly relaxed. It was all too pathetic. Her only danger was that he might fire the gun out of sheer nervousness, or just because his finger was unsteady. He looked ridiculous as he circled the bonnet of the car, pointing the gun at her, and then beginning to unbutton his flies, fumbling for his penis.

She could close both the doors with a flick of a switch, and there'd be no way he could get back in. But he might lose control and fire at her through the window.

Quietly she opened her door a fraction of an inch.

He was trying to pee while still keeping his gaze on her and the gun trained on her. He was standing at such an awkward angle that he began to dribble down his trouser leg. With a muttered curse he tried to edge a few inches to the right, and his foot began to slide over a coating of mud. He slipped, flailed out with one hand, and dropped the gun.

Lesley was out of the car, hurling herself at him. She wrenched his arm behind his back. Urine sprayed across her wrist, and then she was pushing him face down to the ground. She gave his arm a violent tweak that made him howl.

'If you make any move to get away, I'll break your arm. And then your leg, just to make sure.'

She groped for the gun, and released him.

'You stupid bitch.'

'No,' she said. 'As I told you, the police aren't stupid.'

'Police? You're never a copper.'

'In a recent incarnation, that's just what I was.'

'Oh, shit.'

She felt quite sorry for him as she steered him towards the car and into the front passenger seat.

'You know how to use a car-phone, I'm sure. Must have

stolen plenty of them in your time, right? So ring for an ambulance.'

'And what if I don't?'

'I know just where to shoot you in the knee to cause the most discomfort.'

'Police brutality never goes down well in court.'

'Self defence,' said Lesley. 'Now do as I say.'

'I can't tell them exactly where we are.'

She smiled sympathetically. 'I never did think you had much idea where we were going. Just running for the sake of it. All right. You know where Martine is, because you were doing the driving. And I'd estimate you came off the road about fifteen miles south-east of Balmuir, on the Moniaive road. And when you've done that, you can ring the police and tell them that we're twelve miles further on, down the first right turning, with a signpost nobody can read.'

'You're not thinking of driving us back yourself?'

His weaselly cunning was too transparent. 'No,' said Lesley. 'I'm not going to risk an undignified scuffle in the car. We wait here until the cavalry arrives. And to pass the time, you can tell me the rest of your fairy story.'

Defeated, he slumped into the seat, made the ambulance call, and then went on with the plaintive whine of a deeply wronged man. She had heard it so often from villains who were as guilty as hell but still resented being found out.

'For a little while we thought we'd sit tight and go on being Mr and Mrs Maxwell. We were innocent, so why shouldn't we sit it out? But then Martine said she thought . . . well, she couldn't be sure, but . . . look, you want to start asking questions about that Queenie Chisholm.'

'Queenie?'

'Martine thought she'd been recognized. Thought Queenie remembered her. So we'd better get out of there after all.'

Queenie had known who they were, and what their probable plans were? Nick had said how hard it was to imagine Queenie committing a murder. Fey and unpredictable she might be, but she would never have had the strength to lay Brunner low.

137

But she could have told somebody else.

'It wasn't worth the risk, hanging around there,' said Waterman. 'We just had to get out.'

'Why didn't you stay, and tell the police just what you're telling me? Tell them exactly what you'd found? Show them where the body had been, and how you had dragged it up the slope?'

'And who'd believe us? I'd told everyone I was going to get Brunner. And I meant it. But somebody else got there first.'

'So why not give yourself up and tell them that? The police aren't stupid.'

'You would say that, wouldn't you?' He tried a moment of defiance. 'Oh, not too stupid to cover up, I'll give you that. Cover up having lost track of me. Shove me inside, fill in the right forms, case closed, and dash off to the next fit-up before anyone noses in too deeply.'

The rescue party arrived in a surprisingly short time, and in impressive force. Three armed men, padded with body armour and followed by a dog handler with a large Alsatian, sprang out of a white van liberally decorated with the red, yellow and electric blue of the Kyle and Carrick Constabulary, and stamped towards the Laguna.

'Right, Waterman. Come on out with your hands up. Stay quite still, Lady Torrance, and you'll be perfectly safe.'

Waterman slid out of the car, with one backward glance. 'Lady Torrance? Christ, whoever heard of a copper being a lady?'

For the twentieth or thirtieth time, Nick looked at his watch. How much longer before something happened; somebody appeared? He heaved himself up the slanting side of the Escort and into the driver's seat, taking care not to jar against Martine's sprawled right leg and hip.

She eased herself into a more comfortable position. 'Look, if you want to try and get in touch with someone, try to stop him before your wife—'

'I'm not worried about my wife.' Nick was trying to convince himself as much as Martine. 'I think she can cope when the moment presents itself.'

'Yes. I don't think he's capable of killing anyone any more. Not any more.' She sounded almost regretful that Lesley was in no real danger. 'He's past it. All the wind's gone out of him. From the moment I felt we'd been spotted, all he wanted was to be well out of it. Only we left it a bit late. And after all that time inside, his driving wasn't too good.'

'On roads like these, anyone could come off. I was close to it myself, several times.' Absurd, thought Nick, that he should be making soothing noises to her about the driving skills of her long-time villain of a husband. 'Just a minute. When you said you'd been spotted, what did you mean? Who by?'

'Queenie Chisholm. We saw her in the village, and the way she looked at me I thought perhaps . . . well, for a moment I wasn't sure. But afterwards I just got the feeling that she could have recognized me.'

'She did. But I gather she didn't say anything right away.'

'Whenever she said it, it was too risky for us to stay there. The murder was bound to be blamed on Ronnie.'

'You still say he wasn't guilty?'

'He's been guilty of plenty of things. But not of killing Chet.'

On the road above, an ambulance was drawing in to the side. Two paramedics came hurrying down the slope. One put his arm through the open window and gently touched Martine's forehead while his colleague went round to the driver's side. Nick wriggled out to make room for him.

The two men examined Martine as if handling a fragile piece of porcelain. Then one nodded and said: 'Try to let yourself slump down a bit while I open the door. Don't worry, I won't let you fall. Ian, can you see how she's fixed on your side.'

Nick said: 'You've heard from my wife, then?'

'It was a man called Waterman who rang, sir. He told us about his wife here.'

'Didn't he say something about mine?'

'Not that I know of, sir. We just got the message, and got here as fast as we could.'

They lifted Martine on to a stretcher, and carried her up the lumpy slope with a care and steadiness that would have earned

139

the admiration of a fire-walker. As they reached the road, the Laguna pulled in behind the ambulance.

Nick bounded up the hill and threw his arms around her. 'What the hell happened?'

'I overpowered him,' said Lesley modestly, 'then made him ring the ambulance. And then I called the police to come and collect him. Purely routine.'

'Overpowered him? Rough business? I thought you were an academic sort of policewoman. Dealing with art thefts and identification of assay marks, that sort of thing. Never suspected you of beating up suspects.'

'Whatever you do afterwards, your basic training takes in a lot of unarmed combat and some nasty tricks of the trade.'

Martine on her stretcher was being lifted into the ambulance. She turned her head stiffly to gaze admiringly at Lesley. 'He was good at getting other people to do that sort of thing for him. Wish I'd had your training.'

'I'm to pick you up,' said Lesley to her husband, 'and drive us to Ayr. Or you can drive. You've had rather a long break doing damn-all.'

'Why should we want to go to Ayr?'

'McAdam wants a statement. Everything that happened and everything that was said.'

'Into Ayr? Almost back where we started. And by that time . . . have to find a hotel in Ayr, I suppose.'

'No,' said Lesley. 'I've phoned Anna Chisholm. For obvious reasons she has a few days vacant in one of her cottages for a short let this week.'

'But we don't want to go back there.'

'As a matter of fact, we do,' said Lesley. 'Because I'm not satisfied. Too many things were overlooked. And I don't believe Ronnie Waterman killed Chet Brunner.'

'Oh, he's been spinning you the story as well, has he? Like Martine.'

'Yes. And I believe him. We've got a couple of days to spare before we go home. I won't be happy till I've gone all over that ground again.'

'In McAdam's footsteps?'

140

'Ahead of her this time, I hope.'

'I'm sure she'll love that.'

It was all crazy, thought Nick. What an end to a honeymoon. Started out as a love story, then became a murder story, and now it was sheer farce.

13

The phone call from Lesley Torrance, with its news about the capture of the Watermans and the urgent offer to take over the remaining days of their abruptly broken tenancy, had only just finished when the phone rang again. This time the caller was a girl whose voice was as strangulated as Mr Ritchie's. She might have been taught this as a condition of employment in the Haining and Ritchie office.

'Would that be Mrs Chisholm I'm speaking to? Mrs Anna Chisholm?'

'It would,' said Anna.

'Then I'll be putting you through to our Mr Ritchie.' Now there was a reverent, throttled-down quality in the tone.

Ritchie's attitude when he came on was quite changed since their last encounter. He tried to combine obsequiousness with pride in his own achievements, but she wondered why he should sound so fawning rather than cocky.

'Well now, Mrs Chisholm. Ye'll not be saying we haven't been working hard in your interests. I've had a surprising number of enquiries for your cottages. But in the present circumstances, I've felt it my duty to ca' canny – verra, verra careful indeed – in sieving them, if I may put it like that. We'd not be wanting some sensation-seeking undesirables, would we now?'

'We would not. But at the moment I'm not sure that I—'

'Regrettably we've had one cancellation for next week. Of course we shall insist on a cancellation charge. But ye'll be glad to hear that I have personally chosen a substitute.'

'So our recent misfortunes have not, as you predicted, led to a slump in trade?' said Anna drily.

'Och, Mrs Chisholm, we all make the wee mistake from time to time.'

She would never have expected him even to hint at such a possibility.

He went on: 'And there's a respectable couple who'd be happy to take over one of the cottages for what's left of this week, and stay on for next week as well.'

'Nothing doing, I'm afraid. Covenanter's Cottage needs a thorough going-over, and I've just had a call from . . . well, from friends . . . who want to take Stables Cottage for a few days.'

'Could ye be giving me the name of these friends, then, so I can keep our records straight?'

Meaning, she thought, that he wanted to make sure that the letter of their agreement was honoured and Haining and Ritchie would get their usual commission.

She said: 'We'll discuss it later, Mr Ritchie. When all the legal problems concerning the whole estate are clarified, I fancy we'll have quite a lot to discuss.'

'Aye, we will that.' There was a pause, at the end of which he became as awed and deferential as the telephonist had been earlier. 'Mr Haining is also wishing to have a word wi' ye.' It was clear that from the telephonist onwards there was a strict hierarchy, rising step by step to the senior partner.

'Mrs Chisholm?' It was a more confident and resonant voice than Ritchie's.

'Mr Haining.' Anna tried to match his solemnity.

'I am sorry to be telling you that there has been a rather displeasing turn of events. A delicate procedure. Very – hm – delicate. Strictly speaking, I ought not to be contacting you until proper legal formalities have been gone through. Matters of confirmation, you understand. All very regrettable. At this establishment we have not been used to dealing with – hm – people of a certain calibre. We ought not to have been put in this unethical position, but in the circumstances I thought it advisable to be having a word with you.'

Anna glanced at the kitchen clock, wondering how long it would be before Mr Haining considered it ethical to get to the point.

His voice sank half an octave. 'As ye'll no' need telling, Mrs Chisholm, there are strict obligations set upon the legal representatives of a deceased client, and as such representatives of the late Mr Brunner—'

'I didn't know Mr Brunner had dealings with you. I'd have thought he kept his interests in London.'

'The late Mr Brunner has lived in this region for some years now, and rightly considered it more practical to deal in certain personal matters with the most highly respected firm in the said region.'

Probably rather like having a separate drawing facility at a provincial branch of one's bank, thought Anna; but she felt it was not a comparison Mr Haining would relish.

'To be blunt,' he said at last, 'we drew up Mr Brunner's most recent will for him, and it is lodged here with us. The executor he appointed was Mr Alec Chisholm, whom of course you know.'

'My father-in-law.'

'Ah, hm, yes,' said Mr Haining mysteriously. 'We may need to discuss that at a later stage, depending on one's interpretation of . . . that is . . . Ah, well,' he went on with a sudden burst of speed, 'I have tried to telephone Mr Chisholm to warn him, but he does not appear to be on the premises.'

'Probably gone down to the village,' said Anna. Then she said: 'Just a minute. What do you mean – "warn him"?'

'We have had a visit from Mr Brunner's wife – hm – widow, that is. Accompanied by a singularly aggressive person by the name of Hagan.'

Anna could not repress a grin at the thought of Tam Hagan swaggering into the chaste gloom of the Haining and Ritchie office.

'I objected strongly to his presence,' Mr Haining went on, 'but Mrs Brunner seemed, for some reason not clear to me, to depend on him in her time of bereavement. They were both very aggressive, which I found quite deplorable in the circumstances.

As the late Mr Brunner's widow, Mrs Brunner appeared indecently eager to know the contents of his will. She demanded' – outrage welled up – '*demanded* to be informed immediately when she could take over the estate.'

'I imagine she was impatient,' said Anna. 'I can understand your concern, but I suppose she has plans to make, and needs to know her exact legal position before taking any steps. But what was that about warning Alec? She's not going to chuck him out, is she?'

Mr Haining cleared his throat. It was an impressive performance, heralding some world-shattering proclamation. 'Mrs Brunner's exact position,' he intoned, 'is unfortunately less secure than she had hoped.' His words began to sound more like a sermon, and Anna had a vision of him with a huge Bible opened on the lectern before him, preparing the final judgement of a vengeful deity. 'She is to receive a stipulated sum but no part in the property of Balmuir Lodge or properties appertaining thereto. A further sum to be gifted to – hm – a trust for an annual film and television award for' – Mr Haining allowed himself to sound faintly sceptical – 'production innovations of outstanding artistry, to be known as the Brunner Bronze. And the estate itself, including Balmuir Lodge and, as I have said, all land and properties attaining to it, are bequeathed to yourself.'

'I'm sorry. I don't . . . that is . . .'

'To Mrs Anna Chisholm of Balmuir Mains – "as some recompense for the troubles inflicted on her by my son." That is the relevant wording.'

'His son?' Anna's head was spinning. 'Relevant? That doesn't make any sense. I don't remember any troubles from his son. Never even knew he had a son, in fact.'

'That is, nevertheless, the exact phrasing, Mrs Chisholm. Which I may say I chose not to communicate to Mrs Brunner.'

'What exactly did you communicate, then?'

'The simple facts. Her own monetary legacy, the endowment of an award in the cinematographic arts, and your own inheritance of the estate. I fear it put her in a gey combative mood when she left here. I thought it my duty to give Mr Chisholm, as executor, advance notice of a possible – hm – confrontation.

And yourself, of course.' As Anna tried to fight her way out of a daze of incomprehension and demand some explanation of his remarks about Alec, he hastened to conclude: 'I shall be in touch again, Mrs Chisholm, just as soon as it is right and proper for me to do so.'

Anna was sure that every minute of the phone conversation would be meticulously recorded and charged for in due course.

Before she could pour herself a large glass of cold water and sit down to try and make sense of the things she had just heard, there was the swish of car tyres in the stableyard. Going to open the door, she rehearsed the stock phrases. No, we have no vacancies, and in any case we do not deal with casual trade but work exclusively through a letting agency. Or, if it was yet another TV team or a newspaper reporter, she would suggest they got in touch with the police, soaked up the good news, and went chasing off to film the wrecked Ford and interview any available officer.

A Vauxhall Vectra had stopped in the yard. The man who got out of it was ruddy featured and had a commanding air. Anna, used to sizing people up the moment they arrived, assessed him at once as a businessman golfer, a Rotarian, probably keen on shooting or fishing or both, with the assumed military bearing of a chief accountant wanting to be regarded as something heartier.

'Are you the proprietor of this place?' The bossy bluster of his voice tied in with her assessment.

'I am. But I'm sorry, we don't accept bookings from passers-by. They all go through the letting agency in—'

'An agency? And what exactly is that agency running here – a club for two-timers?' He stared at Covenanter's Cottage. 'Yes, that's the one I saw on TV.' He stomped past Anna and hammered on the door.

'Look here,' she protested. 'You've no right to—'

Walter Robinson opened the door. 'If it's any more bloody interviews, we're not . . .' He went pale. 'Oh, hell, no. Richard!'

'So it was you. I might have guessed. You devious . . . you rotten little—'

Sharon appeared suddenly at Walter's side, knotting the belt of her dressing-gown. 'Ooh. Oh, no. Richard, you're not supposed to be here.'

'Neither are you.'

'But how did you . . . I mean, whatever brought you here? I mean . . .'

Richard glanced at Anna. 'Can you imagine what it's like, getting your boots on ready to go out for a day's fishing, and there on the room telly is your wife, half naked on the screen.' He swung back to Sharon. 'That cameraman did you proud, didn't he? Made a real meal of it.'

'I *wasn't* half naked.'

'Staying with your dear old friend Amanda, eh? Liars, both of you. Cheap liars. Both of you having a wonderful giggle about it afterwards.'

He advanced towards Wally, who shrank back against Sharon. 'Now look here, old chap—'

'You bastard. You miserable, cheating bastard.'

Walter bridled. It was the only way to put it. Anna had never seen a man bridle before. 'Hey, now. Just a minute.'

Richard began advancing slowly on him. 'Right, Mr Walter bloody Robinson. The moment my back's turned, you think it's great fun to . . .' He grabbed Walter by the shoulders and pushed him indoors, carrying Sharon along with them in the rush. Anna heard a thud of blows, Sharon whimpering, and Walter yelling. Abruptly the two men came out again, Richard with blood on the knuckles of his right hand, this time dragging Walter with him instead of pushing him. Sharon stumbled after them, howling something incoherent. Walter was staggering in the middle of the yard when Queenie's Fiat swerved in at a characteristically awkward angle. He tried to dodge, and lurched head first into the flowers in the horse trough. Cocky shot out of the car and frisked up to him, making three wild leaps in the hope of getting into the trough so that he could lick Walter's cheek, but just couldn't make it.

Richard turned and jabbed his finger at his wife. 'While I finish with this miserable creep, you can go and make yourself decent. Or as close as you can get. And then come and get straight into the car.'

148

'I'm not going to be bossed about.'

'Oh, yes, you are. And when we get home . . .'

He did not specify what was likely to happen when they got home, but Anna thought she detected in Sharon's stare a dawning interest. All at once she was in quite a rush to pack her case.

'Come on, stand up and let's finish this.' Richard put a hand on Walter's shoulder.

Alec was out of the car. 'That's enough. Whatever's been going on here, we'll have no brawling on these premises. If you don't stop at once, I shall call the police.'

'I've told him to get up, and he's bloody well going to get up.'

Walter emitted a muffled moan. 'My knee.'

'Come on, get up and tell it to take the weight while I get ready to knock you down again.'

'My knee. Oh, Christ, my knee.'

'That's enough. Leave him alone.' Alec's firmness brought him a doting smile from Queenie. 'We've had one murder here already. We don't want another one.'

Sharon appeared in the doorway of the cottage, carrying her suitcase. She waited demurely as Richard strode towards her and snatched the case from her.

'All right. Get in the car.'

She lowered her head and walked meekly towards the car, waiting by the passenger door. Her husband opened the boot, hurled her bag in, and slammed the top down again. He hesitated, glowered; and then came to open the door for her to get in. She smiled even more demurely at him.

'Look here . . . just a minute . . .' Walter at last heaved himself out of the trough, his face smeared with soil and a runnel of blood from his nose. A twisted strand of damp fern drooped behind his left ear. 'You can't just . . .'

The Vectra purred into life, the tyres sprayed grit, and Queenie grabbed Cocky out of the way as it headed for the road and went speeding off up the hill.

Alec helped Walter to his feet. 'I think you'd better go in and have a wash. And then do your packing and drive off home.'

'With my knee in this state?'

'Maybe your insurance company can pay for your transport

home.' There was a flicker of mischief in Alec's voice. 'But then you'll need to find your way back here to pick up your own car when you've quite recovered.'

'Oh, all right. All right. I suppose I have to manage.'

Twenty minutes later he limped out with his case, and eased himself into the driving seat of the Honda.

As soon as he was gone, Anna went in to put the furniture straight after the brief tussle had overturned the coffee table and sent a chair scudding across the room. As she got a grip on the table, she felt a stickiness on her right hand.

'Oh, this is disgusting. There's blood on it. And on the carpet.'

Behind her, Queenie said. 'Oh, do let me help, dear. We've just been down to the village, and I did think to buy some more cleaning materials, so we can set to. And Stables is all right, isn't it? Ready for any new people you can get for next week.'

'For the rest of this week, the Torrances are coming back. They asked for the cottage. Probably thought things would be too chaotic up at the Lodge.'

'Why on earth are they coming back? I thought they'd be well on their way home by now, or wherever it was they were heading.'

'They caught up with the Watermans.' Anna explained what had happened. 'And now they'll be in Ayr, giving a full account to the police.'

'Well, I never. You mean they overpowered Ronnie Waterman? And Martine – it was Martine, wasn't it?'

'It was. She's injured and in hospital. I don't know all the details, but I expect we'll be hearing before long. But that's not all.' She poured herself a glass of water, her hand shaking. 'There's the little matter of Chet Brunner's will.'

Alec frowned. 'But that's one of my problems right now. Keeping the administration ticking over until we get some idea of what he—'

'I think you'd better ring Mr Haining in Ayr. He was trying to get in touch with you earlier.'

Alec went off to the kitchen, where the pay-phone sat in a slot beside the central heating boiler.

Queenie eyed Anna nervously. 'What's this about, dear? Can you tell us?'

'I don't know if I ought to. It's up to Mr Haining to—'

'Oh, blow that old fart. Tell me what you know. Or what you think of it all.'

Anna braced herself. 'It doesn't make any sense. There's some money for Jilly-Jo—'

'Just "some money"? That doesn't sound too good.'

'An endowment for an annual sort of BAFTA-cum-Oscar in his name.'

'Oh, dear. Gracious me.' Queenie wriggled on her chair and giggled. 'That'll give the studios something to quarrel about each year.'

'And the estate, including the house and all this place, cottages and all, come to me.'

'To you?' Queenie put her head on one side like a querulous bird, and then her voice became a trill. 'But that's lovely. What a lovely surprise, my dear. But why you?'

'That's what I don't understand. The way it's worded, it makes no sense. Something about my getting all this "as some recompense for the troubles inflicted on her by my son." That's the way Mr Haining quoted it.'

Queenie had gone suddenly rigid. The twittering, bewildered look which so often seemed an act, put on to get her out of awkward arguments or situations she didn't want to face, was wiped away. She was staring fixedly at something she couldn't avoid any longer.

Cocky, curled up at her feet, whined uneasily.

'I suppose it'll all come out now.'

Before she could say any more, another car swept into the yard. It stopped with a slither of tyres. Cocky began barking as Anna opened the door, prepared again to fend off visitors.

Both front doors of the electric blue Jag opened. Hagan got out of the driver's seat. Jilly-Jo came storming round from the other side.

'Pleased with yourself, are you?' Jilly-Jo's baby-doll face was contorted. There was a fleck of spittle on her lower lip. 'So po-faced, butter wouldn't melt in your mouth, would it? And all the time you were having it off with Chet. In one of your scruffy little love nests down here?'

Queenie squeezed past Anna, raised her arm, and slapped Jilly-Jo so hard across the face that she lurched sideways into Hagan's arms. Queenie winced as if the blow had jarred up the muscles of her arm. Cocky burst out between Anna's feet and did an ecstatic victory lap round the yard.

'If you wasn't a woman, you'd pay for that,' growled Hagan.

'Get out of here,' said Queenie. 'The two of you. This is private property.'

'Oh, you're in on it too?' Jilly-Jo shrilled. 'What sort of a stitch-up d'you call this? After all I've done for Chet. All I gave him. Everything. And all the while, behind my back, you've been fixing things, getting him to sign away all the things that belong to me. His wife. Not just a piece on the side, but his real wife. Not just a . . .' She saw Queenie's arm begin to flex again, and stopped. 'Very well. You obviously know what's in his will, because you've fixed it the way you wanted it. But I'm not going to lie down and let it happen. There's going to be one hell of an inquiry into this, believe you me.'

'We'll be going to law, that I'll be telling you,' said Hagan.

Cocky let out a squeal that was close to hysterical laughter.

'And right now' – Jilly-Jo made an attempt at dignity which was beyond her acting talents – 'we're going back to the house. To *my* house and *my* private suite. You'll be hearing from me very soon. Believe me, you will.'

They waited for the Jag to reverse, swerve, and head for the lane, then went back indoors. Queenie stood still in the middle of the floor for a moment, her face screwed up in a spasm of pain. Before Anna could ask if she had hurt herself, Alec came out of the sitting-room.

'Quite a situation,' he said quietly.

'I still don't understand any of it.' Anna sat in a chair across the kitchen table from Queenie. 'He told you, did he, that stuff about Chet's son and the troubles he'd caused me?'

'He did, yes.'

'But I never knew Chet's son.'

'You did,' whispered Queenie. 'You were married to him.'

152

'Peter? You can't be . . .' Her gaze wandered helplessly from Queenie to Alec.

He said: 'Yes. Peter was Chet's son.'

'But you. . . ?'

'Alec married me in spite of that.' Queenie smiled up as Alec came round the table and put his arm round her shoulders. 'The best thing that ever happened to me.' Her smile faded. 'But I don't see why he had to make that filthy remark about my Peter. What did he mean by him causing you troubles? My Peter never hurt anybody, never . . .'

Alec reached for her arm. 'Let's go and leave Anna to think about things. She does have a lot to think about.'

Anna stared at the trace of bloodstain left by Walter Robinson. Everything else was so unbelievable that she was letting her mind become hypnotized by something real and tangible. Blood on the table.

Worse than marmalade?

14

DCI McAdam had been very properly, politely congratulatory on the behaviour of Sir Nicholas and Lady Torrance. The capture of Ronald Waterman had been admirable, though without actually saying so she managed to imply that there had been an element of luck in it. Since this was true, neither Nick nor Lesley cared to challenge the implication.

They recorded statements, one part of which displeased McAdam. Each of them reported, as closely as possible to the original wording, what Ronnie and Martine had said about finding the body and dragging it away, but not being responsible for having reduced Chet Brunner to the state of a corpse.

'And you believed them?'

'Oddly enough,' said Lesley, 'yes.'

'Me, too,' said Nick.

'I think the weight of evidence will overcome their pretences.' Something in her aggressive tone suggested she might have been talking down such doubts in herself. 'Anyway, thank you again. Your co-operation has been much appreciated.'

'Too late for my wife to be given a police medal?' Nick had asked.

'I'm sure the appropriate authority will want to issue a formal commendation. And of course you may expect a great deal of praise in a number of television news programmes.' She made that sound far from desirable. Shaking hands stiffly, she said: 'Safe journey home.'

'Oh, we ought to mention that if you want to get in touch with us, we won't actually be back at Black Knowe until the week-end.'

For some reason McAdam looked disconcerted to learn that they would be staying a night or two in Stables Cottage. Since things were now virtually wrapped up so far as she was concerned, she would perhaps have been glad to wipe all the supernumeraries off her record.

On the way back to Balmuir, Nick grinned. 'See what I've saved you from? You'd have finished up just like that.'

'She's a conscientious officer.'

'I'm sure. And she's not going to be distracted from her course of duty by niggling little doubts.'

As they went through Balmuir and up the slope to turn in between the gateposts of Balmuir Lodge, Lesley said: 'Hold on a minute. We're supposed to be going to the cottages, not the house.'

'Oh, damn. I wasn't thinking. I'll turn round at the end.'

But when they reached the wide terrace in front of the house, Alec Chisholm was emerging, followed by Jilly-Jo waving her arms and shouting. As Nick stopped and opened his door, the lumpish form of Tam Hagan lumbered out in Jilly-Jo's wake. He set himself beside her, his jacket buttoned up tightly, with the air of a bouncer waiting for any chance to clobber somebody. Lesley, on her way in with Alec, stopped in the doorway like a member of the audience arriving late for a performance.

'We're off to see a solicitor,' Jilly-Jo announced. 'I'm not going to be cheated out of my rights as a loyal wife by some piddling little provincial solicitor.'

Obediently picking up his cue, Hagan nodded. 'I know just the man in Glasgow. Someone who really knows what he's doing. Nobody cheats on me. On us.'

Lesley saw Nick's right eyebrow raised in her direction at those pronouns. *Me . . . us. . .* ? They suggested Hagan's interest in Jilly-Jo was not exclusively an amorous one.

Jilly-Jo headed for the Jaguar parked against the low stone wall, glaring at Lesley as if she were under suspicion as a poten-tial rival. It was quite a compelling performance, striding from stage centre to stage left, lacking only the swirl of a silken scarf, with the added spice of Georgina Campbell coming up the steps to the far end of the terrace at the same time.

'And *you*,' Jilly-Jo blazed. 'You can get out of here before I get back, or I'll have you thrown out.'

'Chet owes me. I'm not just going to clear out without a penny. Something to remember him by,' she snivelled, trying her own brand of calculated melancholy. 'He wouldn't want that to happen to me.'

Hagan managed to eye her up and down as he followed Jilly-Jo to the car.

'Crap,' said Jilly-Jo. 'You were just one of his cheap little trollops.'

'You'd never understand a real sincere relationship, you wouldn't. No wonder he wanted to ditch you.'

'A relationship? We know what sort of relationship you two were in, don't we? But at least the pictures he took of me were artistic. Not like the filth you posed for.'

'I don't know what you're talking about.'

'I've just been going through Chet's drawers—'

'A long time since he bothered to go through yours.'

'You see!' Jilly-Jo appealed to her guardian bruiser, who hastily looked away from Georgina. 'Cheap, vulgar. No wonder he wanted to hide that smut away.'

'Or didn't want my poses contaminated by someone like you getting envious.'

Alec came between Nick and Lesley, and touched their elbows. 'Come on in. Safer to leave them to it.'

'I wonder. We wouldn't want another murder on our hands.'

'Probably only a few scratches, at most.'

He was steering them into the house when Nick said: 'Just a minute. We meant to head for the cottage and settle ourselves in.'

'Do come in and have a dram. Or coffee. I can do with some company.' Lesley had already spotted the grey shadows in the corners of his eyes, and the slight shake in his right hand. 'Queenie's not around.' He sounded shamefully relieved. 'Cocky's gone fizzing off somewhere again, and . . .' He was

157

drowned out by the howl and thunder of a low-flying plane. 'Probably one of those that set him off. Now she and Anna are wandering around the grounds looking for him.'

He opened a cupboard in the small sitting-room, and poured two large malts in spite of Nick's raised hand of protest. When he turned to Lesley, she shook her head. 'I can see I'll have to do the driving from here on. Anyway, Nick does keep taking wrong turnings.'

Nick raised his glass to Alec. 'How's it going?'

'Now that the police and the telly and the newspapers have gone away, and we're rid of most of Chet's house guests I'm trying to sort out some sort of routine. It's high time I went round the place and checked on the state of things. I've got all the keys. But with all this set-to over the will, and Anna not sure where she stands until they've got confirmation, or probate, or whatever they call it, I still have to keep the place ticking over. Not to mention finding out who gives the orders for the funeral.'

Lesley smiled. 'Nick's told me how conscientious you are – as steady as a rock in a crisis.'

'He means a fusspot, I expect. But keeping the show on the road has been my job for so long, eh, Nick? And right now there are bills to pay, the staff to pay, refunds for those guests who've had to leave mid-week and aren't too happy about it. Need to do a full recce. But I don't want anyone coming along later and accusing me of removing things. Or damaging anything.' He took a long, searing gulp of whisky. 'Now there's an idea. Would you both come along with me as reliable witnesses, just in case Jilly-Jo or anybody starts up some snide rumours?'

Lesley was delighted at the idea of a tour of the premises. There was so much she wanted to see, and to fit into place. She ignored Nick's disapproving glance at her, and got to her feet.

'Let's go.'

They had seen most of the main building when they first arrived. Alec led the way through the various rooms, ticking off points in a small blue notebook and in his mind obviously shifting furniture back to original positions.

As they set off upstairs, Lesley stopped at a curve in the stairway. Tucked into a recess was a tiny table carrying what must be a fertility symbol of some kind: a wooden head and shoulders with polished bare breasts and prominent nipples.

'Javanese?'

'Could be,' said Alec. 'I wouldn't know. Could be a copy – a bit of Stuart Morgan's handiwork.'

'Where would he have seen the original?'

'Goodness knows. I know that Queenie's never liked it. Though there's not much about Stuart that she does like, poor lad.'

On the first landing, the ledge of each tall window looking out on to the garden and the hills beyond bore a figurine of some kind: here a jade Egyptian cat, beyond it a crouching mythological beast in marble.

On the right was a line of bedroom doors. Two of them further along were open, and a little girl from the village was tidying them, piling sheets in the passage. Looking down on the heaps of bed linen were portraits of two tall, dignified gentlemen providing a suggestion of ancestors, but certainly not the ancestors of Chet Brunner. Lesley recognized one of them as a copy of a full-length portrait by Lely of the Duke of Lennox. And one of Lady Jean Seton by Cornelius Jansen, from Traquair House.

'Chet fancied keeping good company,' Nick commented. 'Well and truly putting Soho society behind him.'

They edged past a waste-paper basket stuffed with what looked like the discarded jottings of one competitor trying to solve the clues in one of Brunner's games, and Alec tried a door at the end of the passage. It was locked. He hesitated, then said, 'She no longer has any rights in this house,' reached for a bunch of keys at his belt, and opened the door. Beyond lay another, shorter passage leading to a further door with panels bearing heraldic devices.

'Cecil B. de Mille crossed with Walt Disney,' said Nick.

Along the outer wall of the approach, three tomb brasses of armoured knights were set upright into the stone of the wall.

'Not a Scottish tradition,' said Nick. 'Where did he dig those out?'

'Copies of English originals, I think,' said Alec.

'Pretty convincing.'

159

'Done by Stuart in his workshop, I imagine.'

'This Stuart seems pretty versatile.'

Lesley said: 'Is there any way of getting more light on them?'

'All provided for.' Alec reached for a switch, and three precisely adjusted spotlights gleamed down from the ceiling, striking silvery reflections from the breastplates of the knights.

'Oh, dear,' murmured Nick as Lesley examined the brasses from each side, and stooped to make closer examination of the dog recumbent at its master's feet. 'What awful discoveries are you about to make?'

'These aren't copies. I'll swear these are the real thing. This one on the left here must come from about the same period as Sir John de Creke at Westley Waterless. And this one in the middle – I once saw something remarkably like it in Essex.' She straightened up. 'I do think I ought to have a word with the Arts and Antiques folk at New Scotland Yard.'

'It's none of our business,' said her husband.

'Tracking down tomb robbers is everybody's business.'

The heraldic shields on the door swung open on to a small sitting-room with the master bedroom beyond, and a smaller one beside it. Velvet tartan hangings must have been Chet Brunner's preference to medieval tapestries. Two crossed claymores hung above the huge double bed. Against one spread of tartan weave was a small Georgian bookcase.

'Wouldn't have thought of your old pal as being much of a reader,' said Lesley.

Nick grimaced. 'Least of all in the bedroom. Except maybe between wives, or whatever.' He bent down to look at the titles of the volumes, all bound in leather with a gilded CB at the foot of the spine. 'Ah. Bound copies of scripts for all his films and TV shows.'

Through the open door to the smaller room they glimpsed a riot of pink hangings, a pink dressing-table, and a huge blown-up, framed photograph of Jilly-Jo in a cerise boob-tube and black velvet shorts, sprawled over a chaise-longue from which one bare leg dangled languorously. Lesley wondered how long the late Chet Brunner had intended to leave it there before replacing it with a similar portrait of Georgina Campbell.

Nick stared at a small work table, inlaid with ebony and pewter, in the alcove between the two rooms. 'I remember this. It's one of the pieces that went missing from McIver's place at Westerlaw. Some of the stuff was recovered, but not all of it. Not this.'

Lesley, at his shoulder, leaned forward and fingered the surface. 'It's a copy.'

'Then where did the original go?'

'Maybe Brunner knew, or maybe he didn't. So long as it looked the way he wanted it, he wouldn't know an original from a reproduction. But one way and another, he seems to have indulged his artistic tastes pretty lavishly.'

There was a sudden squeal from the far end of the corridor. It had to be the maid's voice. Alec was nearest the outer door, and had turned to investigate when a man rushed towards him, gasped, and tried to turn back.

Alec said: 'Mr Pitcairn. Taken a wrong turning?'

Harry Pitcairn drew himself up and tried to look unfazed. 'I came back to look for something I'd left behind.'

'And what was that?'

'A cravat stickpin. Lost it. It was supposed to be a key piece in one of Brunner's silly games. Only the whole thing was half organized, and then things happened and . . . well, you know what confusion there was. It was a clue that had to be planted somewhere. And I . . . well, I thought I might have dropped it in my bedroom. That was my room,' he added defiantly, gesturing at the doorway in which the maid stood, flustered and indignant.

'And have you found it?'

'No, damn it. Probably been swept up and thrown out by now.'

Lesley was impressed by the steely authority that had come into Alec's voice, fighting off the earlier tiredness. 'Mr Pitcairn, you had no right to sneak into this house without—'

'I was not sneaking. I didn't have to sneak back into a house I know—'

'Know so well,' Alec took him up, 'that you know exactly where to sneak in, and where to prowl – and how to get out with whatever it is you've picked up.'

'I won't be talked to like that.'

Lesley said: 'Mr Chisholm, as custodian of these premises pending confirmation of Mr Brunner's will, and executor of that will, would be perfectly entitled to ask you to wait here until the police have checked your story and—

'And searched me? To find out what I've come back to steal?'

'That would be an excellent idea, yes.'

Harry Pitcairn looked aggressive for a moment. He might well have stormed away along the passage. And whose job was it to stop him? Lesley tensed, uncertain but ready to act on impulse. Then, still trying to be scornful but subsiding with a shrug, Pitcairn said: 'All right, so I did come to collect something I believe belongs rightly to our family.' He made it an accusation rather than a confession. He stooped and rolled up his left trouser leg. Strapped against it was a skean dhu. 'I remember this as a child. I ought to have removed it when I walked out that evening, but I couldn't be sure Brunner wouldn't have spotted it was gone.'

Lesley held out her hand. Warily he put the sheathed, silver-hilted knife in it. She turned it over to read the inscription in the silver. 'James Mitchell Pitcairn.'

'My great-grandfather.'

'Very attractive. It's a copy, of course.'

'What?'

'There's no hallmark. I'd have thought it might originally be an Edinburgh piece. But the hilt is a giveaway. It's—'

'I don't believe you.'

'My wife is an expert on this sort of thing,' said Nick frostily.

'Then where the hell is the original?'

'Quite possiby Mr Brunner sold it for a good price,' ventured Alec, 'but liked it enough to have a copy made first. He put a lot of reproduction work into Stuart Morgan's workshop.'

'Just how many things did he sell off? How much of our heritage has been flogged off to some greedy bloody American, or—'

Alec took the skean dhu from Lesley. 'I think we'll keep it on the premises, Mr Pitcairn.' His voice softened into sympathy. 'But when everything's been settled, since it means so much to you, perhaps we can—'

'It means nothing to me,' snapped Pitcairn. 'A copy means nothing to me. It was the original that meant everything.'

None of them made a move to stop him as he stalked away.

On the way down, Lesley glanced casually out of the window on the first turn of the stair. Below, a grey Volvo was drawing in by the side door. She thought she remembered it as Anna Chisholm's, which might mean that she and Queenie had found the wandering dog and were bringing it home.

Before she could comment on it, Nick was saying: 'You know, Alec, knowing Chet the way we do, I'd have thought he'd have had some security guard on duty round this place. People do seem to be able to come in and out without so much as a by-your-leave.'

'He did, to start with. Two uniformed blokes, clomping around and opening doors and frightening the daylights out of the staff. But then he found they were helping themselves to various perks as they went along. And then a village girl accused one of them of raping her.'

'And did that get into the papers?'

'It didn't get anywhere. The idea of that Wallace girl putting up a fine struggle for her virtue was too much. Never got any further than our Carrick community policeman.'

'So Chet disposed of his strong-arm buddies.'

'He'd have done better with a couple of Border terriers.'

Even so, thought Lesley, there really ought to have been some form of protection. She recalled all the lectures she had given to happy-go-lucky landlords who wouldn't spend a bawbee on security but moaned blue bloody murder when their family treasures went missing.

And how many of them knew when the real thing had gone missing and been replaced by a clever fake?

Maybe tomorrow she ought to pay this remarkably gifted Mr Morgan a visit.

15

A wide circuit along the perimeter of the estate had brought them to the unsightly combination of fence, wall and hedge which Brunner had devised to mark the border between his property and the Pitcairns'. Twilight was seeping like a fine purple dew over what until fifteen minutes ago had been sparkling green slopes. Leaves of a sycamore tree rustled uneasily in a faint breeze, suddenly overtaken by the howl of a low-flying plane splitting the skies.

'It was one of those,' wailed Queenie. 'Must have been one of those that terrified Cocky and set him off.'

They stopped at a ragged gap in the hedge and looked across at the hunched greyness of the mock castle in the dell.

'D'you suppose he might have got through there?' Anna suggested.

They both started as a voice came from beyond the higher point where fencing met the hedge. 'Come to make sure we haven't infringed the late Mr Brunner's boundaries while he wasn't looking?'

Harry Pitcairn emerged from the shadow of the fence and stared a challenge at them.

Anna said: 'We are looking for Mrs Chisholm's dog. It's run away. We thought it might have got through the hedge and gone wandering over your land.'

'Not a lot of it to wander over.'

'All the same, if you do come across him—'

'I'll notify you. And give you details of any damage it's caused.'

He stood where he was until the two women had turned and continued the search down the slope towards the farmhouse and cottages.

'What d'you suppose *he'll* make of the news?' said Queenie.

'The news?'

'About you inheriting. And . . . oh, dear, I suppose it'll all come out now. Everyone'll be sniggering about me and Chet.'

They stumbled on a few more paces, straining their eyes to peer into the distances on both sides. As much to take Queenie's mind off the missing Cocky as to satisfy her own curiosity, Anna said: 'Did it go on for long, the affair? Mean a lot to you?'

'It all seems so stupid now, when you think of it. But we were both a lot younger.' It was hard to tell whether Queenie was peering across the landscape in search of Cocky or looking dreamily into the past. For a moment Anna thought she was going to leave it at that and not stir up memories which by now must be distasteful. But then she went on. 'You've only seen him as a big shot, throwing his weight about. It's not the same as the enthusiasm he used to have. He really did believe in every word he said – while he was saying it,' she added wryly.

'I think he always did.'

'Yes. No matter how crazy it was, he did believe it. Made himself believe his own mad notions. Such as being in love with every beautiful girl he met.' Queenie darted a glance at Anna. 'Oh, I was quite a dish in my day.'

'I've never thought otherwise.'

'And it wasn't just casting-couch routine. He was quite a powerful lover. More muscle than fat in those days. Peter took after him.'

Yes, thought Anna. Peter took after Chet Brunner in every way. Convincing you with every word he was telling you because while he was telling it he was convincing himself as well.

'But in the end of course he turned out to be a bastard.'

Anna was about to nod sad agreement, when she realized that Queenie had gone back to talking about Brunner.

'That thing in the will about Peter,' Queenie went on. 'He ought never to have said anything like that. Peter was a lovely boy, but he was so impressionable. I ought to have realized early on that he needed a firmer hand. I was always too indulgent towards him. And Alec – oh, dear Alec – he always felt that if he tried to take a firm line, I'd blame him for making me feel guilty. So we both of us got on with our own work and sort of pretended that things would be all right.' She came to a halt, breathing heavily and bracing her right leg to keep her balance on the uneven ground. 'I was so pleased when you married him. I really thought you'd be the making of him.'

If there was a hint of reproach in that remark, Anna was not going to rise to it. She said: 'I loved him. And I tried to keep loving him, in spite of the way things . . . well, not going the way I'd wanted them to go.'

'I know you had your difficulties, dear. But he fell under bad influences. Especially that Stuart Morgan.'

'But Stuart was the one Peter cheated on, as well as cheating on me.'

'I don't deny Peter did wrong, but it was that Morgan who played on his weaknesses. And now that you're in for this inheritance, *you'll* be that man's next target, mark my words.'

She set off again, and said nothing more until they reached the farmhouse.

'Come on in and have a cup of tea,' said Anna. 'And then I'll run you back to the house. By the time you get back there, you'll probably find Cocky's lying in a corner somewhere and pretending he's been there all afternoon.'

'I expect so. I do hope so.'

She gasped and clutched her side. Even in the uncertain light it was clear that her face had gone very white, and her other hand was wavering, clutching for a support that wasn't there.

'Are you all right?' It wasn't the first time Anna had witnessed these little wrenching movements. 'Come on, let's get the car and—'

'No, dear, I'll walk up the hill. One last little look on the way, you know.'

Without waiting for any more arguments, she set off. Anna watched her go, groggy but determined. After a few steps she began whistling in thin, piping little bursts; but there was still no sign of Cocky bounding towards her.

As she turned back towards her front door, Anna was conscious that something was missing. It took a few seconds to dawn. Her offer to drive Queenie back to Balmuir Lodge would have been difficult to fulfil. The Volvo was missing. She paced round the yard, absurdly wondering if she might have parked it behind one of the cottages or in the shadow of the wall, even though she never did such a thing.

Indoors, she looked at the phone and thought that the obvious thing to do was ring the police. Yet some stirring of unease made her reluctant to reach out and dial the number.

She hadn't left it up at the Lodge before she and Queenie set out, had she?

She knew damn well she hadn't. Agitated over Cocky's disappearance, Queenie had driven down here in the Fiat to see if he had come visiting, as he so frequently did, and then driven the two of them back to start the search from the house.

Anna had not yet drawn the curtains when the beam of headlights made a bright brush stroke across the sitting-room wall. As she went out into the yard, Stuart was getting out of the Volvo.

'Sorry,' he said. 'Thought I might get back before you did.'

'You're not supposed to drive. You're banned.'

'I know. But this was urgent. I came to see if you'd help me, but you weren't here, and I thought I'd risk it.'

'Risk what? Getting nicked for joyriding without a licence?'

'Not going to offer me a drink?'

He had that slight wheedling note in his voice that usually amused her, but now rang a false note after what Queenie had been saying. Damn Queenie: she would never admit that her precious Peter could really be personally responsible for any misdeeds.

'You've got some explaining to do,' she said as she led the way back into the house.

'Yes' He waited until she had poured him a large whisky, and raised the glass to her. 'I won't risk driving back. Don't want drunk-driving added again to my list of felonies.'

'All right. Just what on earth have you been up to?'

'I came to ask you if we could use the wagon to remove some of my things from the Lodge.'

'Your things?'

'Work I'd done for him that hasn't been paid for. All sorts of oddments, and a recent batch of stuff he never got round to agreeing a price on.'

'But you can't just barge in and remove things from a dead man's house until everything's been thoroughly accounted for. If you'd waited for me—'

'Let's be honest. I wasn't entirely sure you'd agree. Rather glad not to have shoved the responsibility on you. You'd left the keys in the car, as usual. Asking for it. So I drove up, collected what was mine, and took it all back to the workshop. Sorry.' He grinned his most engaging, pseudo-sheepish grin.

'And nobody saw you?'

'No. I do know my way in and out of that dump.'

'I'm glad I wasn't party to it. Not in my line, running the getaway car for a theft.'

'Anna, love, it wasn't theft. That was stuff I'd spent hours working on. Days. And not getting paid. And I reckoned my chances of getting a penny out of that Jilly-Jo creature were zilch.'

'What's Jilly-Jo got to do with it?'

'Well, she'll inherit the lot, won't she? I'd have thought that would have worried you, too.'

'Jilly-Jo isn't going to inherit the lot. Some money, but that's all.'

He stared. 'What are you on about? What do you know about it?'

She told him.

His eyes were blinking rapidly. If Queenie hadn't implanted petty little doubts in her mind, Anna would not have found herself wondering whether Stuart was marking time, thinking furiously, shaping a plan. She made herself shrug them aside. Listening to Queenie had always been a dizzying business.

'Well,' said Stuart at last, 'that puts a different complexion on things, doesn't it?'

'On lots of things, yes.'

169

He drained his glass and stared down into it. Absurdly Anna wanted to giggle. There was a weird resemblance between the tilt of his head and Queenie's when she peered down into her tea mug. Both of them brooding, sorting things out.

'Especially,' he said, 'on the two of us.'

She didn't want him to go on. He was thinking too desperately on his feet, instead of waiting. There was too much to be thought through for it to be tackled right away. But would it be better if he were given more time?

'I don't get you,' she said.

'Exactly. Probably you won't, now. And I won't get you, which I was hoping might happen.'

'Stuart, this is no time to—'

'I ought to have spoken last week. I meant to. It just seemed the time wasn't right. And now I can't say anything, can I?'

'It's all been a bit of a shock for all of us. Let's not make any silly presumptions.'

'It'd look too obvious, wouldn't it? Penniless ex-jailbird cons young widow who's suddenly become well-do-do into marrying him.'

She felt very tired, and unsure of anything.

He was looking at her with that pleading, always loyal and reliable expression of his. He might be waiting for a move. When she said nothing, he kissed her as lightly as ever, and went off.

She had not even offered to drive him back to the village, which she had so often done. But she made no move to run after him and make the offer.

Taking his empty glass to the sink, she realized that she needed a drink herself, and it had to be something stronger than that earlier mug of tea. After she had poured herself a vodka and tonic, she sat staring at one of her own pictures on the wall, only to find that from this angle the glass was reflecting a blurred image which she could conjure into Stuart's face.

Was he sincere? Were any of them sincere? Lying in bed, drifting unsteadily in and out of the fringes of sleep, she found herself surrounded by familiar and half-familiar faces, all of them acting. All of them, from way back. Alec, Queenie, Peter,

Stuart, the Balmuir Lodge guests – all in a perverse production by Chet Brunner. Harry Pitcairn, standing there with his pose of a wronged man done out of his birthright. And what sort of aggrieved, outraged stance would he adopt when he learned who was to inherit the Balmuir estate? Queenie had been right to wonder about that.

It was contagious. All playing a part, each and every one of them. How could you ever tell the difference between the real thing and the phoney?

She was plagued by the question far into her dreams.

Lesley turned over and tried to read the time on the bedside clock. The clock must have been moved. She could see none of the red numerals that ought to be about nine inches away, near the lamp. But there was no lamp on the table either. Then she realized that she was not in the Balmuir Lodge bedroom but in Stables Cottage. From ship to lodge to cottage: it was disorientating.

Morning sunshine was a bright pencil of light between the two curtains. Lesley eased herself out of bed, and immediately banged her right knee. This side of the bed was too close to the wall.

'Huh?' grunted Nick. 'What time is it?'

'The clock's on your side.'

'Oh.' He heaved himself up. 'Good Lord, it's nine o'clock.'

'It's all right, we don't have to fit in with breakfast hours. We're making our own, remember?'

He floundered across the duvet to put his arm round her and drag her back into bed, but she dodged and headed for the bathroom. 'We have some phone calls to make this morning.'

'They can wait.'

'I'm afraid of what might go missing if we wait.'

Nick groaned as she closed the bathroom door.

Anna had provided bacon, eggs and tomatoes in the fridge, and there were three different kinds of tea on the shelf. On his second round of toast, Nick said: 'All right, what's the programme for the day?'

'I want to tell the Arts and Antiques boys at the Yard about

171

those things we saw in Brunner's private quarters.' She looked up at the kitchen clock. 'They ought to be in by now.'

She went to her coat to fetch her mobile; then scowled. There was the faintest little flicker of a signal. They were in a dead spot.

Nick began emptying his pockets of loose change. 'There's a payphone over there.'

The voice at the other end was warm and welcoming. Inspector Percy had an epicene manner in the flesh, and was inclined to coo rather too ecstatically over works of art which he admired, and to tut-tut in too high and indignant a tone when learning of thefts or damage; but he was a devoted pursuer of villains, and generous with praise for those who helped him.

'My dear Lez.' He was one of the few who could call her that without giving her a prickle of distaste. 'Didn't expect to hear from you so soon. Married life palling already?'

'Nothing of the kind. But I have something that might interest Freddie.'

'Alas, you've missed him. He's on his way to an antiques recognition course run by an expert in – would you believe it, my love? – Scotland. Forfar, to be exact. Near enough for you to nip over and see him?'

'Well over a hundred miles.'

'Ah. Looks as if you'll have to manage with me. Only do make it snappy, there's a love. We're inundated at the moment with wild goose chases and rumours about loot coming in from Iraq – or, worse still, getting right past us. But go ahead: what's troubling you?'

She summed up the oddities they had seen in Brunner's private quarters, and her doubts about Stuart Morgan, a furniture restorer who might be too skilful in other directions. Percy made encouraging little grunts at intervals, but did not come fully to life until she reached the subject of the tomb brasses. Then he stopped her with a short, yapping question.

'Hold it. Those brasses – one of them wouldn't have been of Sir Willoughby de Dalyngrunge, would it?'

'Could be. And there are some interesting jewel boxes and some rather fine marquetry. Oh, and' – a picture was snatched vividly from her memory – 'on one landing there was a framed fragment of a painting on wood that might have been a Bodhiattva. Probably a copy. I didn't stop to give it a proper look, but it may have been quite important.'

'Indeed it may. Sounds like part of a wall painting collection that was smuggled out to the States to a museum there, and then went missing a couple of years ago. I'd have to check. But it'd hardly be the original, would it?'

'If it's a copy,' said Lesley, 'where did the copyist see the original? And what happened to the original after he'd finished copying it?'

'This does get interesting, yes.'

'I've no longer any authority to institute an investigation. But you and Freddie can surely cook up an excuse to come and have a look. DCI McAdam of the Kyle and Carrick Constabulary would have to be your starting point. In the meantime I'm going to have a saunter round his workshop.'

When she had put the phone down, Nick said: 'A saunter round the workshop, eh? On what grounds?'

'We're staying in the neighbourhood, aren't we? Time on our hands. Simply going to have a look at some local crafts. You don't have to come if you don't want to.'

'I'm certainly not going to let you walk into trouble on your own.'

'Good. Let's walk into it together, like we did with the Watermans.'

As Nick opened the door, they were confronted by a television camera and a reporter looking remarkably old-fashioned with an ordinary notebook.

'Sir Nicholas Torrance? Lady Torrance? Can you tell us some of the details of your capture of the runaway murderer yesterday?'

'I'm sure the police officer in charge of the case has given you all the facts you need.'

'Yes, but she wasn't actually there, was she? You were there. What was it like, coming face to face with a man you knew to be a killer?'

Nick locked the cottage door and took Lesley's arm, trying to march them towards the Laguna, but found the way blocked by the cameraman, down on one knee to shoot up at them.

'We won't take up much of your time, sir. You really owe it to the public. It's a fantastic story. Pretty brave stuff, I'd say.' Seeing the direction of Nick's gaze as he measured the distance to the car, he added in a voice which was skilled in not being actually threatening but implied possibilities of becoming quite a nuisance. 'We can always follow you and pick up the threads as we go along, sir.'

It was really quicker to run through it and be done with it. Lesley thought this, but did not need to say it. Impatiently Nick said: 'Oh, all right. Ten minutes and no more.'

'We gather that Lady Torrance here was forced at gunpoint to drive Ronnie Waterman away, leaving you and the injured Mrs Waterman behind. Weren't you worried sick about your wife, sir?'

'No. I knew she was trained to cope with whatever happened. Which is exactly the way it turned out.'

'Trained, sir? By you?'

'In a previous incarnation,' said Nick heavily, 'she was a police officer.'

'The chief inspector didn't mention that.'

I don't suppose she would, thought Lesley.

As crisply as possible, the two of them ran through their experiences, matter-of-fact and without emotion. The framing of the questions showed the likelihood of a considerable amount of dramatization before their words, or a version of them, appeared in print. Lesley felt she could read their minds and see the banner headline being set up: LAIRD AND LADY OF BLACK KNOWE OVERPOWER WANTED KILLER. And she was sure she sensed their regret in not being able to repeat their success in capturing a scantily clad young woman in the doorway.

It was closer to twenty minutes than ten when they finally got away.

'Are you sure you want to start meddling?' asked Nick. 'After our last encounter and that interview, do we really want more publicity?'

174

'There's no question of publicity if we're just visiting a local craftsman.'

'Let's hope not. You do still have that ability of some sleuths to attract trouble before anyone else has even considered stirring it up.'

In the village there was a flurry of morning traffic. Several cars were parked outside the general shop, and there was a post-bus blocking the pavement by the craft shop. Nick edged in behind a four-wheel drive smeared with mud and rust. As they crossed the road, Lesley looked back and saw two men heading towards it. One of them she remembered as Harry Pitcairn. The other was older, limping along with a stick. Even across the street, with a car engine starting up close beside her, she could hear the older man growling and spluttering about something or other.

A woman drifting from one table to another in the craft shop was holding on to the hand of a resentful small boy, who reached out now and then to knock something over and then pretend it was his mother who had pushed him that way.

Nick said: 'Is Mr Morgan on the premises?'

'He's upstairs. I think I heard him moving about not that long since.' The shopkeeper was trying to be polite while keeping an eye on the boy as he and his mother disappeared round a tall display case.

'We saw some of his work up at Balmuir Lodge. We were hoping he might have some on show down here.'

'There's that table of models over there. That cat, and that curved lamp standard – that's the sort of thing he does. Only if you wanted to see how he works, I'm sure he'll be glad for you to go round to the workshop. He gets quite a few visitors, and he never seems to mind.' She moved round the case like a sheep-dog urging the mother and boy out into the open again. 'It's at the back of the building. The green door at the side.'

Nick led the way. The door was ajar. He tapped, but there was no reply. Pushing the door open, he took a couple of steps inside.

'Anybody here? Mr Morgan?'

Lesley followed him, ducking past the steep flight of stairs leading up to the top floor. To her right, almost blocking the way

175

round the main workbench, were two large sacks which might have been dragged up and dumped ready to be dealt with later. On the corner of the bench nearest to her were two woodcuts which at a glance looked remarkably like the work of Thomas Bewick.

Nick was sauntering round the other side of the bench, humming tunelessly to himself. Abruptly the humming stopped. She heard his swift, shocked intake of breath.

'Christ! Is this him? Morgan?'

Stuart Morgan was crumpled on the floor, half under the workbench. Blood had flowed thickly across the floor from his neck, and there were jagged spurts of it up and over the edge of the bench. Some tools had fallen from the bench beside him, maybe dislodged in a struggle or knocked over as he fell. The blade of one of them was dark with blood. Only it wasn't one of the tools. It was a skean dhu, and Lesley recognized it.

16

When she was irritated, Detective Chief Inspector June McAdam dreaded the inevitable onset of a sharp stab at each side of her temples, growing from a rhythmic jabbing which became more insistent as both sides pressed inwards to meet at the centre and form a belt of pain right across her brow. Each time it started, she tried telling herself to relax every muscle, to close her eyes and wait for it to ebb away. That rarely worked. Nor did the stress counselling which she had once, reluctantly, been ordered to take. Once the sequence began, there was no stopping it.

It had nothing to do with overwork. She rarely felt stressed when she was at full stretch, driving herself through long hours until she could see the end of the problem, whatever it was, in sight. Irritation clawed at her only when she was confronted by a gaping flaw in something she had been pursuing with single-minded conviction. The stinging pain was even worse now, when something she had considered well and truly wrapped up and off her hands was prompting an awkward doubt. It had all seemed so uncomplicated, pinning Brunner's murder on the obvious suspect, Ronnie Waterman. An open and shut case, in the familiar phrase.

But another murder so soon after that one, and in the same neck of the woods, was a hell of a jolt. And, most irritating of all, this time it couldn't be pinned on Ronnie Waterman. Waterman was in custody.

She vented her twitchiness on her driver. 'Are you sure you know your way? We seem to have discovered some weird roads.

We're not out for a country ramble, you know.'

'It's a new patch for me, ma'am. But I had a good look at the map before we left, and I'm pretty sure I've taken the shortest route.'

Sergeant Elliot was new to her. Her usual sidekick, DS Brodie, had gone off sick with a torn ligament after falling down the station stairs – which made a change, said his detractors, from suspects in his custody falling down those same stairs. His replacement was a strapping young man with sandy freckles and the purple shadow of an old scar down his left cheek. She felt he was the type who could make his weight felt in a tight corner, but even on such short acquaintance she had reservations about him. He had once been in the Midlothian and Merse force, but had divorced his wife after she became involved with a senior officer, and asked for a transfer to get away from a region with too many daily encounters and painful reminders. It was not the sort of thing McAdam approved of. A serving officer should never allow a situation to build up in which one woman could play off two men, one against the other.

Not that she had ever been given the chance of taking part in such a situation.

All in all, she was in no good mood when they arrived in Balmuir village. Things were made no better by her being greeted at the door of the craft shop by the retired DI Gunn, even though she spoke politely enough. There surely lurked a complacent snootiness beneath that courteous voice?

'An odd one this, isn't it? So soon after Chet Brunner's death. And it can't be Ronnie Waterman, because you've got him in custody.'

Sergeant Elliot greeted Lady Torrance with an affectionate familiarity which was quite out of order. 'Hello, guv. Great to see you again.'

'Hello, Rab.'

McAdam made it clear she had no time for civilities. 'I understand you discovered the body of this Morgan. Stuart Morgan, yes?'

'Nearly an hour ago,' said Sir Nicholas.

'It's inside here?'

178

'In the workshop, round the back.'

'What made you go in there? Had he invited you, or something?'

She was sure that Sir Nicholas had shot his wife a warning glance, but it was so brief that she could not guess at its significance. Lesley Torrance said: 'I'd seen some of his work up at Balmuir Lodge, and I wanted to see how he went about it.'

'You didn't move anything? You left everything as it was?'

'I'll bet you can rely on the DI to remember all the old procedures,' said Sergeant Elliot warmly. Under McAdam's fierce stare he cooled down and said: 'Sorry . . . er . . . Lady Torrance.'

'Thanks for the testimonial, Rab . . . er, sergeant.' Lesley Torrance allowed herself the faintest friendly smile. 'You're quite right. We knew it was best to get out rather than obscure any clues by fidgeting about the place. I made sure it was locked up before we left. And then came here and sat around until you arrived.'

'The key?' said McAdam.

'The door was open when we got there. The key was on the inside.' She held out a key wrapped in a sachet of polythene torn from a roll above the souvenir counter. 'And we kept an eye on the door until we could get the local constable to stand guard.'

'Very efficient of you.' McAdam forced the words out. 'Well, I'd better go and inspect the scene.'

As they left the shop and began walking round to the back, a blue Mondeo and a van arrived almost simultaneously. The SOCO team came out and began writhing into their white overalls. Dr Fairlie came out of his car and offered McAdam a curt nod.

'Is there any legend of a Balmuir curse? Some thrawn bogle coming back to spread some malice around? If this goes on, it'll be cheaper for me to rent a holiday home here than do all this travelling to and fro.'

A uniformed policeman provided a hefty presence, blocking the doorway. Flushed with the responsibility of his part in this commotion on his usually tranquil patch, he stared up and down, side to side, determined that not even a passing crow should decide to look for crumbs, or the howl of a low-flying fighter be allowed to take him by surprise.

McAdam led the way, followed by Dr Fairlie and two Scenes Of Crime Officers, one of them the photographer. The constable moved aside, reluctant to give way even to his superior officers. McAdam took a packet from one of the men and drew out two sterile surgical gloves. Gingerly she extracted the key from its wrapping, calling back to Lesley Torrance.

'You say the door was open. How far?'

'A few inches,' said Nick Torrance. 'I was in the lead. I pushed it open, and my wife followed me in.'

McAdam turned the key in the lock, pushed gently, and went in.

After looking down at the angle at which the corpse was lying, and the disarray of tools on the bench, she beckoned the photographer to edge round the other side of the bench and start work. Dr Fairlie came to her side and, stepping and stooping as carefully as herself, bent close to the bloodstained head, taking out his thermometer.

Although she would be the first to insist that everything should be done according to the book, for McAdam it was all going too slowly and ponderously.

'Well? Any idea of the time of death?'

'Within the last couple of hours.' He put his hand out towards the drying stain on the implement closest to the dead man's throat. 'And whose dirk might this be?'

'Can't say. Certainly not a tool for putting fake wormholes into reproduction furniture, or anything of that kind.'

'Mm.' Fairlie winced as he straightened up and eased his back. 'So we've got ourselves a double murder on our hands. But you've got the previous suspect in custody, haven't you?'

'Yes.' McAdam needed no further reminders.

'In that previous case, it would have needed some strength to drive that weapon, whatever it was, into the man's skull. This thing is fine enough to go in nice and easily. Incidentally, have you found the weapon for that other incident yet?'

'No, we haven't. But we're questioning Waterman.'

'Who threatened to shoot his enemy, not bash him with a heavy object.'

Something else of which McAdam needed no reminding. She said: 'We're dealing with the facts in *this* case at the moment.'

'Aye. I think we'll leave the boys to it and continue when they've dumped the pieces in the morgue and the lab.'

They backed out and made way for the SOCO team to do their painstaking work.

The Torrances had disappeared from the shop. 'Who the hell said they could push off?'

Sergeant Elliot said: 'Sir Nicholas thought they'd be more comfortable waiting for you in the pub. Just down the road there.'

McAdam braced herself against the return of that angry ache inside her head. She had a picture of that ex-Gunn woman pumping the locals, overstepping the mark and trespassing on official territory. But for the moment it would do no good to fly off the handle.

She kept it very calm. 'Go and work your way down the street, sergeant. Ask if folk saw anybody going towards the workshop or coming away from it. Especially if they seemed to be in a hurry. Anything that might help. But you needn't go into the pub. You can leave that to me.' She dared him to grin, but he was getting the measure of her now, and kept a grave face.

She approached the counter. 'Now, Mrs . . . er. . . ?'

'McTavish. Brenda McTavish.'

'These premises are your property?'

'Nae, I only run the shop for the Chisholm lass.'

'And the workshop?'

'That was hers and her late husband's. And he was in partnership with Mr Morgan, restoring furniture and . . . och, as if we hav'nae had enough trouble round here wi' the tragedy of young Mr Chisholm, and then that other dreadful business, and now this. Such a bourach . . . aye, indeed, what a muddle. No sense in it.'

McAdam glanced at the tables and display shelves. 'Some of this was the late Mr Morgan's work?'

'Those small wooden pieces, yes. Souvenirs for tourists. But that was only a sideline. You'd find some of his bigger work up at the Lodge. He did do work in the house for Mr Brunner.'

Something thudded faintly against the wall behind her.

'Did you hear anybody in there with Mr Morgan at any time this morning? Or see anybody leaving?'

'I did hear him moving about early on. But then we had a coachload of tourists stopping off for ten minutes on their way to Glasgow. We get quite a good passing trade. The village has got the only public toilet for thirty miles,' she added proudly.

'But some of them came in here?'

'Aye. A lot o' them. So I wouldnae ha' heard anything else while they were here.'

'And you didn't see anybody running away, or acting suspiciously at all?'

Brenda shook her head. 'That I did not. Seen one or two of the usual folk, mind you.'

'Usual folk? Such as who?'

'Och, there was the Chisholms. Mr Alec, anyway, though I suppose Queenie would have been with him. Stocking up in the shop across the way, I'd imagine. And the Pitcairns.' She frowned. 'You don't often see them out together. They seemed to be having a bit of an argument.'

'You've no idea what it was about?'

'Nay, I didnae ken.' Brenda drew herself up and folded her arms across her ample bosom. 'And besides, it was none of my business.'

McAdam walked down to the inn.

Nicholas Torrance stood up and moved towards the bar. 'What can I get you?'

'Thank you, but I don't drink on duty.'

In fact she rarely drank at all, and knew she was always regarded warily by her subordinates at divisional parties.

They sat at a table in the window, all three of them looking out from time to time, knowing that everybody in the bar was studying them and making muttered comments.

'When you arrived,' McAdam began, 'did you see anybody coming away from the workshop?'

Torrance shook his head. 'There were a few people in the street, here and there, but nobody all that close to the craft shop or the steps at the back.'

'Anybody at all you recognized, either before you went up or after you came down?'

'Only that young Pitcairn chap who seemed to have a grudge against Chet Brunner. With an older man. Could have been his father.'

This was the second time they had been mentioned. McAdam scraped her chair closer to the table, propping her elbows on it.

'And they were arguing,' she said.

'That's the way it looked. You know that already?'

'The woman in the craft shop saw them and got that impression. And she confirms that the older man was Harry Pitcairn's father. I think I'll leave your friendly sergeant down here, Lady Torrance, to tie up any loose ends he can find, while I go back to ask some questions in Balmuir Lodge. And a few questions for the Pitcairns.'

'If you want us, we'll be in Stables Cottage.' As McAdam got up, Lesley Torrance added: 'Do you think this is a separate murder, or could it be a double one?'

'Meaning you're keener than ever to believe Waterman innocent?'

'I just thought the question might be an interesting one.'

'Interesting, yes,' said McAdam. 'But for the time being Waterman has been cautioned and is still being questioned.'

As they walked back to their cars, the wrapped corpse was being carried out of the workshop.

Alec Chisholm was cleaning out the interior of the Fiat when McAdam drove up to the house. 'Got filthy, with all this dried mud from the last few days.' Then he registered who she was. 'Oh. Didn't expect to see you back. Thought you'd be away dealing with our killer.'

'Mr Chisholm, have you been down to the village this morning?'

'Yes. Picking up a few things.'

'How long ago would that be?'

'I got back about an hour ago and decided to do something useful. But hang on – what's this about?'

'You haven't heard the news?'

'What news?'

McAdam told him, briefly and brutally. At first he did not seem to take it in, then began shaking his head. He looked ashen grey, utterly drained. When he did speak, it was to echo Brenda McTavish in the craft shop.

'It's too much, on top of everything else. Too damn much.'

'Your wife was with you in the village, shopping?'

'Yes. Right now she's lying down. We've lost our little dog. She spent most of yesterday looking for him. Looked everywhere, and she's very upset. And now this. Oh, for God's sake.'

'Do you think we can go indoors? It looks as if I'm going to ask for the use of the incident room again. It's well equipped, and it'll save us having to bring in a caravan or anything.'

'Well, I don't know. The present owner might not want—'

'That would be the late Mr Brunner's widow?'

'No. The estate has been left to . . . well, it's all very complicated. But until legal matters have been settled—'

'I think I'd better have a word with Mrs Brunner anyway.'

'She's not here.'

'Where is she, then?'

'She and that Hagan character have gone off to Glasgow to look for some legal advice. Somebody Hagan knows.'

McAdam could guess who that would be. She had checked on Tam Hagan during that earlier spell of investigation, and found his record had a lot of smears on it. His involvement in Glasgow turf wars was well known. The boys in Pitt Street had provided her then with the name of a solicitor whose work for Hagan in some legal scrapes had more than once brought him close to criminal charges himself. She wondered whether something now had driven Jilly-Jo Brunner and Tam Hagan to clear off together.

Had they murdered Stuart Morgan before making a run for it? And before that, had they murdered Brunner? If the Torrances had been right to believe Ronnie Waterman's story, then somebody else had to have a good reason for getting rid of Brunner. And Morgan as well? But *what* reason?

She settled herself in the studio and put in a call to Glasgow for someone to check whether Hagan and Jilly-Jo had really been visiting that solicitor. If so, they should be asked – very

184

firmly asked – to return at once to Balmuir Lodge. If they refused, it should be suggested to them that they could be taken into custody to help the police with their enquiries.

Then she called Alec Chisholm in. He looked sick and apprehensive, though she could think of no way of implicating him in either of the killings. Not yet, anyway. Like everybody else, after this new development he had to go back on the list, unlikely as he might seem as a killer.

'Is there a phone in that cottage the Torrances are in?'

Chisholm gave her the number.

It was a call she had to force herself to make. It went against the grain. She needed to see the Pitcairns again, and reluctantly she felt she could do with an expert at her side. During her years in the Force, Lesley Torrance had been top of her field in identification of artworks, fake or genuine. It might be that she could be persuaded to think herself back into being DI Gunn for a short spell. Highly irregular, but she might see something that an untrained eye would overlook.

Steeling herself to be as correct and dispassionate as possible, and fending off the resentful stab within her head, McAdam put in the call.

17

Harry Pitcairn's expression as he opened the door of Glengorm Castle to Lesley and McAdam was far from welcoming. Lesley remembered those contemptuous brown eyes scouring everybody in the hall at Balmuir Lodge. Here they were just as aggressive and impatient.

'What the hell is it this time? I've got to be on the new plantation fifteen minutes from now.'

'We'll endeavour not to take up too much of your time, Mr Pitcairn.'

He stood four square in the doorway for a moment, then moved aside to let them in, stooping to pick up a few letters from the mat.

Lesley was amused by the deadpan formality with which McAdam introduced her. 'This is a one-time associate of ours, Detective Inspector Gunn, who has volunteered to help us in our inquiries.'

'Don't tell me you're going to run me in for daring to reclaim one of my family possessions from that Philistine's lair?' His gaze became puzzled rather than aggressive as he led them into the cramped little hall, tossing the letters on to the oak table and glancing sideways at Lesley in the poor light from the window, trying to place her.

McAdam said: 'Can you tell me where you were this morning, around nine or ten o'clock?'

'I was up in the plantation, over by Harden Sike. But what's that got to do with you?'

'You've had dealings with a Stuart Morgan of Balmuir?'

187

'No.'

'You must surely have come across him. He was a skilled furniture restorer, and I'm given to understand he did a lot of reproduction work for the late Chet Brunner.'

'Oh, yes, I've heard of him. But we had no call on his services in this house. We don't go in for fakes and copies here. So what's the purpose of this visit?'

'He's been murdered.'

Harry Pitcairn had been lounging against the oak table in the middle of the room. Now he straightened up and uttered an incredulous 'Huh?'

'Murdered,' McAdam repeated, 'in his workshop in the village.'

'This is the second time you've been to this house to tell me someone's been bumped off. What the hell is going on? And what the hell has it got to do with me?'

Lesley said: 'You've nursed a few grudges against the late Mr Brunner. And you weren't too pleased to find your cherished skean dhu was a fake.'

'Now I remember you. Detective Inspector be damned. Last time I saw you, you were Lady something-or-other.'

'Torrance. But before that I was just what Chief Inspector McAdam called me, and I'm offering her my professional advice.'

'Mr Brunner and Mr Morgan have both been killed, within days of each other.' McAdam raised her voice to make it clear who was in charge here. 'We're anxious to establish a connection.'

'From what I heard on the news, Brunner was done in by some petty criminal who you managed to round up. After making a lot of unjustified implications against me, and no doubt a lot of other people.' He leaned on the table again, swinging towards Lesley. 'And didn't you play some dashing part in that? Don't tell me the police have let the man escape so he could come back and do somebody else in?'

'Waterman is still safely in custody,' said McAdam. 'But it may just possibly be that he was not responsible for Brunner's death. Somebody else could have got there first. And that might be the same somebody who has just disposed of Stuart Morgan.'

'Good God. You badger a lot of folk about a killing, then arrest somebody else, and now you're not even sure of *him*.'

'We do have to eliminate people who may have had a motive. Or call it a grudge, in both cases. You yourself would be the first to admit, Mr Pitcairn, that you hated Brunner. And you were very upset when you found that the supposed heirloom you were attempting to remove from Balmuir Lodge was in fact only a copy. You were aware that Morgan was in the business of making copies of various things for Brunner's collection.'

A collection partly fake, partly genuine, thought Lesley, without commenting on this out loud. Had Brunner chosen certain items to keep, and others to be copied while the originals were sold off? Or had Stuart Morgan been cheating on him in some way? He had served time in prison, and even if a drunken car accident did not mean he had been an habitué of criminals before, his spell inside might have led him to become one afterwards. Men learned a lot of new skills in prison; and made a lot of new acquaintances who could come in handy when they were out again.

As McAdam continued the questioning, Lesley drifted about the room, examining a pair of ivory elephants on the mantelpiece, and a target flanked by two Lochaber axes on the wall above it. She had just turned to study a large portrait on the wall beside it, picturing a man proudly attired in the uniform of the Royal Company of Archers, when a door opened at her elbow and an elderly man came in.

'My great-great-grandfather,' he barked, just as proud as the figure in the painting. 'Sir James Pitcairn.' Then he peered at her. 'And who might ye be, young lady?'

'Lady Torrance,' said Harry Pitcairn. 'My father, Colonel Pitcairn.'

'Lady Torrance, is it? Delighted to meet you.' His hand clutched hers, but it was a very shaky grip. 'To what do we owe the pleasure?'

'Lady Torrance,' said Harry heavily, 'is assisting the police in their inquiries.'

'What inquiries?'

189

'Apparently some odd character from the village has followed in Brunner's footsteps. Been done in.'

Colonel Pitcairn's hand stopped shaking. He folded his sandy-haired fingers in tightly until the knuckles went white. His flabby lips sagged open. Then he spotted the letters on the table, and grabbed at them. 'Ah, the post. Gets later every day. Lucky if we get them before dusk, eh?' All at once he was babbling. 'None of the old traditions of service apply any more, eh? Don't you find that, Lady Torrance? Och, but maybe you're too young ever to ha' known the really civilized times.'

Lesley could not take her eyes off the portrait. As she stooped to examine the lower right-hand corner, Colonel Pitcairn's voice went rambling on. 'Aye, a fine piece of work, that. By Skeoch Cumming, of course.'

'A very good copy,' said Lesley.

'Copy?' Harry exploded. 'That's an original. Skeoch Cumming was noted for his paintings of the royal bodyguard.'

'I know. And this isn't an original. As I said, an admirable copy. Excellent brushwork. But this bottom right-hand corner's been a bit rushed. Covering up a few errors with acrylic paint. Everything else done so well, but just this little bit botched.'

Father and son were staring at each other. Colonel Pitcairn stumbled an awkward step backwards. Harry thrust out his hand.

'Father. Give me those letters.'

The old man shakily extracted two envelopes to hand to his son.

'And that other one,' Harry snapped.

'This is for me. I don't have to—'

'Let me see it. It's from that bookie, isn't it? You're still at it.' He swung towards McAdam. 'Has it occurred to you that maybe Brunner never did get most of our family treasures? My father here had flogged 'em off to pay his gambling debts – oh, they've always been pretty large, I can assure you – and palmed some copies off on to Brunner. That oaf wouldn't know the differ-ence.' He brought his father back into the line of fire. 'Were you working with that character – Morgan, was that the name? But when did you flog the original of the portrait? That never went to Brunner. Who did it go to?'

190

'This is outrageous. We do not have family discussions in front of strangers. It is none of their business.'

'Oh, but it is,' said McAdam, very quiet after the shouting. 'It is very much the business of the police to know exactly what deals were done with the late Stuart Morgan, and who would have the strongest motive for getting rid of him before he let out too many secrets.'

'I'll no' have the likes of you talking to me like that. Not in my house. I'm still well-kent round here, you know. I reckon the fiscal would listen to me if I laid a complaint against police blundering in and—'

'Whatever he listened to, Colonel, he would also agree that in the circumstances we'd be entitled to hold you and your son for questioning for twenty-four hours.'

'In order to let filthy gossip spread through the community and besmirch our name, what? Dammit, woman, I'd be ashamed to be doing a job as shabby as yours.' His Scottish burr became a pseudo-English hee-haw honking. 'No standards. No breeding. No respect for tradition. There was a time when you would not have been allowed to set foot in these premises. Disgraceful.'

Harry said: 'Shut up, father. You're an old sham. I don't know why I went along with it for so long.'

Colonel Pitcairn tried to splutter, but only whimpered. In Lesley's eyes he became, all at once, the Wizard of Oz. All noise and self-righteous bluster – and then in the end you found him cowering behind a battery of amplifiers, making as much noise as possible to disguise the fact that he was scared of being exposed as a twittering little nonentity.

Jilly-Jo came storming into the house, followed by Hagan, less like a tough security guard and more like a browbeaten, dejected dog.

Alec had been asking Anna if she could keep an eye on the place while he took Queenie away for a much-needed holiday, when Jilly-Jo planted herself in front of him, seething.

'I suppose you've known about this all along? A big joke. And you went along with it.'

'Sorry, I'm not with you.'

'You're the bloody executor of that flaming will. Don't tell me you haven't known what was in it, all along.'

'I was appointed executor, but until recently I didn't know the exact provisos.'

'Come off it. He didn't tell you about the marriage so you could both have a good laugh over it? Big deal, leaving me a bit of money, but I've got no rights as a widow, because we were never properly married. Isn't that a scream?'

Anna risked intervening, afraid that Jilly-Jo was on the verge not just of yelling at Alec but of spitting in his face. 'We were under the impression that you had a very romantic wedding in the Highlands, with all the historic trimmings.'

Jilly-Jo turned on her. 'Historic? It was a put-up job.' She jerked a thumb scornfully in Hagan's direction. 'So much for his brilliant solicitor. A fat lot of good he's done us.'

'He found the truth,' protested Hagan. 'And it didn't take him long.'

'The truth!' fumed Jilly-Jo. 'The sort of truth we could have done without. Just another of Chet's stunts. Phoney setting, phoney minister, phoney wedding.'

There was a shriek of laughter from the door. Georgina Campbell made a gleeful entry like an actress picking up her cue.

'Isn't that just the most wonderful twist in the tale? Good old Chet. Just taking reasonable precautions. And who'd blame him? But at least you get some cash, you bitch. More than I do, after all I did for him.'

Alec spoke with a virulence that took Anna by surprise. It was as if aversions which he had bottled up for years had suddenly blown the cork and come foaming out.

'You.' He flung the word at Jilly-Jo. 'You wouldn't go to bed with him unless he married you, would you?'

'I had my pride.'

'Prick-tease,' shouted Georgina.

'Well, at least he left *her* some money,' said Alec. 'Or palimony, as they call it in the States. Whereas you, you didn't hesitate before hopping into bed with him. So there was no need for a put-up ceremony, and no pay-off.'

192

'The cheating bastard.'

'Well, at least that's something the two of you can agree on.'

Like Alec, Jilly-Jo had been quivering with the pent-up need to attack somebody, only with her it was a physical need. Without warning she launched herself at Georgina. Alec started a vain step to come between them, but was knocked to one side. The two women clawed at each other, scratching and squealing. Anna looked at Alec, wondering whether between them they could put an end to this; or whether it was better to let it run its own course.

Tam Hagan stood to one side, sullen and at a loss.

Suddenly there were two others on the scene, each grabbing one of the women and dragging them apart. Anna had to admire their skill. DCI McAdam's right arm did something complicated under Georgina's shoulder, while her sergeant performed a similar move so that they could separate the two women like two interlocked segments of a metal puzzle sliding apart, once you had the knack. Sergeant Elliot was lucky, though, not to have received a scratch down his right cheek to match the scar on his left.

Hagan was eyeing Georgina appreciatively. Her shoulder and left breast had been laid enticingly bare by a long shred torn from her flimsy blouse.

'What's all this about?' McAdam demanded.

'Nothing to do with you.' Jilly-Jo was tugging her hair into some sort of shape, panting, already poised for another assault. 'What are you doing, still hanging around?'

'Have you only just got back, or were you in the village earlier today?' McAdam was including Hagan in her question.

'What the hell are you on about?' He was reluctant to have his attention diverted from Georgina. 'I've already answered your crappy questions once before. Why are you still picking on me?'

'Some other matters have arisen.'

'While we've been away? No business of mine, then.'

'You haven't answered my question about—'

'And I'm not going to.'

'Mr Hagan, I'm making no charges against you at this stage. I simply want you to help with the answers to a few questions.'

'I don't know what you're trying to cook up this time, but I'm not interested. If you keep on, I want a solicitor.'

'Don't talk to me about solicitors,' squealed Jilly-Jo. 'A fat lot of good they've done us so far.'

'If you want a solicitor, Mr Hagan,' said McAdam, 'I will make immediate arrangements for one to meet us at the nick. But since I'm not yet charging you with anything, wouldn't it save time and trouble for you simply to answer a few straightforward questions here?'

Hagan glowered, shuffled, and then grunted assent. Jilly-Jo flopped into an armchair with a histrionic sigh, still keeping a wary eye on Georgina, who was coyly adjusting her clothes to the best advantage.

'Provided you tell me what the hell it's all about,' Hagan said. 'I'm not going to be trapped into answering dodgy questions so you can twist them into something that suits you. What's all this about something coming up since we left?'

'Another dead body, that's what.' McAdam allowed it time to sink in. 'A Mr Stuart Morgan has been killed. Did you know him at all well?'

'Never heard of him.'

'I remember.' The focus of attention had been off Jilly-Jo for too long. 'He was that weirdo who was always carting bits of furniture and God knows what in and out of the place. Chet's odd-job man.' Even uttering Chet Brunner's name was enough to set her off again. 'Another shifty little creep, as shifty as that fat, cheating bastard himself.'

'Since you have such a clear recollection of the dead man's proclivities, perhaps you'll be prepared to help us with our inquiries. Could you spare me a few minutes in the incident room?'

Anna waited for Hagan to say that he wasn't going to let the police try giving Jilly-Jo the third degree unless he was present to protect her. Instead, he let McAdam and Elliot escort her towards the studio, and turned his attention to Georgina.

'Are you all right?'

'I can cope. I'm so sorry you had to witness that dreadful scene.' Her gaze met his, then dropped shyly. She had practised being spontaneous until she had got it perfect. 'I really must go and tidy myself up.'

She did not look back in protest when he followed her.

Anna sighed. 'You know, I do feel guilty. It's not as though I did anything deliberately, but I still feel guilty.'

Alec put his arm round her shoulders and hugged her, the way she had often seen him hug Queenie. 'What have you got to feel guilty about?'

'Oh, I don't know. The will. Me getting the estate. I mean, he was such a tough type, and it doesn't make sense for him to leave me so much.'

'But of course it makes sense. All those wheeler-dealers in our business, they get where they are because they're in tune with the corniest ideas of the general public.' Alec's fit of hostility was seeping away into mere disillusion. 'Their success depends on their vulgarity. Their brashness, pushiness. Knowing the market, playing it, and believing in it while they do so. But believing – that's the essence. Think of all the illiterate bosses, the Cohns and the Mayers who made Hollywood. Bullying everybody, squeezing the last little drop of blood and talent out of everyone who worked for them, but weeping genuine tears over the concept of a white Christmas. And redneck backwoods Bible-punchers who grow misty-eyed over a Catholic priest provided he's played by Bing Crosby. And our home-grown imitators, all of them like Nazi concentration camp officers: eyes filling with tears as Jewish prisoners played a Schubert quartet, then next day despatch them to the gas chambers. Chet Brunner wouldn't have got where he was if he hadn't had a wide streak of corny sentiment right through that leathery hide. Don't knock it. Your inheritance is the happy ending he could never have contrived for himself.'

Anna gulped, embarrassed by his intensity. Clumsily she changed the subject. 'Oh, Alec – any sign of Cocky yet?'

'No. Which is why I want to get Queenie away for a while, just as soon as I can. She's near breaking point. Not that she'll ever forget him, unfortunately.'

Lesley was taking clothes from the washing machine out to the drying carousel when she heard the car draw up on the other side of the cottage. Nick came round, almost tripping over the laundry basket as he reached to kiss her.

'A couple of bottles of rather ordinary Rioja,' he said. 'But I did find a rather good Macallan that seems to have been languishing in the dust at the back of a shelf for a few years.'

Lesley freed a cluster of pegs from a wire, and began hanging her blouse on the outer edge.

'Any staggering developments during my absence?' asked Nick.

'Nothing. I don't know who to suspect. Or who's above suspicion.'

'Shame. By this time one expects a cut-and-dried solution so that the end credits can roll and everyone can switch off and make a cup of tea.'

'This is real life, not Miss Marple. Real life is untidy, and tends to stay that way.'

'In a decent thriller, that old man you went to see would have been Anna's father, and there would be a symbolic clash between Brunner's love-child with Queenie, and Pitcairn's by-blow with Anna. And for some reason Pitcairn would be able to blackmail Brunner, and—'

'Yes,' said Lesley, 'just a telly play where it all ends in a flurry and you can leave a lot of loose ends and implausibilities without anybody noticing.'

'You wouldn't buy my plot synopsis?'

'No, I wouldn't.'

'You may regret it.'

She took her slip from the basket. 'Amateur sleuths and locked door mysteries are not on the programme.'

'Aren't you an amateur now?'

She was framing some flippant response, but it died on her lips. She peered at a stain on the protruding end of one of the cross struts of the carousel, touched it with her little finger, then drew back.

'What's up?' Nick moved round the laundry basket to her side. 'Found a midge colony lying in wait for you?'

'That mark on the end there.'

196

'Rust.'

'That's what I thought. But this contraption is too new to rust. I think it could be dried blood.' As he instinctively lifted his finger, the way she had done, she said: 'Don't touch.'

'What on earth is wandering through your mind right now?'

'Did he fall,' she mused aloud, 'or was he pushed? Or, rather, was he really attacked, or did he just fall?'

'If I'm thinking what you're thinking—'

'I'm thinking we'd better ask the DCI to get Forensic down here.'

'If I'm thinking what you're thinking,' Nick repeated, this time in little more than an awed whisper, 'she isn't going to like it.'

'No, she isn't.'

18

Forensic confirmed that the minute traces of blood still encrusted on the metal matched Brunner's admirably. Further examination of the ground behind Stables Cottage confirmed earlier theories. In spite of the downpour, marks of one pair of feet coming down the slope and two pairs going back up were distinguishable; and between the two tracks was still the flattened path of a body being dragged up.

Sitting in the cottage and reluctantly accepting a cup of instant coffee, McAdam even more reluctantly agreed that the examination which had already tended to verify Ronnie and Martine Waterman's story was now supplemented by the near certainty of Brunner having met an accidental death.

'Brunner came down here that evening after he had heard Mrs Chisholm's suspicions. Maybe he was going to confront Waterman. Simply bang on the front door and get shot in the guts? Or in the first place try peeking in one of the windows to check if it was really them. Either way, he slipped.'

'He was a very heavy man,' Lesley Torrance confirmed, 'and a clumsy one. Always crashing into things.'

McAdam had to agree that it all fitted. Heavy and clumsy, he had lost his footing on that uneven slope, and gone headfirst into the metal end of the crosspiece. It had driven into him, and then the impact could have set the carousel turning, wrenching him to one side and breaking his neck.

Lesley Torrance opened her mouth, then seemed to have second thoughts. Her husband was less restrained. He said:

'You'll have to let the Watermans go, then. With profuse apologies.'

'By no means. He's broken his licence, which means he goes straight back inside. On top of that he's been guilty of dangerous driving, carrying out a kidnapping' – she nodded at Lesley – 'and threatening violence. Also there's a matter of wasting police time by running off instead of waiting to explain things.'

'The *Daily Mail* isn't going to find that story as exciting as the earlier one.'

No, thought McAdam dourly, it wasn't. And now she was faced with a fresh problem – or would it turn out that things were, after all, less complicated? At the outset there had been the easy supposition that Ronnie Waterman had murdered Brunner. Then the new problem of Morgan's death, for which Waterman could not possibly have been responsible, raising the possibility of a double murder by, in official parlance, person or persons unknown. Now, with Brunner's murder not a murder, there was a single killing to be dealt with.

At least you could be sure of one thing: unlike Brunner, Stuart Morgan could not simply have fallen on to that lethal weapon.

'At any rate,' Lesley Torrance ventured, 'in spite of his hatred of the man, this lets young Pitcairn off the hook regarding Brunner's death.'

'But not necessarily Morgan's death. After all that fuss about forgeries, he could have gone round to drag the truth out of Morgan – lost his temper, especially when he saw that skean dhu lying there, and gone for him in a rage. Can't be ruled out, but we'll have to insist on some fingerprinting to compare with the batch we've now got from the workshop.'

'And what about the Hagan bruiser?'

'In that first case, I did wonder if he and that woman could have killed Brunner on their way back from Glasgow, before playing the innocents when the news was broken to them. Good reason for wanting him out of the way so she could inherit more quickly than expected – and before he changed his mind. They didn't know at the time that he had already changed his mind. If he'd ever been minded in her direction anyway. She wasn't going to get the lot. But they're now in the clear, anyway.'

'And this time?' said Nick Torrance. 'Hagan could be in with so many crooks that he might have established some contact with Morgan in prison, helped draw him into shady business afterwards, then found he was somehow being cheated.'

'Yes, that's one of those possibilities you juggle with. Until you find you can't keep all the balls in the air, and the whole theory collapses. And this one's a write-off, I think. I've double-checked on Hagan. At one stage in his murky career he was connected with shifting quality furniture from fire sales, having set the fires in the first place. Been inside twice. So he could have come across Morgan, and used him. But I'm not sure anything that complicated is his line. Mainly he was so stupid he couldn't help getting caught. He's a thick-ear type, not a smart operator. Even as a heavy, he's a buffoon.'

Lesley Torrance voiced the dilemma: 'So where do we go from here?'

McAdam did not want it taken for granted that the ex-DI was now a full-time member of the team, but before she could summon up a suitably dismissive reply there was a tap at the door. Sergeant Elliot came in to hand over further news from the morgue.

Detailed examination had shown that the first blow of the skean dhu had penetrated Morgan's jugular vein and gone through the neck muscles between the first and second cervical vertebrae. Morgan must have slumped back, and as he collapsed against the edge of the bench he was struck again at an angle from above the left shoulder down towards the heart.

'The blade wasn't long enough to reach the heart,' McAdam read it out aloud, 'but by then he was as good as dead anyway. Quite a cluster of fingerprints. Only Morgan's own can be identified at this stage. Top priority must be specimens from the Pitcairns.'

'Harry Pitcairn did say something about handling it during one of Brunner's murder mysteries,' Lesley reminded her.

'I hadn't forgotten that. But if there were prints over and above Morgan's, that might be interesting.' She stared at Sir Nicholas and his wife over the edge of her coffee mug. 'You definitely didn't touch it yourself, when you discovered the body?'

'No, we did not.'

'You'd never have forgotten procedure that quickly, would you, guv?' Elliot was beaming with what McAdam considered inane affection at his one-time DI. 'Oh, and another thing. An Inspector Percy from the Yard left a message to say that they've established a link between two of the brass thefts – is that right? – and the combine in Glasgow they've been after, and thanks very much and he'll be in touch with you when you get home.'

McAdam said: 'Make yourself useful, sergeant. I noticed young Mrs Chisholm is out there in the yard cleaning her car. Go and keep her company, and sound her out about her relationship with the deceased, will you?'

Lesley Torrance began protesting. 'It'd be a bit distressing for her, quite so soon. Stuart Morgan was a close friend of her late husband and herself, and—'

'Precisely. She can probably give us a much clearer picture of him than anybody else, and without realizing it may offer us just the lead we need.'

The flick of her right hand left Elliot no choice.

After he had gone, she pushed the empty mug away from her. 'Lady Torrance, it's quite improper for you as a civilian to be dealing direct with other police forces without going through the proper channels.'

'Inspector Percy is an old and trusted colleague. I shall be keeping in touch with him as an independent adviser on arts and antiques matters—'

'In the present inquiry, everything should be channelled through myself, as SIO.'

With marked displeasure she cut the conversation short and skimmed down the rest of the report. Some of these specialists were just too meticulous, covering their own backs by including every tiny little speck of what might be evidence.

She let out a snort. 'Honestly, I'm all in favour of being thorough, but this is as bad as a surveyor's report when you're buying a house. A whole paragraph listing all the sharp tools in the workshop, one with a smear of dried blood which turns out to be Morgan's own. What did they expect? He must have cut himself quite frequently during his work. Then there's a crack in the bench into which some instant coffee grains appear to have been spilt. Oh, and mention of a slight trace of animal blood on a shred of sacking on the floor near the door. You suppose Morgan was a poacher as well as a furniture faker?' It was surprising, she thought, that they did not include the number of dead flies on the window-ledge, and whether the curtains would draw or not.

It was only when Sir Nicholas Torrance gave a quiet, some-how ironic cough that it dawned on her that her strictures about people knowing their place applied to herself right now. She was using their private accommodation as an auxiliary incident room.

'Well, I mustn't keep you.' She gathered up her papers. 'Thank you for your hospitality. Once we've got you to sign your statements, I hope you'll be able to drive home this time without further incident.'

Anna had been on her knees in the back of the Volvo with a portable vacuum cleaner, digging into a corner to suck out some sawdust and a few shreds of sacking, when something started knocking. At first she thought the machine was faltering, perhaps clogged with the gunge she was removing. Then she looked up and saw the face of Sergeant Elliot at the side window. She switched off, and backed out gingerly.

'Sorry to interrupt.' He had a nice, shy, non-officious smile that softened the implications of that battle scar on his cheek. 'The guv'nor thought you might help us with a few details.'

'Couldn't we go inside?' If she was going to be questioned, at least she wanted to get the grime off her face and hands, and make some sort of dab at her hair.

'There's three of them in that cottage going over some other bits and pieces. The idea was that I could have a word with you at the same time. Out here in the fresh air,' he added as an inducement.

Anna wiped her hands down her denims. 'Sorry about the mess. I've allowed it to get really grotty in the back there.'

'That's what this sort of war-horse is for, isn't it?'

There was an awkward silence. She sensed that Elliot did not know where to begin, or how sensitive she might be about his questions.

She said: 'I can't contribute much to this investigation, you know. I still haven't got over the shock of the news.' She leaned against the side of the Volvo, while he took a few steps to the left, a few to the right, as if on sentry duty.

'Stuart Morgan was a close friend of yours, wasn't he?'

'He'd been a friend of my late husband. They were partners in a furniture restoration business. Chet Brunner used them quite a lot in the house, and my father-in-law . . . I mean, that is, Alec Chisholm . . . he helped us with these cottages and with the craft shop.' She waited for him to ask about Brunner's legacy to her, but either he had not been informed about this or was too shy to bring it up. 'My husband,' she went on, 'died in an accident.'

'Oh, I'm sorry.' He looked at her in a sad, earnest way. She would almost have preferred some tough, unsympathetic questioning which she could have fought against. 'It must have been hard, running this lot' – he waved towards the cottages – 'on your own. Though you did have help from this Morgan chap.' Was he, after all, cunning rather than amiable?

'Stuart was as devastated as I was. We sort of . . . well, clung together. He helped me at weekends with cleaning out the cottages ready for the next tenants, and did odd jobs, and we . . . well, we just got along.'

'No question of anything more personal? Working so closely together, didn't the question sometimes arise that you might as well—'

'I don't see what connection that has with this inquiry.'

'Obviously you relied on him a lot, so you'd hardly be the one to kill him. But since you did work so closely together, did he never tell you anything that might have led you to suspect he might be in trouble? Some hint about his enemies, or financial problems he was having, or anything?'

'None,' she said curtly.

'You must each have had a pretty regular routine. There wouldn't be a lot of changes around here from one week to another, would there?'

'Depending on Chet's whims. Otherwise, yes, life's been fairly predictable.'

'Did he go away often? Working on some projects away from here? The odd contact in Glasgow, for instance?'

'He was banned from driving for some years yet, so he didn't go anywhere unless I drove him.'

'And. . . ?'

'We used to go shopping in Ayr. He bought a lot of materials there. And sometimes he spent quite a long time with one particular supplier,' she recalled.

'Could you give me the name?'

'I'd have to think back. But I'd imagine there'd be plenty of receipts somewhere in the workshop.'

'Unless it was the sort of business where you didn't much go for receipts.'

'I wouldn't know anything about that sort of business. Certainly it's not the way I run mine.'

He gave her an apologetic grin, and extended his sentry-go into a saunter round the car. 'How will you cope now he's gone?'

'I haven't got round to thinking about that yet.'

He glanced towards the farmhouse. 'Have you got a hose?'

'Yes. Why?'

'I thought I might help you with cleaning this up. There's more muck on the outside than inside.' He stooped over the front bumper, and narrowed his eyes. 'Hit any stray cats recently?'

Anna came round to join him. The front bumper had encountered a few objects in its time, but was as sturdy and undamaged as ever. But there was a coating of mud along two-thirds of it; and at one end a small tuft of hair was stuck into the mud, with a few wiry strands curled over the top.

'Oh, no,' she breathed.

Before he could ask what was worrying her, the door of the house opened and DCI McAdam came out.

'Everything OK, sergeant? Hope you've been able to cope with him, Mrs Chisholm? Best be getting a move on.'

Elliot gave Anna a warm smile as they headed towards the police car and drove off. Anna stood well back from the Volvo for an interminable minute, then forced herself to look more carefully at the bumper. Then she remembered some of the shreds that had been sucked up from the interior by the cleaner. Again she went on her knees into the back of the car, and prodded with a finger to see if there was anything left in the corner.

There was still a stubborn shred of sacking which had resisted being gobbled up. The stain on it might have been rust, red earth, or dried paint. But she knew it wasn't. It was blood.

She edged her way out, slammed the hatchback shut, and hesitated for a moment, half wanting to go over to Stables Cottage and tell Nick and Lesley Torrance what she had just discovered. But wouldn't it be better for the news to come from her rather than be spread among other people before Queenie was told?

One way or the other, sooner or later, Queenie had to be told.

Anna slept only fitfully that night. If she told Queenie first thing in the morning, that would ruin their holiday before they had even started.

Or would it make sense to tell her then, so that she would have the holiday to get over it?

Or to tell her afterwards, when she was refreshed from the holiday and better able to bear the news?

Just before dawn, Anna found herself questioning her own interpretation of what she had found. Those fragments could have been any stray animal. There could be absolutely nothing to tell.

Any stray animal, a bit of it smeared on the bumper. But that trace *inside* the the car?

In the morning she found herself blurting it all out to the Torrances.

206

19

Lesley had begun hoovering the kitchen floor when Anna tapped at the door and was brought through by Nick. She at once uttered a protest and began easing the cleaner out of Lesley's hands.

'That's my job. You're on holiday.'

'That's not the way I'd put it,' said Nick.

'Leave it. I'll do it when you've gone.'

She was fussing from one surface to another, straightening a pot of flowers on the window-ledge, moving the toast rack, peering suspiciously at a nearly empty jar of marmalade as if waiting for it to explode or play some silly trick on her. Yet Lesley was quite sure there was something else on her mind.

At last she came out with it. 'I don't know what to tell Queenie. Whether to tell her before she goes on holiday, or afterwards. Or not to tell her at all. Only I think I have to.' To Lesley she sounded not unlike Queenie herself in one of her scattier moods.

'I'm afraid you've lost us,' said Nick soothingly.

'Oh, sorry. I'm so sorry. It's just that I'm so confused about what to do for the best. You see, Queenie's lost her dog, Cocky. Absolutely worshipped it. And now I think I know what happened to it.'

Lesley pulled a kitchen chair out from under the table, and Anna sank into it, half in a trance.

'You've found the dog?'

'No, but I think it was run over. By my car. Only it wasn't me driving the car. It was Stuart, on his way back with stuff he was removing from the Lodge. I found traces when I was cleaning the mess out of my car, and that nice young sergeant spotted blood and dirt on the bumper. Only how do I tell Queenie that? She never had any time for Stuart. And it was my car, and he ought not to have been driving it, but she's bound to go on at *me* about it.'

'You're sure about this? In a police investigation,' said Lesley gently, 'we're always wary of jumping to any conclusions if there isn't an actual corpse.'

'I think it's been . . . oh, dear, I can't make up my mind one way or the other, but I do think he must have ditched it well away from where he ran over it. In one of the lochans down the glen there, maybe. And she'll never know where to find it now.'

Nick sounded very firm and positive. Lesley knew that Anna needed an inarguable decision right here and now, and she loved the confident way he shouldered the responsibility, sympathetic but unyielding. 'Save it until they get back. It'll give you time to sort it out in your own mind, and know exactly how much is evidence and how much is speculation. And,' he finished earnestly, 'time to decide how much you really need to tell her. If anything at all.'

Anna nodded. She sat quite still for a moment or two, then emerged shakily from her trance. She blinked and looked around. 'I've no business lumbering you with all my woes. I really just came in to see you before you leave. Any problems?'

Now it was inconsequential chat about the cottage, its amenities, the few scraps of food and one unopened bottle of wine the Torrances were leaving for the next tenant or for Anna herself.

When she had gone, Lesley strolled through to the bedroom and dragged her case out of the bottom of the wardrobe.

Nick said: 'All that talk of dirt on cars – have you had a look at ours in the last day or two? We've got a sizeable helping of rural deposits all over it. While you're doing your bit of packing, I'll run it into the village. They've got a power hose behind the garage there.'

'Leaving me to do all the last-minute chores here? Very cunning.'

'Save stumbling over one another as we pack.'

'You sound very experienced in that direction.'

'Not at all, my love. Just that I remember you bumping into me every few seconds in that cabin. Pleasant enough experience, depending on which part of your anatomy was doing the bumping, but—'

'Oh, do go and squirt some foamy water all over the car.'

He kissed her, and went out to the Laguna.

Lesley stood by the window, watching the car swing out of the yard and hearing the familiar purr as it accelerated out of sight. Instead of getting back to her packing, she went on staring out across the yard at the bonnet of Anna Chisholm's Volvo which she could just see in its slot at the end of the farmhouse. As if by just staring at it she had managed to provoke it into life, she saw it begin moving out across the yard, and turning in the opposite direction from Nick, heading towards Balmuir Lodge.

Long after the sounds of both vehicles had faded, there was a sound scratching at the back of her mind. Something was ringing a bell somewhere, demanding her attention. Where had she seen a bloodstained fragment of sacking? Only of course she hadn't seen any such thing. She had merely heard of it, somewhere.

Then out of those recesses of her memory she heard McAdam's voice complaining about the overload of details she had received from examination of Stuart Morgan's workshop. A reference to sacking in there, too. And a trace of animal blood. Instead of throwing the bloodied corpse of a dog he had just hit into bushes or a ditch beside a road much used by locals, had Morgan decided it was safer to dump it temporarily in his workshop and later dispose of it further down the glen, where it was unlikely to be found or identified? Hastily bundling it into a sack along with all the other items removed from Balmuir Lodge, he intended to get rid of it at leisure.

Had he had time enough for that before he was killed?

Once she had finished her packing, there was nothing to do in the cottage. Even making a cup of coffee would mean dirtying a cup and having to wash it up again. Having tidied the cushions on the sofa in the sitting-room, she absurdly didn't want to sit down and disarrange them.

The sun was shining. She would have a last stroll. On the last day of a holiday, there was often a brief interlude during which you wanted to have a quick last look at some of the places you had enjoyed, the corners which would linger in your memory. Though, as Nick had said, this had hardly been a holiday. As she went out she glanced at the carousel where Brunner had met his end, and then her footsteps took her up the slope past the spot where he had lain. Not reminiscences which merited any holiday snaps. She continued round the swimming-pool, and in an arc round the Lodge to the Chisholms' wing.

She had not been aware of the existence of a tiny garden in the shadow of the wing. As she came upon it now, Queenie was standing with her back to her, striking a crooked, stooped pose and holding a small trowel above her head.

Play-acting again, poor dear.

'Who would have thought the young man to have had so much blood in him?' She raised the trowel like a monstrance.

Lesley said instinctively: 'Haven't you got that wrong, Queenie? Surely it's "the old man"...?'

Beyond Queenie she saw a hummock of freshly turned earth in the centre of the patch, covered with little knots of cut flowers. Some terrible urge drove her past Queenie to stoop over that little mound.

Anna had been worried about bringing sad news to Queenie. Lesley knew with an awful shiver that there was no need to break such news.

Behind her, Queenie's voice raged with a tragic intensity she had probably never achieved before. 'Don't you dare touch! Who asked you to come here? Can't you leave well alone?'

Nick was puzzled, then mildly annoyed before becoming mildly worried. Where the hell had Lesley got to, without leaving even a scribbled note on the coffee table? He strolled over to the farmhouse, expecting to find her chatting to Anna; but there was nobody there. The Volvo was missing, so probably Anna had gone up to the Lodge to wish Alec and Queenie a happy holiday.

Would Lesley have gone with her, in too much of a hurry to leave a note? It was not as if she was particularly close friends with them – less so than he himself was.

He phoned Alec's number, but there was no reply.

Torn between annoyance and an indefinable apprehension, he went back to the Laguna, sparkling after its bath, and drove up to Balmuir Lodge. At the entrance to the drive he had to swerve on to the verge to avoid a Jaguar coming out into the middle of the road. The driver glared at him; the woman in the passenger seat looked perfectly happy. It appeared that Tam Hagan and Georgina Campbell were leaving Balmuir behind them.

As he got out of the car, Jilly-Jo was standing in the middle of the terrace screaming at anyone who would listen. Unfortunately for her, there seemed to be no audience whatsoever. Queenie's Fiat was not parked near the Chisholms' wing, so the holidaymakers must be on their way to wherever they had chosen. Hagan's Jag, as he had just seen, was on its way to pastures new – if Glasgow could be regarded as coming into that category.

Jilly-Jo came ranting towards him. 'D'you know what they've done? D'you know what they've *done* to me?'

'I'm sorry, I came here looking for my wife. Have you—'

'Locked me out of my own suite. I've been cheated by every rotten bastard, every little floozie, every . . . I tell you, this place stinks. I'll make somebody pay for this. But I can't get back into my suite to collect my clothes, or my cases, or . . . or *anything.*'

'Who's got the key, then?'

'I don't know. Maybe those two. Getting a big laugh out of it.' Her breasts were heaving up and down, and there was a trickle of sweat forming along her throat. Her breathing slowed gradually, and she tried a completely new approach, switching from raging harridan to helpless maiden in distress. 'Do you think you could break the door down for me?'

'I'm sure I couldn't.' Nick tried not to make it sound too dismissive.

'Oh, sod it. Couldn't you at least come and have a look?'

Reluctantly he followed her indoors and up the stairs. The door to what had presumably been Chet Brunner's apartment was open. In one wall was a heavy oak door. Jilly-Jo stabbed her fingers at it as if hoping an 'Open Sesame' would work this time.

211

Nick tried the huge brass knob, and shoved hard. The door did not even creak.

'It's pretty substantial for a bedroom door, isn't it?'

'That's the way Chet wanted it. The walls are solid stone, you know. And no window. As near soundproof as anyone could wish.' He avoided looking at her too intently, wondering what sort of noise she and Chet had made that needed soundproofing. 'Sort of cosy little prison,' Jilly-Jo went on. 'Chet liked to think of it as an eastern what-d'you-call-it. You know, a place for his woman to be kept secluded ready for when he wanted to come to her.' For a moment she was simpering, back in the past with a memory of Chet. Then she came rushing back into the present. 'The bastard. Treacherous fat bastard.'

Nick pointlessly beat a tattoo on the door with his knuckles.

Were there voices on the other side? Then there was a faint but unmistakable rapping.

'I think that's my wife they've shut in there.'

'Why the hell should anyone do that?' Jilly-Jo was in no mood to have the dramatic emphasis shifted from herself.

Nick set off downstairs again, intent on phoning for someone with the equipment for breaking down that door. On the turn of the stairs he looked down from the window and saw a Volvo in the shadow of the building. Anna Chisholm's, surely. But when he got down and strode across the hall to the door, there was neither sight nor sound of Anna.

Nor of Lesley.

Had they both been locked in that room?

It took him five exasperating minutes to find a telephone directory and start looking through for a local builder or some shop in the village that could recommend someone for breaking down a door – which would undoubtedly lead to an outbreak of succulent gossip round the village.

Just as he had found the number of the village shop, he heard the sound of a car outside, coughing and hiccuping. He put the directory down and went out, to see Alec Chisholm getting out of the yellow Fiat, gripping the edge of the door to steady himself. His face was ashen, and when he moved away from the car he was staggering as if he had just come off a ship which had been rolling for hours in a terrible storm.

When he saw Nick he came stumbling towards him, starting to weep.

'We should never have set off. She wasn't up to it.'

Nick put an arm around his shoulders, and looked past him. It was the second time within a few days that he had seen a woman's head slumped against a car window.

'Queenie? Is she all right?'

Alec slipped away from his grasp and slumped down on to the low wall fringing the terrace. He put his head in his hands. When he spoke, still shaking, all that came out at first was an incoherent murmur. Then he forced himself to look up.

'She's dead. It was all too much for her.'

'Alec, I'm so sorry. I thought the holiday was going to be just what she needed. What both of you needed, after all the turmoil.' He took a step towards the Fiat, but Alec put out a hand to stop him.

'There's nothing you can do. She wanted us to turn back. Said she wanted to be near Cocky when it . . . when she . . .' Again words failed him.

'She'd been ill. You could see that. I didn't know how serious it was.'

'She'd suffered from atheroma for quite a time, and it was getting worse. Deposits of cholesterol in the lining of an artery, you know.' He had fallen into the plodding rhythm of a recitation. 'She had several fainting fits before we found what it was. Tried taking anti-coagulant drugs, but they seemed to aggravate it. The specialist kept warning her against emotional stress, since that made things worse. Only when Queenie gets emotionally stressed, of course, she gets stressed, and that's that.' He was trying to smile, and trying to get Nick to smile sympathetically with him. Then the smile faded. 'Oh, Christ. Nick, I'm sorry. The girls – honestly, we didn't mean them any harm, but we had to have plenty of time to get away.'

'Get away?'

'Your wife. And Anna. We were going to phone you when we were sure we were well away, and tell you the key's in the drawer beside the microwave, in the kitchen.'

213

'You mean *you* locked them in?'

'Between us. I suppose,' said Alec pitifully, 'that stress, on top of everything else, didn't do Queenie any good.'

Nick stormed away, into the kitchen of the Chisholms' quarters. It was not difficult to find the key. In keeping with Chet Brunner's flamboyant tastes, it was a huge piece of brass with a haft of some intertwining Eastern design. He snatched it up, and went back up the stairs two at a time.

Lesley threw herself into his arms and would not let go.

'How did you find us?' asked Anna at last. 'I mean, how did you know about the key, wherever it was?'

'Alec's just told me.'

'Alec? But it was he and Queenie who shoved us in here. They'd already asked me not to tell the police, and when I said they'd have to face up to it, they bundled me in here. And then they rushed your wife in as well.'

Nick held Lesley away from him, his hands biting into her shoulders. 'You must have been taken well and truly off guard.'

'The woman was mad. I couldn't believe how much strength she could summon up. I've known some nut cases before who suddenly seemed to have the strength of half a dozen. But yes, Queenie got me quite by surprise. And Alec' – she forced a tremulous laugh – 'poor Alec, he kept apologizing.'

'It's dreadful,' said Anna, 'but you'll have to tell the police to get after them. And stop them before something else happens. The state Queenie's in, there's no telling—'

'Queenie,' said Nick, 'is dead.'

They followed him back into the open air. Alec was still hunched on the low wall, staring at the Fiat but making no move to get up and go towards it.

Lesley said: 'I'm sorry about Queenie. But, Alec . . . she did kill Stuart Morgan, didn't she?'

He looked at her and nodded quite calmly.

'I shall have to ring the police,' said Nick. 'You do realize that, don't you?'

'Of course. And to save you time, that woman detective was in the village as we came through. I nearly stopped, but somehow I felt I had to get here so that Queenie could be near Cocky for the last time. Even though she was past knowing by then.'

Nick went to his car phone and came back to find that Lesley and Anna had joined Alec on the wall, sitting almost companionably on either side of him. It was a bright morning; somewhere two starlings were chattering, and a long way away a dove uttered a plummy, repetitive coo.

In an apologetic tone, as if he felt it a duty to fill in time for them while they awaited the police, Alec began a bald, direct recital of events which seemed too far away for him really to believe in them.

Queenie had always hated Stuart Morgan. Like all Queenie's moods, the hatred came and went; but its embers were always there, smouldering away, ready to be fanned by a sudden mood or a sudden bit of news, misinterpreted. She was sure Morgan had planned the death of his wife and of Peter. Had fixed Peter's car somehow. Queenie had been in a few TV thrillers where cars came off the road and burst into flames, and it turned out to be somebody fiddling with the brake cables or something – she was never mechanically minded enough to know precisely what.

She was determined to steer him away from Anna. Quite sure that now he knew Anna was coming into the estate he would be pursuing his campaign to win her. Queenie couldn't bear the thought. She went round to see him at his workshop, to have it out with him.

'And she found Cocky.' For the first time Alec faltered in his narrative. 'Just dumped there, a mangled, bloody body stuffed into a piece of sacking and left on the floor. Why he hadn't just thrown it into the bushes after hitting it, God knows. Though I suppose it's a pretty bare stretch of roadside there, along the edge of the moor. Might have been seen from the road, and traced to him and the Volvo. Do him no good – in trouble, driving without a licence. And Queenie had enough counts against him, without that on top of it all. He was quite right about that.'

'So,' said Anna, 'Stuart wrapped the corpse up and put it in the back of my Volvo, and took it indoors along with all the other items he had collected from the house here. Intending to get rid of it as soon as possible. But he didn't get the time.'

215

'No,' Alec continued sombrely. 'Queenie rolled up to challenge him over his intentions towards you, and the first thing she saw was the remains of Cocky. She grabbed the first thing that came to hand, and stabbed him with it. And then ran out, excited, dithering . . . and came to me. But she didn't tell me right away.' He stared wonderingly up at Nick, hardly believing his own words. 'We just carried on shopping. She was steamed up, but she was often like that. Could get very dramatic over a kilo of potatoes that had what she thought was a bad one in the middle. Or catch a headline in a paper that displeased her, and declaim a ranting political speech until I bought her a bar of chocolate and led her away.' Now it was becoming too real and vivid. Tears flooded his eyes again. 'And when she did get round to telling me, we decided we had to get away. I'd been talking about a holiday anyway. Only it was stupid, wasn't it? We'd never have got away with it.'

'Too much like the Watermans.'

'Yes. Only they were innocent.' Alec shrugged and managed a sad smile. 'We'd probably have lost our way anyway. Take too many wrong turnings.'

'It's been known,' Lesley agreed.

'It was Queenie who said she wanted to come back. She was the one who saw that it was hopeless. Said she'd sooner have a last look at Cocky's grave and then be arrested, and let them do what they liked. But she didn't even make that.'

A police car was coming down the drive. As if to protect Queenie against the immediate impact, Alec got up and went towards the Fiat. Over his shoulder he said: 'Maybe it's best this way. With Cocky dead, she wouldn't have had much to live for. He was her best audience. Whatever part she played, he adored her. I did my best, but . . . well, she knew that I knew her failings, and I loved her for them, but it wasn't enough. Cocky didn't care whether she was a quite good Mrs Mopp or a lousy Lady Macbeth. For him she was star quality all the way.'

He dried his eyes and watched quite stoically as DCI McAdam approached. She halted near Nick. 'Thanks for your call. Though I did think you'd have been away by now.'

'So did we,' said Nick grimly.

'Were you involved in any way with events this morning?'

Nick told her. When it came to the point of Anna and Lesley being locked in Jilly-Jo's suite, Sergeant Elliot moved protectively closer to Anna.

'In that case,' said McAdam as Nick finished, 'I'm afraid we shall need a statement from you.'

'Meaning we still can't go home?'

'I'm afraid not.' With an undertone of malice, McAdam looked at Lesley. 'I'm sure that with your past experience, Lady Torrance, you'll be the first to realize that strict procedures have to be adhered to.'

'Yes. But could we please get through it quickly?'

'I do think that you ought to be able to get away first thing tomorrow morning, unless of course there are some snags which crop up as we go along.'

She acknowledged the arrival of Dr Fairlie, who said, 'I don't believe this,' and went towards the Fiat and its contents. Then she turned back towards Alec Chisholm.

'Now, sir. Perhaps we'd be more comfortable inside while you tell me exactly what has been going on.'

20

Again the sun was shining. And again they had done their packing, and this time the luggage was stowed away in the boot of the Laguna. Everything was in order. But Lesley was still wary, unable to believe that this time they would really be allowed to drive away.

The fact that DCI McAdam was there first thing after breakfast was not reassuring. She was perfectly capable of thinking up a whole new lot of questions which would involve further delays.

Instead, she said: 'I thought you'd like to know we've had a message from your friend Inspector Percy at Arts and Antiques. The Skeoch Cumming . . . is that right?'

'Skeoch Cumming, yes,' Lesley confirmed.

'Apparently it has shown up, along with the Raeburn from the Westerlaw burglary, in Antwerp. Seems to have been shipped six months ago from Rosyth to Zeebrugge, and then on to Antwerp.'

'That's great. Thank you.'

McAdam hesitated a moment before putting her hand out to Lesley. 'I think it's a pity you didn't stay with us. You obviously have so much to offer.'

'I'd never have made the grade.'

'That's not the way I hear it.'

'I'd never have been ruthless enough.'

'So you think I'm ruthless, DI Gunn? If I may call you that for a few minutes?'

'You're dedicated in a way I never could be.'

' "Dedicated"?' McAdam mused on this, and seemed to like

the word. Then she said brusquely: 'Well, mustn't keep you. I've said goodbye to you once before, Sir Nicholas. And you, Lady Torrance.'

'And this time,' said Nick, 'you're praying it really is goodbye.'

'Have a safe journey home,' said McAdam, cool and correct. She was already drawing her old armour around her.

'No wrong turnings this time,' he promised. 'And provided we don't run into any more escaped prisoners, or highwaymen, or Border reivers on the rampage, maybe this time we can get home without incident.'

As they drove out of the yard, Anna waved to them from her front door. Sergeant Elliot was standing attentively nearby.

'Wonder if he's any good at mounting security on self-catering cottages?' said Lesley.

'Or helping to turn Balmuir Lodge into a hotel, instead of catching villains?'

There was a few minutes silence as Nick concentrated on the turns in the road, and slowed to make sure that the next signpost bore a legend that made sense. When they had at last reached something with pretensions to being a main road, heading due east, he relaxed.

'What do you suppose will happen to poor old Alec? They can hardly let him off, can they? Accessory after the fact, or something – isn't that the jargon? And imprisoning you and Anna, obstructing the course of justice. If he needs a good lawyer, I'm inclined to offer him all the backing he needs.'

'Of course they can't turn a blind eye. It'll all have to go before the procurator fiscal. But at a guess I'd say he'll get a hell of a roasting in court, and a sentence of two, maybe three years in prison. Suspended.'

'I hope so.'

Lesley was unwinding the tangle of recent events in her mind. One odd strand got itself snarled up. 'It's just struck me, whatever's going to happen to Jilly-Jo? She's a bit of a loose end in all this.'

'In real life there are always loose ends. But I somehow don't think Jilly-Jo will be on the loose for very long.' Nick reached for his sunglasses as they breasted a rise and came face to face with the morning sun. 'And on the subject of real life, what the hell did you think you were doing, walking into trouble all on your own? Sneering at Miss Marple and Poirot and those sort of plots, and then doing what every professional knows you don't do.'

'I was never in any real danger.'

'Oh, weren't you? Every silly thriller has a moment when a silly woman goes on her own into a dark cellar or a deserted warehouse only to find it's not deserted. Not waiting for back-up, or letting anyone else know,. You of all people – a so-called professional!'

'Ex-professional,' said Lesley sheepishly.

'And from now on you'll stay that way. No more dabbling.'

'No, sir.' She brooded for a minute. 'Though mind you, if I'd been in charge down at that workshop, the first thing I'd have checked on would—'

'That's enough.' Nick accelerated so vigorously that she was jolted in her seat. 'Let's get way, way out of here before you get done for impersonating a police officer.'

He drove fast but carefully. All at once he was desperate to get home. Not so that he could lord it as the laird of Black Knowe and be surrounded by his own sycophants, the way men like Brunner wanted the world to be run. It was simply that he wanted to be at home with his wife, and they could be arranging that home and living in it at their own pace, amid their own belongings. Simply living – and loving.

They stopped for coffee at a wayside cottage which also sold vegetables, herbs and duck eggs, but Nick was impatient to be on the road again, veering south-east until, as they approached the Borders, a welcoming castle of clouds soared into pinnacles and distorted battlements.

'Do you suppose they'll really have finished the work on the house?' said Lesley.

'They'd better. Though I'm wondering' – he was keeping his eyes on the road but grinning – 'if it was wise to start, after all. Will we be able to combine that with other heavy responsibilities?'

221

'What responsibilities?'

'Oh, I was just thinking. I wouldn't want a repetition of the muddled way I came into the baronetcy. You know, someone dying childless, a brother coming in from the side and all the rest of it. I'd prefer the inheritance to be straightforward.'

'What are you getting at?' But she was beginning to smile herself.

'It would save a lot of hassle if we could be sure of Black Knowe staying in the direct line without problems.'

'A daughter might be a problem?'

'Oh. Ah, yes. Though I wouldn't mind having a couple of them. And one could keep trying.'

'*One* could?'

'Well, two would have to keep trying.'

'I don't think one should look on that as an arduous responsibility.'

'So long as you agree.'

'Oh, I agree,' said Lesley as the car came over the crest of the hill and they saw the tower of Black Knowe bathed in sunshine on its knoll ahead of them.

Then they both let out a groan. At the foot of the tower was a huge skip filled with strips of wood and plaster, lengths of twisted piping, and some shards of broken glass.

'They haven't finished,' said Lesley. 'They're still at it.'

As Nick stopped a few yards away from the skip, young William Kerr came round from the side door.

'Sir Nicholas. Good to see you back, sir.'

'You haven't finished,' Nick accused him.

'Oh, but we have. Sorry about the skip being still here. It'll be gone twenty minutes from now. McRobert is fetching the loader right now.'

Lesley breathed a sigh of relief.

'No problems?' asked Nick. 'You didn't unearth any hidden treasures, or a priest's hole, or some hidden corpses, or anything?'

'Well, now.' Kerr looked at him slyly. 'Now you mention it, there were some corpses.'

Nick felt a chill down his spine. Hadn't they had enough trouble, this last year, with a murdered body found down the flue of Kilstane Academy? He looked at Lesley and could tell that she was chilled by the same memory.

'You mean there was more than one?'

'Twenty-four, actually. Starlings. When we were putting in the new flue pipe for the heating in the old fireplace, we found them. Mummified. Must have sat on top of the lum to warm their backsides, and the fumes made them drowsy. And in they went.'

Nick took Lesley's hand and led her through the main door into the lower hall. 'Let's go and look at our new quarters. And,' he added warningly, 'there's no need for you to start worrying about whether those starlings did, after all, meet a natural death. No need to call in Forensic.'

'Farewell, Detective Inspector Gunn,' whispered Lesley.

Anna had made her last inspection of the Stables Cottage kitchen and checked that it was re-stocked with the basics she provided for every newcomer. She was about to go through and give a few final flourishes with a duster when the doorway was blocked by a solid, impressive figure.

'Sergeant!'

'Er . . . the name's Rab, actually. Rab Elliot. I just dropped in to say goodbye. The boss is wrapping things up, and I don't think we'll need to bother you again. I'm . . . Mrs Chisholm, I'm so sorry things went the way they did. It's been rotten for you.'

'I'll cope,' said Anna stiffly.

He edged into the kitchen and looked round it with an appreciative nod. Did he think there were still some clues to be found, something that would impress his DCI?

He said: 'I'm due for some leave soon.'

For a moment she thought he was going to have the nerve to suggest a dirty weekend. Then he went on:

'I rather like the look of this place. I can do with a quiet week to think things over. I've had rather a hectic time recently.'

'I'd have thought a bracing week at the seaside, or a walking tour round the Summer Isles, was more in your line.'

'I do enough walking in the course of my duties, even though I'm not in uniform any longer.'

He was treating her to an awkward, puppyish look while at the same time running his hand along the work space beside the sink. There was a slight hiss as the new, full pot of marmalade she had placed there went skidding along the surface, to cannon off the electric kettle and fall to the floor.

She held her breath, watching it go and envisaging the sticky mess she would have to clean up yet again.

The jar rolled a few inches and came to a halt, unbroken.

Maybe that was a good omen.